DRIFTER'S VENGEANCE

DRIFTER'S VENGEANCE

Max Brand

DODD, MEAD & COMPANY
NEW YORK

ISBN: 0-396-06626-7
Library of Congress Catalog Card Number: 72-1540
Printed in the United States of America
by Vail-Ballou Press, Inc., Binghamton, N. Y.

PART ONE

CHAPTER 1

Mike was annoyed. In the first place, One-eyed Mike did not believe in such follies as "straight" roulette wheels; he never had advised this one, and he hated to watch it in operation, controlled by blind chance only. In the second place, he was troubled when he saw a patron winning honest gold in his employer's gambling house. Above all else, it drove a knife through his heart when a fellow who was obviously nothing but a lazy loafer started raking in hundreds of dollars.

"Loafer" was too mild a word, really, to be used upon the stranger. He was simply a tramp in rags, a youngster not much over twenty, with a darkly handsome face and a flashing smile.

Now, laughing at his own good fortune, cheerfully advising his neighbors at the roulette wheel to follow his betting chances, the lad spread his elbows at the board, so to speak, and so momently increased the loathing that filled the manly breast of Mike Doloroso.

The name of the stranger irritated Mike more than all else.

Shoving some money toward him with the long wooden rake, he had asked: "Here—this is for you—What's-your-name."

"Thanks. Speedy is my name," the stranger had answered.

"Thank me for nothing," said One-eyed Mike gruffly. "Where did you pick up that moniker and why?"

"I really don't know the reason. I only know the name," said Speedy.

"You're a polite cuss, anyway," said Mike Doloroso. "You been your mother's pride, I reckon. And joy, eh?"

His sarcasm brought wide grins from the other players, but Speedy was not offended. It was plain that, like most other tramps, he had no trace of manly pride in him. The disgust of Mike increased. He presently saw two hundred dollars go down on a combination of four. A thousand and eight hundred dollars had to be taken from the bank and shoved across the hand-polished board in the direction of Speedy. Mike Doloroso felt his face turn hot; his neck swelled; there were sensations of strangling in his throat.

Finally he turned the wheel over to an assistant and went to see his employer, Sid Levine.

When he had waded through the crowd of prospectors, laborers in the mines, teamsters, idlers, all the riff-raff that collects in a mining camp like froth below a cataract, he banged on the door that said in large letters: PRIVATE.

And a voice from within, the voice of his master, Sid Levine, answered: "Keep out of here, I tell you!"

"I ain't gonna keep out," said One-eyed Mike. For his chief pride was his familiarity with the great man, Levine. He was one of the half dozen who, in this world, ventured to call him Sid.

"You keep out, Mike," called Levine. "I'm busy."

"Who you busy with?" asked Mike.

"I'm busy with the sheriff," said Levine. "Go away."

"Yeah; the sheriff is what I wanta see," declared Mike.

2

He turned the handle of the door; it was locked. But presently a step crossed the room inside and the lock turned; Mike Doloroso walked in.

It was the sheriff, Buck Masters, who had opened the door. Levine, fat as a carved Buddha, a Buddha of pale-green jade with a great jaw and a greater hook of a nose, sat immovable, as usual, behind the table, a cigar fuming in his hand.

The sheriff was another type. He was a great, swarthy man. He had been a singer in his youth; he still sang, generally after midnight. He had gone from singing into the prize ring, and he had made more money at the latter game until years and a bad reputation had ruled him out of the business. After that he had taken his blunt jaw and his gleaming eyes to other parts of the world, and finally he had drifted to the West, and wound up, in the middle of the gold rush, in Sunday Slough. There he met Levine. When Sunday Slough grew up so far that it needed an official representative of the law, Levine, who owned Sunday Slough, caused Buck Masters to be elected sheriff, because he was the kind of sheriff that Sid Levine wanted.

He was the sort of sheriff that One-eyed Mike wanted also. And now, measuring the man of the law from an equal height, Mike said to him out of the twisted corner of his mouth: "Move over and let me in."

"What call boy went and paged you?" asked the sheriff.

Mike shifted slightly the patch of leather that covered his missing eye.

"I went and called myself," said he. "Get out of the way, Buck, will you?"

"Gunna have this big stiff in?" asked the sheriff without turning his head.

"Aw, leave him come in, then," said Levine. "He's always butting in. He ain't got any sense about where he's wanted."

The sheriff stepped to the side and closed the door behind Mike. There was no false pride about the sheriff when he was

3

among his intimates. Then he returned to the table and sat down again. Mike was leaning a hand on the table top, looking at the wad of papers which Sid Levine clutched and moistened with his fat, sweating hand.

"Lookit," said Mike. "Whacha talkin' about, you two? What kind a crooked game you cooking up? Whacha got on the table?"

"Hands," said Sid Levine. "Now you go on and tell us what's biting you. I was talkin' private with the sheriff. But you gotta go and butt in. Now talk yourself to death."

This sneering abuse pleased Mike. He knew what cold dignity could be in his employer, and it tickled his fancy to have the great boss speak in such terms to him.

Said Mike: "There's a bird out there that something's gotta be done about."

"Drunk?" asked Levine. "Why don't you bat him on the jaw and throw him out, then?"

One-eyed Mike looked affectionately at his burly right hand, which was now supporting his weight against the table.

"No, he ain't drunk," said he, "but he's wrecking the roulette bank."

He turned to the sheriff. "Say, whacha know about a guy like this Levine that has to go and put in a roulette wheel without no brake on it? Whacha know about that, eh?"

"Yeah, that's pretty cute, ain't it? said the sheriff. "But I'll tell you what, he's law-abiding. That's what Levine is. He's afraid of the law, is what he is."

He laughed. All three of them laughed at the good jest. "Yeah, I'm afraid of the law, all right," said Sid Levine. "I'm afraid of the sheriff, too, because he's got the law behind him. I uphold the law because I uphold you, you big stiff. That's what I do."

He grinned, an act that caused his nose to lengthen and his pointed chin to rise.

4

"Go on," said Buck Masters. "What about the bird that's breaking up the roulette bank?"

"Aw, what I mean," said One-eyed Mike, "he ain't nothing but a bum that's crazy with luck. He calls himself Speedy."

"I went and heard that name somewhere," said the sheriff thoughtfully.

"Yeah, you maybe think you heard it because it sounds familiar," said Mike. "But you never heard it about him. He's just a kid; kind of a smiling fool. Just a bum; just a tramp. That's all. He's having a crazy run of luck, what I mean."

"What kind of a run?" asked Levine, flicking the ashes from his fat cigar.

"What I mean," said Mike, "he bumped the bank for eighteen hundred the last spin of the wheel. You gotta go and put in a wheel without no brakes. That was bright. I told you it was bright to do that!"

Levine flicked his cigar again, though there was no ash on the glowing tip of it.

"Eighteen hundred, eh?" said he.

"Yeah. Eighteen hundred, I said, and eighteen hundred I mean," answered Mike.

"Well, we gotta do something about it," said Levine.

"That's why I come and talked myself to death," said Doloroso.

"All right. You kind of showed some sense," declared Levine.

He turned his massive head toward the sheriff. Buck Masters acknowledged the glance by yawning.

"We was talking about something important," he said. "You gotta go and drag in a low bum like this Speedy," commented the man of the law.

"Whacha been talking about?" asked Mike.

The sheriff looked up quickly at Levine.

"Aw," said Levine, "he's inside. Mike is inside. He's a friend of mine."

5

The sheriff turned his glance upon Mike again.

"We was talking about Cliff Derrick," said he.

A wave of excitement spread across the damaged face of Mike. "Derrick!" he gasped. "What's he gone and done now?"

"He's gone and bedded himself down on this here range," said Buck Masters.

CHAPTER 2

The single eye of Mike looked up and far away. It was clear that he was seeing things in the past.

"Derrick!" he murmured again.

"Yeah, Cliff Derrick," said Levine. "That ain't so easy to say, neither."

"No, it ain't so easy to say," murmured Mike. "It ain't so easy to take, neither."

"Neither is dynamite, or lightning, or arsenic," commented Buck Masters.

He looked down at his right hand, spread it, folded it into a fist, admired the row of knuckles, and yawned. He always yawned when he grew interested. He felt that it was unmanly to betray excitement.

"Well," said Mike, "Derrick is dynamite, all right."

"He's arsenic, too," said Levine. "He's slick, is what he is."

"Yeah, he's slick," said the sheriff. "He's poisonous slick, is what he is."

"What's he mean, coming out here?" asked Mike.

"Air, maybe," suggested Levine gently. "Wanted a change of air. I guess that's what he wanted. He wouldn't be bothered none wanting the free and easy that's floating around this here camp."

"Look at here," said Mike. "He ain't gone and come into town, has he?"

"Aw, he ain't that much of a fool," said the sheriff. "Say, Levine, is he a friend of yours? You ain't told me that."

Levine puffed carefully at his cigar, which was almost out. At last, abstractedly, he answered: "We never done no business together."

"Then he ain't been trimmed," said Mike.

He and the sheriff laughed loudly. Levine smiled broadly with gratified vanity.

"What I mean," he said, "we got some mutual friends. That's all. I dunno nothing about Derrick. I read the papers. I dunno nothing about Derrick personal."

"The papers is enough," said the sheriff. "Even the papers can't go and lie all the time."

"Yeah," said Levine, "I guess he's pretty tough."

"Like a boiled owl, is all he is," said One-eyed Mike. "Say, where's a drink around here?"

"You always gotta drink," remarked Levine. "It makes me sick, the way you always gotta drink. Aw, go on over there and help yourself, then. You know where it is. You take Mike," he added to the sheriff, "he's always gotta be sliding something past his front teeth. That's a fault of yours, Mike. Some day I'm gunna fire you. I ain't gunna have a lot of booze hounds around my place."

"Make it two," said the sheriff as Mike opened a filing cabinet and pulled out a bottle. "Yeah," he went on, "there's some people that ain't ever satisfied unless they're half tight. You gotta be a man to drink like a man oughta. You gunna have a shot?"

"I'll have a taste," said Levine. "Not them glasses, you dumbbell. Them are for the ladies. You take a skirt, they can't hold no liquor. They ain't got any head, that's the trouble with 'em. Well, here's how, boys."

7

Mike lowered his glass and smacked his lips.

"Whacha always gotta have a chaser for, Sid?" he asked. "There ain't any use having a drink if you can't let it smoke a while."

"He's gunna teach me how to drink, too," commented Levine coldly. "That's all he's gunna do. He knows how to drink, is what he knows. What I mean about Derrick, is he the kind that stands in or is he the kind that stands out?"

"He'll stand in," said Mike wisely, "but he's a hog."

"He wants it all, does he?" asked Levine with a sad eye.

"You gotta throw a bluff with Derrick," said Mike. "That's all you gotta know; but you gotta throw it big. Know what I mean? He's wise, is what he is."

"He's the kind," said Buck Masters, "you sock him on the chin and then you help him to stand up again. That's the way to get started with him."

"You sock him on the chin, you go and bust your hand, that's all," said One-eyed Mike. "Who's gunna go and sock him on the chin, what I mean?"

"Oh, I dunno," said Levine, "anything can be managed, one way or another."

"Don't you go and make any mistake," said Mike, frowning with the intensity of his belief. "You better declare Derrick in. You better give him a cut. It'll save you money any time before you're done with the game. But there's a roulette wheel in there without no brakes on it. What're we gunna do about that?"

"The wheel's all right. The wheel'll take care of itself," said the great Levine. "About the guy that's running in luck, we better do something about him. What about you, Buck? What about you doing something?"

"Well, what would I do?" asked Masters. "I gotta have a charge agin' him before I can go and slam him in the hoosegow."

"I'll give you a charge," said Levine. "He's a bum. Go and

sock him in jail for vagrancy."

"And him with five or six grand in his pockets that he's just taken out of the roulette?"

The sheriff shrugged his shoulders as he asked the question.

"Well, whacha want?" asked One-eyed Mike. "Ain't that the kind of fish that you wanta catch? Two minutes after he's been pinched he won't have any five or six grand, I guess."

The face of the sheriff grew still, and his eyes burned.

"Roll him?" he suggested.

"Why not? Half for you and half for the house," said One-eyed Mike.

"Half for the house?" echoed the sheriff, frowning.

"Well, you hunt on our land, so you gotta pay a commission. It ain't every place in the world that the gamekeepers holds the game by a halter while the hunter comes up and gets the kill."

"You ain't such a dumbbell, Mike," murmured Levine. "You got a kind of a brain in your head, at that. Fifty-fifty, Buck."

Masters shrugged his powerful shoulders.

"I don't mind," he averred. "Fifty-fifty is all right. But it's kind of raw rolling a gent for vagrancy when he's got five, six thousand bucks in his jeans. Never mind. I'll slam him in the hoosegow, but I hate to bother the judge with that kind of a deal. I know the judge is fixed, but he don't want to be bothered except for something big. He don't wanta be bothered by no vagrancy dope."

"Aw, whacha talkin' about the hoosegow for, anyway?" asked One-eyed Mike. "What I mean, slam this bird, trim him, and give him a run out of town. Make it so hot for him he won't stop running for a coupla weeks. That's all I mean to do."

"Well, all right," said the sheriff. "I'll go and do it now. So long, Sid. See you later, Mike."

"Say," said Mike, "I'll be on hand when you shake him

9

down—just to see what falls. Besides, two do a better job than one. You sock him on that side and I plaster him on this side."

"Maybe you're right," agreed the sheriff. "I never say no. I don't seem to have no mind of my own no more."

"You're just growing up, brother," declared Sid Levine. "Go on and roll that baby, and come back and tell me about it, will you?"

"We'll come back with something more than talk," said One-eyed Mike.

And he led the way out of the room.

The sheriff, half a step behind him, said: "Travel heeled, you guess, this bird you're talking about? This Speedy?"

"Him? He never seen a gun except in a window. He ain't nothing. Nothing but lucky. He's the kind that the women like. Soft and sweet, is all I mean."

"All right," said Buck Masters. "I'll just give him a squeeze and let the dollars fall where they may."

"Sure," said One-eyed Mike, laughing. "Hew to a line, is the idea."

He returned to the roulette wheel at the very unpleasant moment when Speedy was drawing in a five-hundred-dollar win.

One-eyed Mike began to perspire. It seemed to him something approaching a moral sin when he saw good money going to waste as rapidly as this.

Besides, others in the crowd had begun to follow the choices of Speedy and were placing their money on the same numbers or the same color, or odd or even. A regular run on the game was starting.

In the midst of this excitement came the sheriff. He moved with the long and easy stride of a very powerful man, and as he walked he waved a jovial hand to right or to left singling out some one of his acquaintances.

At last he came through the crowd to the place where

Speedy was standing, and instantly he laid a hand on the shoulder of the boy. That is to say, he started to lay his hand on the shoulder of that young man. But he failed to do so. Speedy, at that very moment, glided a little to the side, laid a bet on the odd, turned and faced the sheriff with a polite smile.

"I want you, brother," said Buck Masters.

"Want me?" asked Speedy, his brows lifting.

"I'm Sheriff Masters. You come along and don't make no fuss, is all."

"But why do you want me, sheriff?" asked the boy. "What have I done? It isn't because I've been winning money at roulette, is it? It isn't because Mr. Levine has sent for you, is it?"

He said these words in a slightly louder voice, and they drew instant attention from the crowd.

CHAPTER 3

A mining crowd is never gentle and never dull-witted. This group of men was instantly irritated.

"Look, Masters," said one of them, "what kind of a raw deal is this? Can't Levine lose a few grand without bringing in the police?"

The sheriff arched his black brows and roared: "What kind of a gag are you pulling on me? What kind of bunk is this? Back up, will you, and leave the way clear. Kid, face around and get out of here before I throw you out!"

"Oh, I'm going out, all right," said the boy. "It was simply that I wondered what I'd done."

"Why, you're a bum, you're a tramp, for one thing," said

the sheriff. "And—well, you know what your record is, you worm!"

As he broke into this tirade, Speedy seemed to shrink away through the crowd in fear and trembling, and the sheriff followed after him.

The crowd did not follow. After all, arrests were common in Sunday Slough.

As Mike turned the roulette wheel over to his assistant and hurried in pursuit, the sheriff reached again for the shoulder of the boy, and again missed his grip. He thought that was odd—as though the youngster had eyes in the back of his head and knew when to side-step without turning to look!

They came out the rear door of the dive. Suddenly it was quiet. The voices inside of Levine's Grand Palace were shut behind a stout wall, and the noise of labor up and down Sunday Slough—the clinking of double and single jacks on drill heads, the calling of orders, and the rumbling of wagons over the roads, deep with white dust—came thickly through the mountain air.

Mike came out behind the sheriff and Speedy. His face shone with sweat; his eyes shone with hungry expectation. He saw the sheriff poking a big, capacious Colt revolver in the direction of Speedy's stomach.

"Stick up your hands, brother," said the sheriff.

Speedy lifted his slender brown hands, hardly larger than the hands of a child.

"What do you want?" he asked. "The money I've won?"

"Fan him," said the sheriff.

Mike fanned him.

He got a stuffed wallet, a bundle of money out of an inside coat pocket, and some more money from a trousers pocket.

There was a small sewing kit, an undersized pocket knife, a pair of handkerchiefs extraordinarily clean, and nothing else.

The sheriff almost laughed aloud.

"Tramp royal is about all you could say of him," said he. "He travels light, all right. Got a hoss?"

"Yes, I have a horse."

"But maybe you'd as soon walk as ride when you leave Sunday Slough?"

Speedy did not answer, because it was fairly obvious that no answer was required. He looked with gentle, helpless eyes from one face to the other.

"Well, give him a start," said the sheriff.

"I'll start him, all right," said Mike.

He had stepped around so that he was just opposite the man of the law, and now he gathered his strength and launched a pile-driving blow at the back of the boy's head.

Unfortunately, at that moment the youth stooped a little and stepped to the side, so that the great, balled fist of One-eyed Mike whizzed past the head of Speedy, missing it by a mere fraction of an inch, and shot straight up at the sheriff.

It was a beautiful punch, long and straight. It very nearly reached the face of the sheriff! In fact, he had to throw up a sudden guard, and his left forearm was bruised by the violence of the blow.

"Why, you big ham!" said the sheriff.

And then he himself, putting up the revolver, stepped in to flatten Speedy with the practiced might and skill of the prize ring.

Once an artist always an artist! It was a short and snappy left hook that he tried on the boy, who stood blinking and bewildered, with his hands at his sides, hanging loosely. It was plain that there was so little manhood in Speedy that he did not even know the first elements in the art of self-defense. Not even enough to lift his arms!

He was so paralyzed by fear that he was even unable to turn and run. The sheriff, on second thought, might have refrained from striking such a helpless target, but he was not using second thought just now. He was too irritated by

13

the ache in his left arm, where Mike's fist had grazed him. Therefore he struck with the precision, with the lightning speed of a cat's paw.

It seemed as though the wind of the blow preceding it knocked the boy back upon his heels, and the good left fist of the sheriff jarred home on thinnest air alone. He grunted as his own shoulder and stretching side absorbed the shock.

But he balanced himself and stepped in with a long, overhand right smash.

The boy staggered again, and literally fell to the ground in helpless fright. But it so happened, just as he dropped, that One-eyed Mike came charging in with furious violence. Over the kneeling form of Speedy he tripped and pitched with violent impetus into his friend and comrade, Buck Masters.

They were heavy men; they rolled in headlong confusion upon the ground, while over them hovered the slender form of Speedy. He told them that he was sorry for their fall; but when the sheriff regained hands and knees and then feet, he found that a pair of big revolvers dangled from the hands of the boy.

He held them as though he had never seen such weapons before. "Look out!" gasped the sheriff. "That's hair trigger, that one of mine."

"I hope that nothing happens," said Speedy.

In his other hand he held a considerable wad of paper money and his own wallet.

"I took this," he said. "I thought you had had it long enough to know what it was all about, sheriff. Am I wrong?"

"Sleight of hand, eh?" said the sheriff. "Circus stuff, jujitsu, and all that, eh? That's all right, kid. You made a good play. But don't you think that I'm done with you!"

One-eyed Mike had been stunned by the violence of his fall.

Now he got to his feet, reeling. His brain was ringing with

mighty bells; the leather patch had shifted, and the horrible, dark cavern of the missing eye was visible.

"Leave me get at him, Buck," he pleaded.

"Why, I ain't holding you back none," said the sheriff. "Go and catch him if you can, but don't let him drop a gun on your toe while you're chasing him around. That's all. Sail right in and catch him, brother!"

"You ain't funny," said One-eyed Mike. "Hold on! Gunna let him go sneakin' off?"

"I won't sneak far," said Speedy cheerfully. "When you really want me, just send for me."

"Give back that gun," said the sheriff. "You leave that gun behind!"

"I forgot which is yours and which belongs to Mike," said Speedy. "But I'll do my best to find out which belongs to which!"

He moved away as he spoke, and the sheriff leaned a hand against a tree trunk and stared gloomily after the lad.

"He's a slick one, all right," said he.

Mike rubbed his hand across a troubled brow.

"He's so slick," said he, "that he's gunna get all roughed up before he leaves this here town. You hear me talk?"

"I hear you talk," said Buck Masters in some disgust. "I seen you fight, too. You can knock a hole in the air, all right, you can!"

"You're all thumbs when it comes to kidding," said One-eyed Mike. "But I'm gunna point out something to you. Except when I fanned him, we ain't either of us laid a hand on him."

"No," said the sheriff, "we ain't, as a matter of fact. I wanta see that kid again."

"I'm gunna see him again," said the gambler, "if I gotta walk miles and swim rivers all the rest of my life to get at him. And the guns, too. Walkin' off with our guns!"

Young Speedy, in the meantime, had sauntered into the

15

main street of Sunday Slough until he came to one of the most flourishing shops in the street. It was a place where one could buy anything from dynamite to drills. Every whim and fancy, whether for the hunter of bird and beast or the hunter of man, could be satisfied there. Shotguns in one long rack and rifles in another begged to be handled and used.

Speedy, once inside the door of this shop, paused a moment to admire the display. Then he found an idle clerk and laid the two revolvers on the counter.

"I picked up this pair of guns," he said. "Who owns 'em?"

The clerk frowned at them. Then he jerked up his head with a start.

"Why," he said, "that's the criss-crossing that the sheriff cuts into the handles of his guns to roughen up the grip. And this here with the sight filed off, wouldn't that belong to One-eyed Mike?"

"I don't know," said Speedy. "I suppose the right men will come to claim those guns."

With that he walked out of the shop and went on down the street, regardless of the clerk, who followed him as far as the entrance and then stared after him agape. It seemed that the clerk had many things that he wanted to say, but all stopped on the verge of his lips. Then he saw the editor, reporter, business manager and sales agent of the Sunday Slough *News*.

"Hey, Bill!" he cried. "Come here and get a story!"

CHAPTER 4

Bill Turner came to get the story. There was plenty of news in Sunday Slough, running from cheerful gun fights to new gold strikes up and down the canyon. But the appetite of Bill for new items was an amazing thing.

"What's the idea, Pete?" he said. "Got a new kind of a gat in stock?"

"Say," said Pete, "tell me the moniker of a kid all kind of dressed up in rags and patches, with a sad kind of a soft look about his eyes, which, once you'd seen him, you'd remember."

"Yeah, I seen him in the Grand Palace," said the reporter. "I seen him making a run on the roulette wheel. Five, six grand was what he picked up. Along comes the sheriff and gives him a run. Slugs him in the hoosegow for vagrancy, they say."

"Ain't that kind of thick?" said the clerk. "Slugging a gent in the hoosegow for vagrancy when he's got all that kale in his poke?"

"Yeah, kind of thick. But they're deep, some of the people around this here town!"

"They're deep, all right," said Pete. "But they didn't slam the kid in the hoosegow, after all. Lookit here. Did anybody go along with the sheriff when he run the kid in?"

"Yeah. There was one went."

"Was it Mike Doloroso?"

The reporter started. "Who told you that?" he asked.

"Leave that be," said the clerk. "The name of this kid—who does he call himself?"

"Speedy."

"Lookit," said Pete. "Maybe there's something to him besides his eyes."

"There's luck to him. I saw him have that run at roulette."

"Maybe there's something more than luck. Come here!"

He took Bill to the counter and showed him the pair of revolvers.

"There's the sheriff's cannon. And that one belongs to Mike Doloroso or I'm a one-eyed sucker," declared the clerk.

"What are you doing with them guns?" asked Bill.

17

"Speedy left 'em here. He says that he found 'em in the street. Is that likely? No, it ain't likely. He brought 'em in and says I'm to hold 'em till they're claimed. Now lookit here. The sheriff and Mike go out to run Speedy into jail. Instead, he walks off with their guns. If you're a bright guy, you might find a story buried in that somewhere."

"By Jove, this is one of the best!" cried the reporter. "But if I print anything, Mike and the sheriff and the whole inside gang will cut my throat."

"They won't," declared the clerk. "Lookit what I do. I put them two guns in the window, and I put a big show card under 'em, and on the card I say that Speedy left these two guns with me, and anybody that claims them can have them. That's gunna bring every gent in Sunday Slough to look at the guns. And everybody's gonna know, before night, who really owns those guns. And everybody is gunna be asking questions how Speedy got 'em. All you do is to write a little item in the paper."

Bill writhed with pleasure.

"It's worth a three-column head," he vowed. "It's a beaut. But they'll murder Speedy. The thugs, I mean!"

"Yeah, and maybe they tried to murder him before and instead he just takes their guns away from 'em. Who is this here Speedy, anyway?"

"I dunno," said Bill, "but I'm gunna find out!"

In twenty minutes he found Speedy in the Best Chance Saloon, far down the street. The sounds of sweet singing and the twanging of a guitar drew Bill Turner into the place, and there he found that a good-sized crowd had already gathered. They leaned their backs against the bar and faced toward a lad who sat cocked back in a chair in a corner of the room, with his battered hat on the floor before him and a guitar across his knees.

It was Speedy, singing songs of old Ireland, and the crowd listened, hushed and respectful. It does not take many drops of Irish blood to color all the rest in a man's body. And every one of these listeners, though the names might have ranged from Russian to German and Portuguese, gave reverent heed as though to the songs of a fatherland.

Showers of big silver and dollar bills fell into the hat at the end of each song. But Doc Wiley took firm hold of the ceremony at this point. He was a prospector whose flaming red hair was gradually being dulled to gray; but his shoulders were as ample and his voice as huge a roar as ever in his famous youth. For a famous man he had been up and down the range, following his fortune wherever he could find it, and throwing it away again as fast as found.

Now he said: "I got three hundred dollars, kid, and I'm gunna hear three songs. Tune up, you wild cat, and lemme hear you yip good and loud!"

He named his songs. They were sad and wailing affairs, every one of them, and they proclaimed the miseries of the green island and the cruelty of the oppressors, but some day, far away, happiness would return again. So Speedy sang them to great applause, and after every one of them he threw in a whirling, jolly, dancing tune for an encore.

Then Doc Wiley, the prospector, very drunk, but very solemn, crossed the room and put his three hundred dollars in the hat.

He said: "Kid, if I'd ever been in old Ireland, these here songs would put me right back there again. And I tell you what I'm gunna do. When I make another pile, I'm gunna pull out and go to Ireland and buy me a dog and a potato patch, and be as Irish as any of 'em all!"

He turned around and made a slow, stately way toward the door. Just as he reached it, Speedy, on noiseless feet, overtook him, and the three hundred dollars glided from his hand, unnoticed, into the pocket of the big man. Then Doc Wiley went out into the street.

The Best Chance Saloon broke into deep-throated murmurs. It is easier to take three hundred dollars, after all, than to return it, and Speedy would have been heavily plied with liquor had not Bill Turner, of the *News*, got the lad into an obscure back room.

Said Turner: "Speedy, I'm a newspaperman. Sit down and tell me about yourself."

"I'm poor newspaper copy," said Speedy. "You ask me questions and I'll answer 'em."

"Tell me, where you from?" asked Turner.

"Over there," said Speedy, with a gesture that included half the points of the compass.

Turner grinned.

"I see," said he. "What's your line?"

"Everything but work."

"No work, eh?"

"Never a stroke."

"Gentleman of leisure, Speedy?"

"You can call it that if you want to."

"What brought you out here, anyway?"

"Travel," said Speedy.

Bill Turner laughed.

"That's the way most people get around—by traveling. Been on the stage?"

"I prefer blind baggage to a stage," said Speedy.

"Usually travel around and pick up your money singing?"

"I don't care how I get money," said the boy, "so long as there are no sweat stains on it."

"About the sheriff and One-eyed Mike—"

"What about 'em?"

"What did you do to them?"

"Nothing," said Speedy.

"Hold on! Down there in the shop window there's a pair of guns. You took 'em from the sheriff and One-eyed Mike. The town's gunna be buzzing about it, Speedy. You might as well tell me the straight story."

"There's nothing for me to tell you, partner," said Speedy.

"You did nothing to 'em, eh?"

"I didn't touch them."

"Just persuaded 'em to give up their guns?"

Speedy shrugged his shoulders. "I just found the guns," said he.

"You don't have to touch a man if you get the drop on them," suggested the reporter.

"The drop? Oh, I never carry a gun," said Speedy.

Bill Turner rose slowly to his feet, as though lifted by an unseen hand.

"You—never—wear a gun?" he echoed.

"No, never."

"Well, I'll be dog-gone!" said Turner. "Is that all you're going to tell me?"

"I can't think of anything else to say."

Turner looked steadily upon his companion.

"Speedy," said he, "you won't talk, but I'm gunna tell you something. After that story of the two guns gets around, they're gunna make you walk the plank. You better leave Sunday Slough."

"I can't," said Speedy. "I'm too interested in cleaning it up."

"Cleaning it up?"

"Yes," said Speedy, "I want to help the sheriff do his job!"

CHAPTER 5

Turner had plenty of news to print day by day, but as has been said before, he rarely had such a feature as he carried that evening. It was read by every man in town. The edition was sold out before dusk. He printed a new edition, an extra, and charged twenty-five cents a copy. He sold out that edition, too, and ground his teeth because he had not made the printing twice as large.

However, it was a good day, a grand day, for Bill. He was not in the newspaper game to make money merely. He was an artist, and he had built out of Speedy a new feature, and one that would be remembered. He wrote a good head in the first place.

BETTER SUNDAY FOR THE SLOUGH

OR

A BETTER SLOUGH FOR SUNDAY.

SPEEDY ARRIVES TO CLEAN UP THE

TOWN!!!

Under that beginning he wrote that Speedy had come to Sunday Slough, found money easy in the Grand Palace, and had then been arrested on a charge of vagabondism by the sheriff, assisted by formidable Mike Doloroso.

But something had happened. What was it?

On the way to the jail the sheriff and Mike had lost their prisoner and both their guns! Could they explain?

Perhaps the guns would offer an explanation. And they were both on view in the window of the gunsmith!

Yes, it was a story that made Sunday Slough gasp, and then laugh loudly, though somewhat up its sleeve, for no matter what might have happened to the sheriff in the course of this misadventure, he was known to be a formidable man.

His humor was not of the best the next morning as he sat in his office blinking whisky fumes out of his brain. A cloud was still drifting before his eyes, and through that cloud appeared, with increasing brightness, the image of Speedy, the tramp entertainer.

Mike Doloroso came down the street at this moment and

22

paused to scowl at the sign beside the sheriff's door.

It read: "Wanted, a deputy sheriff, a man who knows this range, his horse, and his gun."

The pay was high, but even forty dollars a week no longer tempted men in Sunday Slough. They had seen too many others apply for the job, get it, and then disappear from the tale of the living at the end of a few days. Sometimes the people of Sunday Slough referred to these fellows as Buck Masters' seven-day men. That was about the average of their incumbency. After seven days they faded from the picture, and the pay they drew was just about enough to pay for their funeral. Therefore it was generally said that a deputy sheriff in the Slough was working for his grave.

One-eyed Mike eyed the sign with disfavor, also with thought. He had come with evil will to call upon the sheriff, but now he remembered that though the deputies came and went with the weeks, Buck Masters had remained in Sunday Slough for twenty times that long and still he was alive. Neither did he assign the hardest jobs to his assistants. In fact, there was nothing that Buck liked so well as a brawl, and his favorite diversion was meeting an out-of-town bad man and beating him at his own game of general, all-around badness.

So, having considered these things, One-eyed Mike came into the office with more respect than he had intended to show.

He merely said: "We turned up an ace yesterday, Buck."

The sheriff puffed at his cigar, and instead of looking at Mike, seemed to be regarding only the bad taste in his mouth.

"I been by the window and seen them guns," said Mike. "Everybody else has seen 'em, too. That cross hatching, it stands out pretty strong on the handles of that gun."

"What about the filed-off sight?" asked the sheriff sharply.

"Yeah. You can see that, too. How are we gunna roll this

bum, what I mean?"

The sheriff turned his head slowly away and looked out over the ragged, staggered roofs of Sunday Slough, with the bright smoke of the sun already rising from them, and beyond the roofs he saw the cliffs of the upper valley, gleaming gold or blue. He loved that valley, and he loved that town. His twenty weeks in it had been profitable; more than that, they had been happy weeks. He felt that his finger was upon the main pulse of life at last, and that he mattered vitally to many people.

At last he said: "The dirty bum is by way of makin' a fool out of me!"

"Me, too," said One-eyed Mike. "It was a funny thing, what happened yesterday. I dunno that I understand it."

"Sure, it was funny," said the sheriff. "It's so funny that just remembering of it gives me the gripes."

"I dunno what happened," said Mike.

"You never heard of a fool that was crazy with luck, I guess?" suggested the sheriff.

"Yeah, I've heard of that, too. He was crazy with luck, all right."

"Then shut up and let me think," said the sheriff.

Nevertheless, Mike went on: "What I mean to say is that this bird, with five or six grand in his jeans, he goes and gives a show in the Best Chance and pulls down some small change and does a song and dance. Doc Wiley is tight and slips the kid three greenbacks, and every one of them says a hundred dollars, soft and tender and true. And the kid passes them back into old Doc's pocket as he goes out the door. What I mean, the brat is still in town, and he's staged a gun show in a big window, and I dunno what he's all about."

"He dunno what he's all about, either," said the sheriff. "He's just kind of dizzy with himself, and he's pulling a grand stand just now. Pretty soon the floor'll jump up and sock him in the chin so hard he won't ever wake up."

"Yeah, he's gotta be rolled, I guess," said One-eyed Mike.

"Rolled? He's gotta be rolled and plastered, picked up and dropped. I'm gunna crack him wide open. Only, I was just thinking how."

"So was I. So was Sid," declared Mike.

"Didn't Sid have no ideas?" asked the sheriff wistfully.

"He didn't have no good ones," said Mike. "If you take and pinch the kid a second time, everybody in town will know that it's just a grouch. And what can you pinch him for? Vagabondage? Not with him so flush and the whole town knowing it. Resisting arrest? You couldn't bring him up for that, because you and me would have to tell what happened, and we couldn't do that."

"So that leaves what?" asked the sheriff.

"A rap over the bean is all, I guess," said Mike.

"Yeah," suggested the sheriff. "Or a fake gun fight in any saloon where he's working, and the only bullet that hits anything but air is the one that splits the wishbone of this kid. This Speedy, this what's-his-name, has anybody else found out what he is?"

"He ain't nothing but a greasy bum," said One-eyed Mike. "Nobody don't know anything at all about him. And we got people here from all over the world. He won't talk about himself."

"That's nacheral enough with a lot of gents," said the sheriff, who sometimes drew a curtain over sections of his own life. "I bet he's done time."

"Most of Sunday Slough has," said Mike. "What of it?"

"Nothing of it," said Buck Masters. "That ain't anything against a man. Anybody's likely to run up against a piece of time, I guess."

"I guess, too," said Mike. "But we ain't no nearer to rolling this here bum."

"We're gunna roll him," said the sheriff. "But I dunno. Something kind of holds me back."

"Like what holds you back?" said Mike.

"Him not packing no gun, I mean."

"What makes you think that he don't pack no gun? Him saying so?"

"Yeah, him saying so. It kind of stuck in my craw. Suppose that I go out and salt him down with a handful of lead and then they turn him over and find that he don't pack no gun. It wouldn't look so good. We didn't find no gun when we fanned him."

"He's sleight of hand, is what he is," said the other. "You can't tell about a guy like that. They can do funny things."

"They can't put a Colt .45 into a hollow tooth," objected the sheriff.

"I dunno; they can do funny things. You wouldn't believe your eyes," said Mike. "And don't you worry about that baby. If you sock him between the eyes, nobody is gunna go and say that you've robbed the cradle none."

"Put on the brakes and skid to a stop," said the sheriff. "Here comes that ham-and-eggs deputy marshal, Tom Gray, the honest man—Honest Tom. What's he coming butting in for around here?"

"Federal officer?" asked One-eyed Mike, his eyes enlarging.

"Yeah, shut up," said the sheriff. And just then the deputy marshal came in.

CHAPTER 6

The deputy marshal looked far from an important or a fighting man. He was short, stoop-shouldered, and very gray. He wore a close-cropped mustache, as gray as the hair of his head, and his upper lip twitched nervously. Only his eyes were steady; very tired, patient, and sad eyes.

"Hello, Masters," he said. "You haven't forgotten me?"

Masters summoned a smile and a handshake.

"How's every little thing?" he asked. "This is Mike Doloroso."

The marshal turned about and looked quietly, earnestly at One-eyed Mike.

"I know Mike," he said, "but Mike doesn't know me."

That was his only greeting to the gambler; then he turned back to the sheriff.

"I've come hunting for help," said he.

"Have you?" asked Masters, surprised. "What can I do you for, Gray?"

"Cliff Derrick has jumped into this part of the world," said the marshal.

"Has he?" asked the sheriff innocently.

"Yes, he has. Know him?"

"I dunno that I know him. I've heard about him. But this is away off your beat, Gray."

"Yes. It's off my regular beat. But I go where the men I want have gone. I want Derrick. I want all of him, and I want him forever."

"Life, eh?"

"Yes. Even if he had nine lives, I'd want all of 'em."

"Yeah, Derrick's been a busy boy," commented Mike, who kept on the outskirts of the conversation.

"He's what I'd call a handy man to have around the house," said the marshal. "Anything from running Chinks to smuggling dope across the river. He's not particular. He goes where his luck leads him, and he covers up his trail with the handiest thing that comes his way—something red, usually."

"Derrick's a killer, they say," remarked the sheriff. "That's all there is to it. He's a killer."

"That's all there's been to it so far," said the marshal. "I

27

hope to add something to the story, though, a sort of a con-clusion. And I thought you and your boys might help me, Masters. We haven't always been friendly. But I forget the past. I take men the way I find 'em. I hope you can do the same."

"Sure, I can," murmured Masters with a certain air of relief.

"Derrick is no particular help to any one," said the mar-shal. "And though you're policing a big county, Masters, I dare say that you'll be crowded for room now that Derrick has moved in."

"I reckon that I might be," said the sheriff. "Where d'you reckon this Derrick to be hanging out now?"

"Somewhere around the Castle Ford."

"He would be," nodded Masters. "That's a regular hole in the wall."

"That's what it is," said the marshal. "Do you stand in with me?"

"Of course I do. I'll give Castle Ford a stir and see what comes to the top. I'll let you know."

"That's all I want," said the marshal. "Glad I've seen you. So long. So long, Mike. Be a good boy."

He went out into the fiery sunshine of the street with his short, quick, impatiently stumbling step. Like many a horse-man, he was uncertain on his feet.

When he was gone, the pair inside stared at each other, and Mike spoke first, cautiously.

"Well, whacha think?" he asked.

The sheriff removed his cigar and snarled his lips around the issuing cloud of smoke.

"That snake give me the run once," he said. "Like I would throw in with him now! I could eat him sliced for cold salad, is what I could do."

Mike grinned. He actually sighed with relief.

"Like you would throw in with him instead of a man like

28

Derrick!" he said. "There's thousands in a fellow like Derrick. Thousands is just small change for him!"

"Sure. I know that. It ain't the money, though," said the sheriff. "But this Tom Gray, he gave me the run once. I don't forget a thing like that. Now he comes around and finds me in the saddle, and he wants to ride on the same horse. He can go to blazes. I don't work with his kind. I work with my own kind."

"Sure you do," said Mike. "This gives you an easy break with Derrick, too. You can tip off Gray's hand to him. Levine will give me a day off. I could carry a note from you up to him."

"You couldn't carry no note for me," answered the sheriff, sneering a little at this absurdity. "I don't write messages to birds like Derrick. But you can go and tell him what I think. It's only about six miles to Castle Ford. You can be back pretty soon. Try to find out how many men are with him, and what they're like. He don't play a lone hand ever. And if—"

He stopped.

"Now, dog-gone my eyes," said the sheriff, "because I don't believe what they're tryin' to tell me!"

He stared as he spoke. Through the door of his office came none other than Speedy!

He stood just inside the doorway, and taking off his ragged hat, he smiled upon the two.

"Here we all are again!" said he.

One-eyed Mike arose and stepped back toward the wall, a strategic post of importance. The sheriff leaned forward in his chair and drew open, a silent inch farther, a certain important drawer of his desk.

"Yeah," said he, "it looks like we're all together again for a while. Just come in to pay me a little call, brother?"

"I came in to laugh with you about that newspaper article," said Speedy. "What an impression that gives—as though somehow I had managed to manhandle you both!"

He was as good as his word, and broke into the most cheerful laughter as he said this. He took a chair and tilted it back against the wall. One-eyed Mike moved closer, stepping sidewise, like a spider.

"Yeah, that was the impression that the story gave, all right," said the sheriff, his teeth set so hard that the jaw muscles bulged.

"That was the impression," said Speedy. "I knew that you'd be laughing about it, and so I dropped in to join you. There was something else on my mind, too."

"Oh, was there? And what was it?" asked the sheriff softly. "Something about the gun show down the street, maybe? Or the cleaning up of Sunday Slough?"

"You know," said Speedy, "I don't like steady work very well, but I thought that forty a week sounded like pretty good pay."

Both of them stared at the lad with bewilderment. At last One-eyed Mike said hoarsely: "Do you hear him? He means nothin' but the deputy sheriff job!"

"He don't mean that," said the sheriff.

"You know how it is," said the boy. "I understand that the deputy sheriff would have to do a good deal of riding. I'm not a first-rate rider, but I like the open air pretty well. Never feel quite healthy unless I'm well tanned."

The sheriff moistened his tight lips as far as the bristles of his unshaven beard.

"You wanta go and be deputy sheriff, do you?"

"Why not?" said the boy.

"Well, why not? Know what they call a deputy sheriff here?"

"A seven-day man?" asked the boy. "Yes, I've heard that. But they must have been rash people. A little tact will get one around all sorts of difficulties."

The sheriff pointed his forefinger as though it were a gun.

"What's your phony game?" he demanded. "What aces have you got a deal off the bottom of the pack? What's all this about cleaning up Sunday Slough?"

"Well," said Speedy seriously and gently, "you know how it is. Every man ought to have some civic interest in his life. And it seems to me that I might take a hand with Sunday Slough. You agree?"

The sheriff leaned back in his chair. "What would you do to Sunday Slough?" he asked.

"I'd make it quiet at night," said the boy. "I could hardly sleep last night, if you'll believe me."

"Well, I'll be—" began the sheriff.

He broke off to remark: "Yeah, I'll believe you. Son, if you wanta be a deputy, it means signing a paper and swearing an oath to do your duty and execute the law!"

"I know that," said the boy.

"I have a paper here. You slap your name down on this line—that's right—John Smith is what you call yourself, is it? Well, that's all right, too. Now, here's a Bible to swear on. Where's that book? Here it is. You lay your hand on this and repeat after me."

So, hand raised, Speedy repeated the oath of service.

When he had ended, the sheriff swallowed hard and said: "Now you're my man. The law's man, I mean to say."

"That's correct," said Speedy.

The sheriff cleared his throat. He looked down to the desk to keep the burning delight from showing in his eyes.

"You can start on the job right now," he said. "Up at Castle Ford there's a man I want brought into town. His name is Cliff Derrick. I'll write out the description for you!"

CHAPTER 7

The written description of the famous Cliff Derrick did not amount to a great deal, but the running comment with which the sheriff eked out his written phrases was interesting.

He wrote down: "Height about five feet eleven, weight a hundred and sixty-five, complexion fair to medium, features average, habits quiet, no scars or distinguishing marks. Age, anywhere between twenty-eight and forty."

Then he said aloud: "You see that he's kind of an average. He looks tall to a short man and average to a tall man. To you he'd look about the right height, Speedy. What I mean, he wouldn't seem either tall or short. Now you take his complexion, there's a lot of difference of opinion, and I've seen some that said he was sandy and some said golden-haired, some brown and some black-haired."

"Yeah," said Mike, "I met up with a gent from Carson once that said he knew Cliff Derrick personal, and knew him well, and he said that Cliff was a dark gent that had black hair and black eyes."

"Perhaps he dyes his hair or wears a wig," suggested Speedy with an amiable smile.

"How would he go about dyeing his eyes?" asked the sheriff rather sternly. Then he added: "No, he's just kind of average all over. He's the kind of a gent that'd lose himself in any crowd as quick as he entered it. He dresses the same. In town he's like any ordinary townsman. And out here on the range he just looks like a kind of a rusty cowpuncher, is all. Understand?"

"He must be a clever fellow," said Speedy, nodding.

"Clever? He's Cliff Derrick!" said One-eyed Mike. "Don't forget that. You write that down in your books, will you?"

"Yes, I'll write that name down in my mind," agreed the boy.

The sheriff stood up, brusquely ending the interview.

He said: "You get paid off at the end of each week. But you get traveling expenses and the price of a hoss, cost of hoss to be charged agin' you unless it's used up logical and right in the execution of business."

"For instance," said One-eyed Mike in kind explanation, "suppose that Derrick was to choose to dump your hoss before he dumped you, that would be regular execution of your duty, eh?"

"Yes, I'll have to get a horse," said Speedy. "How much should I pay for one?"

"About a hundred dollars ought to get you a high-grade mustang—really high. Hosses are dirt cheap around here. You can get a ride for twenty dollars. But I'm talkin' about a hoss that might be able to follow Derrick's dust for a coupla miles."

"Where shall I look for a horse?"

"Down at Seeman's place. He's always got a flock of hosses on tap. You go down and try him. So long, Speedy. Here's luck to you."

"Thanks," said Speedy. "I hope the talk dies down and the newspaper chokes before I get back from the trail."

"By the time you get back," said the sheriff, "there won't be any more talk. Don't worry about that! When you come back here with Derrick in your pocket, there won't be any more talk at all!"

They watched the youth through the doorway, and One-eyed Mike was rubbing his red knuckles still redder against the side of his trousers.

"I dunno how it is," he said, "but every time I see the

33

mug of that kid I want to take and sock him on the jaw."

"It's a kind of a nacheral instinct," agreed the sheriff. "The butt of a gun would suit me as well as a fist, though."

"Leave Derrick to do a better job than we'd do," suggested Mike Doloroso. "The beautiful part about Derrick is that he don't care what tool he uses. He's choked men with his bare hands and he's knifed 'em in the back. He's shot 'em down in fair fight, and also from behind a rock or a bush. I wish that he would use all of them methods on that kid—all of them together. That's what I wish."

"I hope your wish works out," said the sheriff. "Now, you climb the frame of the best hoss you got and slide up the trail to Castle Ford. You find Cliff Derrick and you tell him that there's a deputy of mine that's got out of hand and that is sure going to gun for him. Give him a description of the fool, and leave the rest to Derrick. Now, you mush, and don't quit galloping till you see Derrick face to face. When you get near the ford, you start whistling two notes, one high and one low. They say that that's the call for Derrick. Beat it, Mike!"

In the meantime, Speedy had gone not to the corral of Seeman, the horse dealer, but to the hotel where the Federal marshal was staying. Thomas Gray never refused to see a man; he saw Speedy now, and the boy said to him: "Marshal Gray, I've heard a lot about you, and I've come around to ask some advice from you, because I've been appointed deputy sheriff here, and I want to know what I should do to follow in your footsteps."

The marshal heard this odd speech without enthusiasm. He said: "Are you another one of Buck Masters' seven-day men? Well, son, tell me, were you born in the saddle? Can you shoot, too?"

"I can hit the side of a barn when it's not too far away," admitted Speedy.

"Are you being funny?" said the marshal.

34

"No, I'm saying the truth, and nothing but the truth. I can stay on the back of a horse so long as it doesn't run too hard. When it comes to bucking, the first jump slams me on the ground."

The marshal mastered his sense of scorn.

"Let me see your guns," he commanded.

"I don't carry any guns," said the boy.

"What!"

"Guns go off and hurt a lot of people by accident," suggested Speedy by way of explanation.

"Yeah, they hurt a lot of people," said the marshal. "You're planning to go out on the trail and catch men when you can't ride a real horse and can't shoot with a gun? You mean a revolver. Of course, you're at home with a rifle?"

Speedy had come near. He talked after the fashion of those people who seem incapable of expressing themselves in words unless they have buttonholed a victim. The marshal shrank twice from this close approach, until the wall was at his back. Then, in great disgust, he was forced to remain in his place.

"No, I'm not at home with a rifle, either," said Speedy. "I don't believe in bloodshed, Marshal Gray," he added with a frank smile. "I couldn't use either a knife or a gun on any man."

"Boy," said Gray, tormented almost beyond endurance, "you dunno what you're talking about. Either you're a born fool or a fool by cultivation. I tell you what. Some of the men that have to be chased on these mountain trails would turn around and swallow you. About one in three of them would as soon die as be caught by the law. And every man jack of them can ride anything that walks and shoot the eye out of a turkey's head at a hundred yards."

"You don't think that I'm worth giving advice to?" asked Speedy sadly.

"Son," said Thomas Gray, "I hate to be rude. But I also hate to waste my time. I'm a busy man. This is right in the middle of a busy day. I've got to say good-by."

"That's all right," said Speedy, and left the room at once. He even paused in the doorway to nod and bow and regret that he had come at the wrong moment; the marshal watched these pretty manners with increased contempt until Speedy suddenly bowed to the floor, exclaiming: "Hello, what's this? Somebody leaving gold watches instead of calling cards at your door, marshall?"

He came back, carrying the massive old watch in his hand, the great chain with huge links dangling far down.

And he said: "Who could have done this, marshal?"

Gray found something very familiar about the look of that watch and chain, and now he fumbled at his breast pocket. His fine old watch was gone, and so was the heavy chain and the bar that kept it attached to the buttonhole in the lapel of his coat.

He exclaimed: "What in blazes!" Then he reached out and took the watch. It had belonged to his father before him; he loved it as the apple of his eye.

"And this pencil was lying there beside the watch, silver case and all," went on Speedy. "To any nothing of this lapis lazuli stone and the scarf pin that it's set in."

Marshal Gray took back his property, item by item.

Finally, he uttered a great sigh, went to the door, slammed it, and came back to his guest.

"Now," said the marshal, "who are you, anyway?"

"Just a fellow with a friendly feeling and idle hands," said Speedy. "That's all. One must have occupation for the fingers or the mind practically dies of boredom. Am I wrong?"

"You could keep a whole crowd entertained," said the marshal. "You oughta do this thing on the stage."

"I left the stage to find excitement," said Speedy. "I want you to show me how to get it around this town. D'you know?"

36

CHAPTER 8

The marshal was a man with a sense of humor, though as a rule his smiles dawned but slowly. On this occasion, however, he grinned very widely, and afterward he said: "Now, Speedy, since that's the name that you choose to be called by, tell me just what your game is. What is this stuff of yours about going after bad men? What do you want, Speedy?"

With his ingratiating smile, the tramp said: "The fact is that I'm working as a sworn deputy sheriff. It wasn't a hard job to get, either. And I want to hold that job until I've cleaned up Sunday Slough."

The marshal grew sober and nodded.

"What sort of cleaning up?" he asked. "Or is this just a little lark for you?"

"I'll tell you the story in short," said Speedy. "I've never worked with my hands. I never intend to. And the same feeling is what puts a lot of fellows on the bum."

"The very same," said the marshal, while his teeth clicked on the last word and his eyes glinted.

Speedy did not seem to notice these signs of disgust.

He merely said: "Some of the boys who go overland, like the life. They never tire of it. I'm one of that kind. But some of them don't take to it at all. It goes well till the first frosts, as you might say, and then they wish that they'd been ants instead of grasshoppers. I knew a big Swede of a lad by the name of Pier Morgan who was on the bum for two years because he wanted to be President of the United States and didn't wish to start in by selling newspapers. Maybe you've met that kind yourself?"

"Yeah. I've met 'em," said Thomas Gray with another click of his strong, short-ground teeth.

"But after he'd been a tramp for two years," said the boy, "he decided that there was nothing in travel except a pain in the head. He decided that he'd go to work. I told him that he ought to go back East, where there's more law than order, so to speak. But he wanted the West because he was Western. He picked on the new mining camp, Sunday Slough. He told me that the West was the land of opportunities and new-made lives. I agreed with him, all right. But I told him that Sunday Slough was also a place where he would have plenty of opportunity to get a knife in the back or a bullet through the head. He listened, but he wasn't impressed. He was one of those fellows who trust the strength in their hands. He never hit a man when he was down, and he never used a club or a gun or a knife, not even on a shack. Personally, I'd make an exception against the brakies. Wouldn't you?"

The marshal could not avoid another smile, but he put it out like a snuffed candle.

"Go on," said he. "What happened to Pier Morgan?"

"He came out here and struck it rich," said the boy. "For three months he worked like a sailor and rolled up a big pile. Then the crooks got hold of him. A thug jumped his claim. He asked the law to help him. The law dumped him in jail! Then he tried to fight his way out, and the law brained him and put a couple of bullets through him. It threw him out on the junk heap, and there I happened to come along and find him. So I packed him to a safe place."

"What place?" asked the marshal.

"A place out of town," said the boy calmly. "And spent the time in between seeing how a tough lad could beat a smashed head and a high fever when he only had about a quart of his blood left in him. It was a good show, and the last I saw of it he seemed likely to get well. When I saw that,

I thought that I'd come into Sunday Slough and see some of the wheels that run it. I mean, I wanted to see Judge Bertram Daly, and Sheriff Buck Masters, and Sid Levine, who owns them both. I haven't seen the judge yet, but I've heard a good deal about him."

He paused.

"You mean," said the marshal, "that you think these men double-crossed your friend?"

"I mean," said Speedy, "that Sid Levine owns that mine today through one of his hired men, that the sheriff rolled poor Morgan for his wad, and that Judge Daly put him in jail to keep. I mean that Buck Masters beat up Morgan when he tried to get away, and shot him up just for fun afterward, and threw him out on the junk heap, as I was saying."

"What do you mean by the junk heap?" asked the marshal.

"I mean the hospital. You know they have a hospital. It isn't a place to cure a man. It's a place to show him the quickest way to the grave."

"Speedy," said the man of the law, "I'm afraid that you're one of these fellows who thinks that every sheriff and judge in the land is a crook."

"You're wrong," said Speedy. "I've had a good deal to do with sheriffs and judges here and there in my day, and I've found them pretty hard, but pretty fair on the whole. My own hands follow their own way to a living, but I admire the fellows who go it straight."

"You're a queer fellow, Speedy," said the marshal, knitting his brows. "I don't think that I'll ever find another of your type."

"I'm not a type. I'm a new kind of business," said the boy.

"Let it go at that. But what is your idea in being made a deputy sheriff?"

"I'm going to get a hold on this town. I'm going to get such a hold on public opinion that the sheriff and the judge and even Sid Levine can't throw me out. So I angled for the deputy-sheriff job, and the first thing I'm to do in that capacity is to go after Cliff Derrick."

The marshal shook his head. "I see how it is," he said. "You're still young enough to daydream. Derrick is a wild cat. A wild cat with brains better than his claws, even. He's a graduate student, my lad!"

Speedy merely said: "I'm going after Derrick. I don't want your help to get him. I want your help to hold him."

"Say that again," suggested Thomas Gray.

"These thugs who run Sunday Slough," said the boy, "will never keep a fellow like Derrick in their jail. He has too much money to oil their hands. They couldn't keep their grip on him! But you could. Would you do it?"

Said the marshal: "There's nothing that I want more in the world than to lay hold on Cliff Derrick. He's poison in the world's system. Particularly in the part of the world that I know."

"Good," said Speedy.

"My lad," said Gray, "I'll tell you what I'll do. I'll ride with you!"

"That's a compliment," said Speedy, "that I appreciate a lot. But the fact is that I have to play my game alone or not at all. I can't explain. But I have to ride my own way. I just want to know if you're with me; if you'll take two steps in my direction in case of a pinch, and if you can take over Derrick on a Federal charge when I bring him in. Later on, if I should corner the Levine gang, would you back me up to the limit? I supply the men and the evidence. You simply stand at my shoulder to show people that I'm on the right side. Can you do that?"

"It's the strangest suggestion that I ever have heard," said the other. "I'm to be your ace up the sleeve. Is that it? Well, Speedy, if you act the way you talk, you can play me for all I'm worth."

Speedy smiled gently on him.

"That makes everything twice as easy for me," said he.

"Except," said the marshal, "that I still don't see why you should risk your life by trying to capture Cliff Derrick, when the men you really want to get at are the ones here in Sunday Slough."

"Now," said Speedy, "I'm nobody. But suppose that I could manage to land Derrick; the Slough would know me then. And all the Levines in the world couldn't discharge me unless I wanted to lose my job."

At this the marshal nodded. But he was still frowning.

"I've heard of many strange things," he said, "but I've never heard of saving a town for law and order in spite of itself. There are ten crooks here for every honest man. But try your luck. I hope that everything goes smoothly for you. But if you were a son of mine, by thunder, I'd throw you into an asylum for the insane!"

"Oh, I know how it is," said Speedy. "And nothing is any good until it works! Good-by, Marshal Gray, and thanks a lot."

He left the marshal and went toward the horse yards of Seeman, the big dealer.

He found that worthy in person and in a softened humor because he had just succeeded in selling a dozen Mexican mules for double their real value.

"Well, whacha want, son?" asked Seeman.

"What's the wisest thing on four feet?" asked the boy. "Something that can't step in a gopher hole, or step on a rock that's likely to roll over, or get dizzy with height, or lose a trail in the dark."

"What about speed, good disposition, and such things?" asked the dealer, yawning. "Want them things?"

"I don't care about 'em," said the boy. "I don't want a beast that bucks. But it can have a mouth like iron, and a pace like a snail. I don't care, so long as it doesn't mind a guitar jangling on its back and a rider that doesn't keep a tight rein."

"You've give me the word picture of a mountain mule," said Seeman, grinning. "An old mountain mule. There's one over there. Forty dollars' worth of him. He's eighteen years old. He'll never work in a team. But he'll carry a rider or a light pack. Is that long-drawn-out piece of nothing what you're looking for?"

"He's mine," said the boy, and counted the money into the hand of the dealer.

A twenty-dollar excuse for a saddle completed the picture. Speedy loaded onto his new purchase himself, his guitar, some jerked venison, and some parched corn. Indians could travel on such rations, and so could he.

When all of these preparations had been completed, he moved out of Sunday Slough mounted upon the back of the gray mule, a back as stiff and twice as high as a hurdle.

But he was quite content, and as he reached the open trail beyond the town he unlimbered his guitar and sang to himself and the great mountains as cheerfully as a lark.

CHAPTER 9

For a mile they stumbled up the trail toward Castle Ford in this fashion, the gray mule going slower and slower, but at last the rider abandoned the mule altogether, seeming to prefer to walk in the woods or the shrubbery at his side.

The gray veteran of many a whip stroke strove vainly to understand this. He knew men in all their moods, he felt, but never before in his experience had he encountered such a master as this!

Even when the man was on his back it had not mattered

whether he went fast or slow, until at last his progress had simply been from one bunch of grass on the trail side to another.

Now the man abandoned him entirely to his own devices.

The gray mule felt lonely. For he knew how to employ wile against wile, and endure brutality until he had a chance at the year's end to repay it all with a single stroke of the hoof. On one occasion, above all others glorious, he had kicked a fat and cruel master straight through the side of the barn. For that coup he had waited and planned for weeks and months.

Now, however, he was introduced to a master of a different kind. If he wandered from the trail far to either side, or if he attempted to turn back on the way, he was quickly herded back in the desired direction. But on the whole, there was no point in turning back. The trail was dim with the grass that grew upon it. What a luxury it was to eat one's way through the working day, so to speak!

So the gray mule contentedly marched ahead. Now and then he paused for a mouthful. Now and then he even defied almost certain fate, as it seemed to him, and stood deliberately still, chewing the last bite and looking about him with his red-stained, cat-quick eyes.

No, it seemed literally that the blow would never fall. In fact, nothing that he did mattered very much, as it appeared, to this young master who drifted through the tall brush and the woods to the right of the trail.

The gray mule began to grow mildly excited. It was impossible that real hope could ever again warm that scarred heart of his, but he was filled with wonder; he wanted to know when the catastrophe would occur.

Presently he thought that he had the answer.

He had gone on into the golden end of the day, when the sun was almost ready to sink behind the western mountains. And now, when the woods were growing as dark as thickly rolling smoke, out of a copse came a rider, moving cautiously on a horse of fine fettle that threw up its head and danced over the ground.

The mule paused, and would have sneered except that his upper lip was crammed too full of grass. He despised horses even more than he hated men. For horses were the willing servants; they were stupid brutes who would not rebel against whip or spur.

He tossed his head, which was rather lightened than weighed down by this consideration.

And now the rider came close and peered at him, and rode still closer and lifted the flap of a saddle pocket. He pulled out a strip of dried venison, sniffed at it, and then threw it away with an oath of contempt. It was apparent that he himself lived upon much better fare.

He was a big man on a big horse. He had a rough black mustache that thrust out on either side of his face, almost as far as the edge of the brim of his sombrero.

Now he cursed again and shrugged his shoulders.

"This oughta be the mule," he said. "That son of a gun, that Mart Ransome, he's cut in ahead of me and snaked the kid out of his saddle. I'm gunna give Mart Ransome a good bust on the jaw for that trick!"

He sat his horse again for another moment, pondering, hand upon hip. Should he take in the mule? Well, there was no use in taking the mule. His orders were for the man, not the saddle he rode in.

So presently, with a shrug of his shoulders, he rode on up the trail at an easy dogtrot, the supple fetlock joints of the horse so bending that the rider did not stir in the saddle. And in this manner he reached a point not many yards ahead of the patient mule, where the brush grew up close on the righthand side of the trail.

Here a shadow arose softly and suddenly upon his right hand. He did not really see it. He sensed it, as a man of hair-trigger nerves will receive indications from the very corner of the eye. And in one instant he leaned forward, spurred his horse, and snatched out a revolver.

He was turning his head about, naturally, in the very same instant, when he saw a lithe youngster springing at him, already shooting through the air as if jumping from a spring. Then, like the flick of a whiplash, a lean, hard, sinewy arm jerked about his throat and hurled him backward over the croup of his saddle, with all the more force because his mount was springing away under the stroke of the spur.

He landed hard, but he was not knocked senseless by the fall. He was a rugged fellow who had had plenty of falls before this, and now he loosened his muscles and fell with an inertness that distributed the shock instead of concentrating it with bone-breaking force upon the point of the impact.

He landed and rolled as he landed. He strove to roll on top of the assailant, but hand and knee missed the mark. In his second effort he succeeded, for the stranger had concentrated an instant too long in getting hold of the gun hand of the rider close to the wrist.

Yet, just as the man of the black whiskers struggled on top of his foe a strange thing happened, for it seemed as though a band of hot iron contracted around his right wrist and then twisted. It was exquisite pain, for the tendons rubbed against both the surface muscles and the underlying bone. His senseless fingers were forced to abandon their hold, and the gun fell.

It was picked up at once, and the hard muzzle of it pressed against him.

He was brave, he was rough, he was experienced in many battles. But, like the little boy when the blood from his own nose stains his hand, he knew when he was licked.

He grunted: "That's enough."

"All right," said Speedy. "Take yourself off of me, then, will you? Wait a minute!"

Reaching his other hand inside the coat of the man on top, he pulled out a second gun.

The latter arose slowly. To the last instant he was hoping against hope that the confidence of victory would dim the hawklike coldness of the eye that watched him. But that eye did not dim, and like a wise man who cares something for his own scalp, he stood up and watched the youngster rise slowly and shake himself, getting rid of the dust of the trail just as a dog would have done.

"Well, here we are," said Speedy, "and I take it that you know me, but that I don't know you!"

"Name of Doc Morris," said the other. "And I don't know you, brother. What made you jump at me like a ferret jumps at a rabbit?"

"What sent you down this trail as far as a gray mule and then back again?" asked Speedy.

"I had the bad luck to meet up with Bud Henderson," said the other, "and Bud, he said that there was a crook that had stole an old gray mule from him, and that he didn't mind the mule, but that he'd give a hundred bucks to the gent that brought in the thief. That's all, partner. Who are you?"

Speedy regarded him for a moment with those dangerously gentle eyes of his. Then he said: "Did my friend Derrick only offer a hundred dollars to you for bringing me into camp? Is that all he offered?"

"Derrick?" said the other. "Derrick's got nothing to do with it. Derrick ain't in this part of the country, is he?"

"Where is he, then?" said the boy.

"Why, he's down Tucson way. That's where he is."

"Is that where he is?" said Speedy. "But I think you'll lead me to him this side of Tucson just the same."

CHAPTER 10

The big man scowled. Then he said: "Look here, brother. You've handed me some strange language. As if I could tell you where Derrick is! As if I could lead you to him!"

He put a great deal of astonished and half-scornful emphasis into the last remark.

Speedy lifted one of the guns which he was now carrying, balanced it in his hand, and advanced the muzzle until it was only a few inches from the breast of the other.

Then he said: "Why should I hold off? If I hadn't seen you first, you would have made hash of me, eh? Or else you would have taken me back to Cliff Derrick. I'd like to stay here and bandy lies with you. But I haven't the time. I've got to be quick and mean, and that's hard luck for you. I know it, and I'm sorry about it. But facts are facts. I'm telling you a fact now. If you can't talk, say your prayers. Make them short, because I don't know how long it'll be before another of your gang pops up on the trail."

He fingered the trigger of the gun as he spoke, and the big man suddenly groaned, and his knees sagged.

"Don't do that," he whispered, as though loud speaking might touch off the explosion. "Don't do that, because those guns shoot by looking at 'em. They really do. Quit monkeying with 'em, will you?"

"Do I care if I put a slug through you?" asked Speedy.

The other replied: "Do you care if you hang for it afterward?"

"After I collect the reward on you," said Speedy, "I'll have to be hung for some other job."

"Reward?" gasped the big man.

He seemed to wilt, like lettuce under hot water.

"Why d'you think I'm here?" said Speedy scornfully.

"Why, you're trying to get at Derrick like a—"

He stopped himself. He realized now that he had already said too much.

"I'm here for Derrick," said Speedy, "and you're the fellow to lead me to him. Or else you're the man to drop right here on the trail. I'll collect on you after I've handled the rest of the job."

He jerked the gun a trifle higher.

"You poor fool," said Speedy, "d'you think that I value your life for a nickel? You're wanted, and you're wanted badly by those who will pay for your scalp. I'd as soon shoot you as shoot a coyote in a trap!"

The other raised a hand and pressed it against his face.

Then he said: "I reckon you would. I didn't know that anybody in this part of the world knew me. I didn't know they knew the price on me. But bad news will jump a thousand miles of range like an open ditch. Only, you tell me who sent you after Sam Morrison, will you?"

Speedy could hardly refrain from smiling. He was rather glad that, as the sun began to set, the rosy glow was somewhat of a veil over his features.

"You don't expect me to talk, Sam," said he, "when you're the one who ought to answer questions? I told you before what I want. Now give me an answer. You're walking the tight wire, but you're not dropping off it yet."

"Ask me again what you want," said Sam Morrison. "You see how it is. I'm kind of dizzy. I dunno what struck me from the time you jumped out of the ground and exploded a ton of dynamite under my nose. What is it that you want to know?"

"The way to Derrick."

"I dunno," said Morrison.

48

"Sam," answered Speedy, "I'm trying to be patient, but every minute I know where you ought to be, and every minute I'm trying to keep myself from putting you there. Are you going to use sense or are you going to bury yourself here?"

He added: "I don't much care. Perhaps I ought to bump you off for a beginning and take on the trailing job myself later on. I couldn't trust you. You're a liar now, and you'll still be a liar five minutes from now."

The big man sagged again.

He said: "Speedy—that's what they call you, isn't it?— Speedy, you've got me cold. I don't want to turn the chief in, but it's either him or me!"

"What would he do if he were in the same pinch?" asked the boy curiously.

"Maybe he wouldn't double-cross nobody," admitted Morrison. "He's kind of funny that way. He sticks to his words, all right. They say that he'd sooner die. But I'd like to see him in a pinch like this. You'd get some chatter out of him then, I lay my coin. Speedy, I'm gunna come clean. I'll take you inside of a hundred yards of Derrick's camp. After that you can find your way. Is that a bargain? I take you there and then you turn me loose!"

"You'll have to talk a little more, first," said the boy. "Our friend Derrick, what are his plans about Sunday Slough?"

"Well, there's a lot of easy pickings over there in the Slough," said Morrison. "You know that, or I guess you wouldn't be there with your song and dance. Why shouldn't Derrick clean up on some of the easy dough, eh?"

"Why not?" murmured Speedy. "Who does he hook up with?"

"The bums that tipped him off that you were coming."

"The sheriff?"

"His pal, One-eyed Mike."

"Oh, One-eyed rode all the way out here, did he?"

"Nothing but One-eyed. He don't like you much, brother."

"No, he doesn't like me much," agreed Speedy comfortably. "Did he go back to town?"

"Yes."

"Who else is with Derrick?"

"Nobody but Joe Dale and Lefty Quinn and Ray Parker."

"Aha!" murmured Speedy, to whom all the names were new.

Morrison misunderstood the exclamation. "Yeah, he don't carry no army along with him, but he goes pretty well heeled, all the same."

"He had you, too," said Speedy.

"I'm only the roustabout in that camp," said Morrison. "You know that. I've made my little play here and there. I ain't done so bad, but over there in the Derrick camp the positions don't go by seniority. They go by order of merit. That's the way that they go. Little Joe Dale; of course, he's the kingpin. He's only eighteen, but he's got him a man a year for the last five years. You know Quinn and Parker, too, I guess. They figger pretty high in any society. That's all that you'll find over there in the camp, besides Derrick himself."

"Thanks," said Speedy, "it looks as though we can do a little business together."

"Yeah," said Morrison. "I'll tell you the way it is. I never liked the business none too good. I always wanted to be on the other side of the fence. But I got in a pinch. You know how it is."

"Yeah, I know how it is," said Speedy with sympathy in his voice. "If you decided to open up, you could tell something, Morrison. Everybody knows that."

"If I come all the way clean," said Morrison loudly. "I could wreck a lot of camps. I dunno that I'd come all the way clean, though. It'd have to be worth my while. You know how it is. I'd have to get a stake big enough to make a new start in life. Somewhere in the South Seas, say. That's about where I'd have to go!"

"Well," said Speedy, "there are all sorts of ways of arranging. About Derrick—it was Tom Gray that made him pull in his horns and try to find a new pasture, wasn't it?"

"No, it wasn't Gray," said Morrison. "He don't care about any one man."

"Doesn't he?" said Speedy dreamily.

"He don't give a dog-gone for any one man," insisted the other. "But it was Tom Gray and a lot of others. They was all bringing a lot of pressure to bear. Running Chinks is a good game. But it wasn't good enough finally to run all the risk."

"But Derrick kills them and lets them lie where they fall," said Speedy. "I should think that he would have cleaned out the bunch that have been following him."

"Kills them and lets them lie? Who's been telling you that, Speedy?"

"I've heard people say it."

"Sure, every fourflusher in the land is always giving everybody the low-down on Derrick. But it ain't true. The fact is he don't like killings. He says that one killing is worse than stealing a million dollars. It's the one thing that leaves a trail so rank that a sheriff can follow it. Even a sheriff!"

He laughed, but not heartily, for he still was not feeling quite up to himself.

"So he didn't try to shoot himself out of the trouble?" said Speedy.

"No, that's what he didn't do. Some of the boys said that with Tom Gray gone the rest would scatter, but he wouldn't see it that way. He said that he wanted a change of air, anyway. And maybe he did, because he's always working pretty hard. That's the way he is. Got his nose to the grindstone all the time."

"I see," said Speedy, somewhat vaguely.

Then he added: "Lead off, old son, and I'll follow. I want

to get to that camp a little after sunset. Is there time, do you think?"

"Plenty of time, and the shooting light will still be pretty good," said Morrison.

He added: "You know, I can tell you a lot more later on, while we're riding in."

"You've said enough, Sam, already," said a quiet voice.

And Speedy remembered afterward that big Morrison screamed as he heard the first sound of the voice, screamed before the report of the gun, before the bullet could possibly have reached him. Then he toppled slowly backward, his arms flung out, and seemed to be trying to touch the ground behind him with his hands, like an acrobat. Then he collapsed along the grass.

CHAPTER 11

There were two guns in the hands of Speedy, but he made no attempt to use them. His reason was, first of all, that he knew the man who had spoken behind him was beyond doubt a master of such weapons; in the second place, he had never used a gun, and it was written in the strange list of his principles that he never should.

The gunman in the rear did not speak. Sam Morrison lay on the ground with one arm twisted under his head, as though he were asleep. From that sleep, Speedy knew, the man would never awaken.

Then he said: "If you don't mind, I'll turn around and take it from in front."

"Why do you care about that?" said the quiet-spoken stranger from the rear. "You'll fill the same spot in Hades whether you go there backward, or face first, or upside down."

"It's a question of tombstones," said Speedy.

"There's still a bit of light good enough for shooting," said the man to the rear. "Tell me the riddle about the tombstones."

"What are they going to do back there in Sunday Slough?" asked Speedy. "I mean, what will they do for a fool who was shot while he was running away? Why, they'll simply put a half-rotten shingle at the head of his mound of earth, and then they'll write on it in pencil the name and the date. That's all. But suppose that I'm shot between the eyes? They'll wrap me in silk and put up a chunk of granite half the size of a house and write on it with chisels about another of Sunday Slough's seven-day men, gone in the good cause."

There was a breathless pause.

"You're a wit," said the man behind. "I came near laughing at that, Speedy."

"Besides, you ought to consider yourself," said Speedy. "If you get me from behind, you're just a thug. If you nail me from in front, it's another good scalp to dry over the smoke of your lodge fire. You ought to think of that, Derrick."

"You know my voice, do you?" said the other.

"I don't," said Speedy. "I know your ways, though."

"Turn around and tell me what you know about my ways," said the stranger.

Speedy turned, and he saw a form which did not at all conform with what he had heard about Derrick from the sheriff. Rather, this man was neither tall nor short, but distinguished by a sense of animal strength and adroitness, as perceptible as it is in a wild cat about to spring. He carried his gun not more than hip-high, but it was plain that even from that position it would not miss its mark.

"Nobody else would have been so sure," said Speedy as

53

he looked at the outlaw. "When men have a double target, they make the second shot come tripping on the heels of the first one. But when you had Morrison out of the way, you preferred to wait for me."

"Why didn't you drop and start shooting from the ground?" asked the other, calmly curious.

"There would have been no good in that," said Speedy. "You would have split my backbone before I'd dropped halfway to the ground. I know how fast a fellow shoots when he fans a gun. Even if you missed dead center with the first slug, it would roll your man over and rattle him while you got in the second wallop. No, I'm pleased enough to be standing here for a few seconds, and to get the pepper in the eyes instead of behind the ears."

"You have your own viewpoint," said the outlaw. "We might even have a chat together, you and I, if you wish to. Mind you, at ten o'clock I have to be riding, and before I ride, you're going to be a dead man, Speedy. Is that clear? But if you want to sit about a while and chat, you're welcome."

"Of course, I'd rather come along," said Speedy. "You know how it is. We all have plenty of time to push the daisies, but not so long for talking with a Derrick or a Speedy. You want these guns, I suppose?"

"Just drop them on the ground," said Derrick, "and then turn about and walk straight ahead. Morrison had started you on the right track."

Speedy obeyed. And behind him he heard his captor following close and closer. It was the golden dusk just before twilight that filled the air and filtered among the trees. Overhead he heard the last chattering of squirrels, the sleepy murmurings of birds, and above all, the raucous yell of a blue jay as it dipped across the treetops.

They went on through the trees for hardly more than half a mile, and then they came very suddenly on the ruins of a cabin. Inside the house, a light burned; a fire glowed outside it.

Before they quite reached the place: "Hello!" sang out a voice.

"It's all right," said Derrick.

"It's the chief," said the other, and stepped out into view. He was carrying a shotgun, a fellow who looked very much like a cowpuncher. He walked with a limp, and he had shoulders so broad and hips so narrow that the belt seemed to be pinching him in two.

"Who's this?" he asked.

"This is Speedy," said Derrick.

"You got the man-catcher pretty pronto," said the other without excitement.

"This is Lefty Quinn," said Derrick, by way of introduction.

All three of them went on toward the shack together, and outside it, at the fire, they found two more men busily roasting meat on the ends of small sticks. The fumes of coffee were fragrant in the air.

"This is Joe Dale," said Derrick, pointing to the smaller of the pair, a quick nervous boy. "And this is Ray Parker."

The latter was a handsome fellow in a dark, rather greasy fashion. He smiled and nodded as he heard the name of Speedy. But Dale said: "What's the idea of leading up a sheriff to mug us all, Derrick?"

"My idea is that he'll never report the good news," said the chief.

"But what—" began Dale in a complaining voice.

"Aw, don't be a fool," said Parker. "He means that Speedy is gunna—well, he's gunna put on wings before very long."

"Some time before ten o'clock," said Derrick, "but he wanted to see us before we parted. He's not like most of the others we've had on the trail here and there. I'm glad to feed him before he passes out."

Then he added: "Look here, Lefty. Back there you'll find Morrison's horse, and Morrison, and a gray mule. Drag Morrison over to the first patch of rocks south of the trail and drop him in a crevice. You might use a stick of dynamite to blow some stones over him and make him a grave."

"Did the kid, here, kill Morrison?" asked Lefty angrily.

"No, I did." answered their chief.

"It's a dirty job you've signed me up for," said Lefty, more gloomily than before.

"You can reward yourself," answered Derrick. "He still has something in his pockets."

"He owed me forty dollars," said Ray Parker. "Don't forget to set that aside for me out of what he has, Lefty."

"He can pay his own debts," muttered Lefty Quinn, and left the camp, swinging with a creak of saddle leather onto the back of one of several horses which stood in readiness for instant use.

As he disappeared, Parker said: "I don't like that. Morrison owed me forty dollars. I oughta get that money out of him."

"You should have got it living," said the chief. "The loot that's on him belongs to Lefty Quinn, now. I said it did."

"What about his horse? That ain't 'on' him," suggested Parker.

"That's a four-hundred-dollar horse, but you have it to pay back the forty," answered the chief. "I'll tell Lefty when he brings it in."

"Lefty'll be wild," suggested Parker, grinning.

"No. There's a two-hundred-dollar watch on Morrison, and those emeralds in that ring of his are worth four or five thousand of anybody's money."

"Great Scott!" cried Parker. "You letting Lefty go west with all that loot, and for nothing but chucking a stiff among some rocks?"

"That's all. I have to pay my men high to keep them contented," said the chief. "You've had your turns here and there, Ray. You'll have more turns later on."

Joe Dale had taken no part in the conversation. He remained squatting on his heels, taking charge of the turning of half a dozen of the spits, on the ends of which large chunks of meat were smoking and roasting, black and brown.

Into that rising smoke he exclaimed suddenly: "Whacha go and kill my partner for, Derrick?"

There was a ring of cold animosity in his voice. He did not look at Derrick, but he did not need to. That voice was the last growl of a dog before it jumps for the throat.

Derrick regarded the angry boy with a faint smile, as though he enjoyed this attitude of the lad.

He said: "I never knew that Morrison was a special partner of yours. I've heard you curse him pretty hotly now and then. I never knew that he was a partner of yours."

"You know it now," said Dale in the most offensive way. "Whacha go and kill Sam for, Derrick?"

"Because he'd double-crossed all of us, and was bringing Speedy in to bag us," said the chief.

Dale jumped to his feet.

"You lie!" he cried.

CHAPTER 12

It is almost the only word that cannot be used in the West. You may curse a man in ancestral terms and still remain within the terms of familiar conversation. You may, indeed, call him all sorts of a liar in the most colorful vocabulary. But never, if you are wise, use the verb. Never tell a man that he lies.

And now Speedy, with a spark of growing hope, watched the pair. If they fought, he would wager his chances at better than even that he could get away during the tumult.

Perhaps Derrick realized it, also. At any rate, he controlled himself. The flash of a gun would have been justified at that moment, but instead he said: "You're letting that meat burn, Joe."

Dale barked: "I'm gunna have an answer."

"You'll be answered when your hide is full," said Derrick.

Dale was as small as he had been described. But it was the smallness of a bull terrier. No mastiff could bully him with impunity. Now he shivered and shook like a dog with his beastly desire for battle.

"I'm going to be answered!" insisted Dale, but his voice had grown more quiet, and he sank down on his heels to tend the meat again, scowling.

Ray Parker, from the farther side of the fire, looked on complacently at this scene, as though he would enjoy the fight, even though it meant the end of the gang's work. He even shrugged his shoulders with disappointment when he saw Dale sit down again.

But the latter was not finished.

He said presently: "What makes you think that Morrison double-crossed us?

"By hearing him talk," said Derrick, as calm as ever.

And yet, in some strange manner, he had not in the least compromised his dignity. Without lifting his voice, without betraying the slightest emotion, he seemed as ready to put a bullet into Dale as the boy was to shoot his leader.

"You hear him talk? To whom?" demanded Dale, turning the spits, blind with anger.

"To Speedy," said Derrick.

"It don't sound likely," said Dale. "It's hard to believe."

"You've called me a liar once," said Derrick.

There was only a shade of emphasis on the last word, but

that shade was deadly enough. It made Dale look up fiercely, as though ready to spring. But he checked himself long enough to ask: "What made him talk? What made him talk to Speedy? Was he out for blood money? Is that what you mean? Tell me what you mean!"

"I mean," answered Derrick, "that he was caught by Speedy, snaked off his horse, and threatened. When he was threatened, he yelped like a dirty yellow hound and started to tell everything he knew."

"Dirty—yellow—" began Dale, enraged more than ever. Then he altered his voice and muttered: "You say that this here—this kid, here—he snaked Morrison off his horse? Speedy may say so, but he never done it!"

"Speedy did it. I saw him do it," said the leader. "What's more, he worked from the ground, and jumped Morrison and jerked him off his horse. Morrison landed on top, and had a gun in his hand. Speedy took the gun away from him and shoved the Colt against Morrison's hide. Then Morrison gave up and begged."

The boyish face of Dale twisted with passion. But he was silenced for a moment. Only his harsh breathing was audible. Then he said: "I guess it ain't all made up. I guess that it's straight. But it sounds dog-gone strange to me! That's all."

The chief smiled gently on Dale.

"Furthermore," he went on, "Speedy could do the same thing to you."

"He could do the same thing to me?" asked Dale.

He jerked his head around. The cords of his thick neck stood out. His broad, blunt jaw thrust forward.

"He could do the same thing to me?" he demanded again.

"He could tie you in knots," declared Derrick calmly, obviously enjoying this bit of torment.

"Me on a hoss and him on foot?" gasped the other. "There ain't a man in the world that could do it. Guns or no guns, I'll bet you all I got that there ain't a man in the world that

59

could do it!"

Derrick smiled again.

"So you say," he remarked.

It was plain that the insulting conversation which he had endured from Dale had got under his skin.

Speedy leaned a mere trifle forward and watched.

Derrick said: "We'll call that horse of yours worth a thousand. With the money you got, you can bet three thousand. I'm going to put up that much cash against you. Parker, you can hold the stakes."

He counted out a sheaf of bills, and Joe Dale, panting with eagerness, snatched out a wallet and hurled it toward Parker.

"You know where Betsy is standing hitched," said he. "Here's my wad. Now, get the kid out here."

Speedy had been sitting on a fallen log. Now he rose and stretched himself, bit by bit, as a cat does when it thinks of night trails and night hunting.

"You know, Derrick," said he, "that I've heard a lot of talk about how much you'll get from Dale, here, if I win for you. But what do I get for myself?"

Derrick smiled his cold, thoughtful smile. "You'll get," said he, "an extra fifteen minutes. I'll delay my start till ten fifteen."

"Well, that's a bargain," said Speedy. "It won't take me more than two minutes to put down your wrestler, I suppose."

He came closer and looked from his full height into the eyes of the other. In spite of the much more powerful build of the other, Speedy seemed to look down upon a lesser man.

He said: "Are you ready, Joe?"

"Ready, and crying to go," said the other.

"That's pretty good," said Speedy. "But you'd better get on your horse first. You'll need that much height added to the little that you've got."

Dale threw back his head and strove to laugh. The sound

strangled in his throat.

"I'll need it, will I?" said he.

"Yes, you'll need it," said Speedy. "Give the word, though, Derrick, whenever you want us to start."

"He'll need a horse to help him get away," said Derrick scornfully. "This lesson will do you a lot of good, Joe. It ought to help make a man of you."

Parker came back, leading a magnificent baby filly with a beautiful head and a wise and kindly eye. "I've put the money in this here saddlebag," he said. "Either way the fight goes, the mare goes with it!"

CHAPTER 13

The preparations were not yet complete, however. For Lefty Quinn now returned with his errand accomplished, leading the horse of Morrison and the old gray mule. He came with his singing voice as a herald flying before him. It was plain that he had found much of value on the body of the dead man.

Now the tale of the wager in the camp had to be explained to him. He had no hesitation in plumping on Joe Dale.

"I've got four or five hundred that ain't doing a thing, Ray," he said to Parker. "I'll bet it all on Joe."

Parker wistfully, as one who loves a sporting chance, looked at Speedy and shook his head.

"He ain't got beam and muscle enough to please me," he said. "And I know what's in Joe's arms and back muscles. If he was stripped, the fight would be over before it started. Speedy would be scared to death."

"All right," said Lefty Quinn. "It looks like for once in

my life I've gotta stand by and watch a fight without having a bet on it or a hand in it."

"You may have something to do before the wind-up," said Derrick. "You and Parker are going to help me referee this fight, and if Speedy wins and seems likely to slip away, I want you to help me shoot into him. He's a tricky cat, but I think that our three guns ought to be enough to bring him back if he starts running. If he should get off, I'm going to be on Betsy, here. You don't mind me riding her, do you Joe? She's the best horse in the world when it comes to dodging her way through timber."

"She's the best horse at everything else, too," said Joe Dale. "Supposing what ain't gunna happen, happens, that the kid, here, busted loose from me and got into the woods; why, she'll run him down like a bloodhound."

"That's why I want to be on her," said Derrick.

He mounted as he spoke.

"You're gunna bust your heart because you can't win her," said Joe Dale. "Nobody's ever been on that horse without wishin' that he could pay some of his heart's blood to get her."

"That's what you felt, Joe, when you first sat on her," said Lefty Quinn. "That's why you stole her, eh?"

"Stole her? You lie!" shouted Joe Dale, now quite mad with rage. "I—I'll have a word to whisper in your ear, Quinn, you thug, when I get through with this set-up."

"All right," said Quinn, "but you'll never talk to me with your hands, you poor little man-eater. I've seen you work with 'em before. It'll be guns between us, baby!"

"I've talked till I'm blind in the face," said Joe Dale, "and now I'm gunna finish this little lunch and then—"

He did not wait for the word of signal from his leader, but making a long, light step forward, he suddenly drove his fist into the face of Speedy.

At least, so it seemed. But though the balled hand seemed

to drive straight through the head of the more slender fighter, Speedy had dipped his head to one side.

As Joe Dale, with a grunt of wasted effort, whirled about, Speedy stumbled the wrong way—stumbled toward his formidable foeman, and reached out a long left arm as though for support. The hand struck the face of Joe Dale. It struck him upon the root of the nose and bobbed even his thick head back a little.

He did not mind punishment. But it seemed to him that the slender fist of Speedy must be made of iron.

Now he came in dancing, in the style of a true pugilist. But he had changed his mind somewhat. He would not merely strive to batter his enemy with fists. That was, to be sure, the most satisfactory style. Then the work could be seen and admired by others. Instead of that, he would try a long lead, follow with a short-arm punch, and then, if neither of them stunned the youth, he would close and set his iron clutches upon Speedy.

So he came in lightly, gracefully, in spite of his bulk. He was like a toe dancer. He floated over the ground with a sure and light footing, and before him Speedy retreated, or seemed to retreat. It was hard to tell where his wavering and uncertain, fumbling steps would take him.

Only once, Derrick, from the back of the mare, cried out: "If you get that close to the edge of the trees again, Speedy, you'll take a leaden pill through the brain!"

"Oh, all right," said Speedy. "I'll watch that."

How did he dare to turn his head as he spoke? How did he dare, when such a tiger was drifting in toward him?

Joe Dale, with a brutal gleam of joy in his eyes, tasted the satisfaction that would soon be his before he had actually reaped it, and gritted his teeth as he smashed for the head with his right.

He missed the target. Yes, strange to say, the turned head jerked down at just the awkward moment, and as Joe lurched forward behind his punch, a fist circled up from nowhere, as it were, and finished its looping, overhanded course by landing again exactly upon the end of his nose!

Again he felt as though some one had struck him with a solid section of lead pipe not even masked in a rubber bit of hose. His head jerked back. He tried to clear his brain, but again and again and again that same section of leaden pipe whanged across his face!

He staggered. Dimly, out of the distance, he heard voices calling to him. But the voices were as nothing compared with two things that he saw in shadowy fashion.

The one was his chief, sitting on the back of his beloved Betsy and smiling his faint, derisive smile. The other was his antagonist standing in the middle of the firelit circle, with one hand carelessly resting upon his hip.

He was not smiling. No, he seemed far too bored for that expression of contempt. And the fire of that great anguish, self-scorn, cleared the wits of Joe Dale as if by magic.

He heard Parker's voice saying: "Science, that's what it is. He knows how to hit."

"It's footwork," answered Lefty Quinn. "I never seen such a pair of feet dancin'; never in my life."

Let them talk. Joe Dale could endure words, but he wondered if he could endure many more of those lead-pipe concussions of the brain. Suppose that a punch found a resting place upon the point of the chin?

He heard his chief saying: "Now, Speedy, tap him on the button and put him to sleep. I'll count the ten seconds. I'm going to make it an extra half hour for you, Speedy, instead of an extra fifteen minutes. I knew that you'd lick him, but I never dreamed that you could do it in thirty seconds!"

Thirty seconds! Was that all that had elapsed?

During that interval Joe Dale had crossed a whole continent of wretchedness and self-abasement.

Yet he had faith in himself; if not in his schooled powers

as a pugilist, at least in those hands of his, for when had their grip been broken by any antagonist, even by lumberjacks made of iron and twice his size?

He looked out from his jaw, running in with a high guard close to his face, and saw Speedy standing with a negligent hand still upon his hip.

What trick was coming, what sudden dodge?

Joe Dale hesitated as he ran, swerved like a snipe in a gale, and then, confident, leaped forward with both arms stretched out to take a wrestling hold.

Yes, there might be magic tricks of boxing, but in wrestling sheer, solid might of body and hand would be sure to count.

To his amazement, he found that the youth stood for the charge, and his thick-ribbed body struck that of Speedy and bore him back before the charge—far back toward the perilous verge of the fire, where Derrick, sitting the lovely mare beside it, called out to his champion to beware or he would be stepping soon on live coals.

But Joe Dale, laughing drunkenly, deep in his throat, had secured a grip, a plain round-the-body hold. The game was his! Then he felt something like a whiplash and a club stroke combined across the upper part of his right arm. It bruised the muscles to the bone. That was not all. It bruised the nerves as well and broke the grip in which he was so secure.

He looked up, bewildered and baffled, and saw the face of Speedy without a trace of the stain of battle rage upon it, a calm, thoughtful face. He saw the lean hand of Speedy raised, not as a fist, and not as a grasping claw, but rather as a cleaver, with the hard and seasoned rim of the palm as the edge of the cleaver.

It is said that the Japanese, by long practice, so toughen this part of the hand, and so perfect the science of delivering the blow that they can break a rounded bar of stone an inch thick.

It was such a blow that fell, now, high on the left side of

Joe Dale's tensed neck, where the big cords begin to stand out just before the neck joins the head.

And the head of Joe Dale flopped to one side as the head of a flower drops when struck by a child's stick.

Then followed a singularly light shoulder hold, aided by a tripping foot, and Joe Dale fell on his back straight into the center of the fire.

He rose again like a rocket, screeching, right under the nose of the mare, which reared high. As it reared, Speedy, or a great cat that bore his semblance, sprang upon the back of Betsy behind Cliff Derrick.

CHAPTER 14

It was not that Derrick failed to see the flying danger. He had it well in mind and eye, but just at that moment Betsy, the amiable mare which never had been known to have good manners, was trying to cakewalk, and even leaning a little backward in her effort to stand straight. He had to employ his hands to keep his place, and in the half second of the crisis, as she began to pitch down toward the ground again, Speedy landed behind the saddle and gave to the great Derrick almost exactly what he had given to Joe Dale.

But in this case the cleaver edge of his palm struck more carefully at the base of Derrick's head rather than behind the ear. He managed to draw a gun that simply fell out of his useless hand. Only vaguely his darkened eyes saw the shadowy trees flutter past, and his ears heard the crackling of bullets that pursued them.

Bullets were not the thing. What was needed was an instant riding in pursuit, for shooting from any distance was all too precarious by such a light as this.

The pursuit began. As his brain cleared a little, he could hear shouting, and then the horses crashing through the brush.

The best man of all was out of it now—Joe Dale, who must be wallowing in the cool of the mud, trying to get that coolness against every part of his seared flesh at once.

But the others were good men. Parker was a man in ten thousand, and Lefty Quinn was one in a million. If for no other reason, they would ride their horses hard and well in that pursuit because each of them was mounted on a nag given by Derrick himself.

In fact, he heard the noise of that pursuit speed closer. They were gaining fast, as in fact they were bound to do, considering that the good mare carried a double burden.

It gained, it burst full upon the ear of Derrick as he regained full consciousness, and then it swept on by him!

Amazed and bewildered, at first, after a moment he understood the simple thing that had happened. Speedy had merely taken the grave chance of pulling up the mare suddenly into the deeper shade of a thicket. His trick had borne fruit, for in the dimness of the trees the two riders had rushed past. There was something else for Derrick to think of now.

He found his hands tied behind his back, and his feet bound beneath the mare. A gag was passed between his teeth, and the cord that secured it lashed securely around his head.

A momentary hope came to him. It was the looming of a figure at the side, but now he recognized it as the old gray mule which had accompanied Speedy up the trail to the Castle Ford. Now it had followed again, and arriving at the place, it fell contentedly to grazing.

On its back Speedy mounted, hitched a rope to Betsy, the peerless mare, and went on at the dragging pace of a mule walk toward distant Sunday Slough.

He unslung a guitar that was incased at the side of the

mule, and on this he began to strum softly and to sing in a voice softer still:

> "Julia,
> You are peculiar;
> Julia,
> You are queer,
> Truly,
> You are unruly,
> As a wild Western steer!"

The great outlaw had heard that song before. Never had he heard it so well sung as at present, and never had he enjoyed the singing less. He saw the implication. He saw, moreover, the picture he would make if he were brought in this fashion into Sunday Slough, tied hand and foot!

They did not take the main trail up the valley, but obscure cattle paths that meandered back and forth, getting on at the gait of a lazy worm rather than a mounted man.

Would intelligent fellows like Lefty Quinn and savage Ray Parker surmise such a thing as this? Would they not rather feel that they had simply been outdistanced by the uncanny strength and speed of the mare and left hopelessly behind, even though she was carrying double?

Yes, in ten minutes they had probably given up the ride, or at least when they came close to the shining lights of the town.

Cliff Derrick groaned. He looked back over the course of events as they had befallen between him and the boy. It was true that he had recognized in the lad an enemy of peculiar powers. Yet it seemed that he had taken all reasonable precautions. He had sat his horse, armed to the teeth, ready to strike down the tramp with a bullet during that fight with Joe Dale.

And surely such an opportunity to give fiery Joe a lesson

was not to be wasted. Keen as a whip, ready for any emergency, brave to a fault, all that Joe needed was a severe lesson in order to make him the most valuable man that had ever worked under the leader.

It was only that he, Derrick, had failed to foresee what the mare might do, faultless as she was, if a fiery rocket exploded under her very nose!

That was the turning of the tide, and he wondered in bitterness of heart if the thing had been an accident, or if Speedy had deliberately planned it. Yes, he felt that it must have been a plan, because that would explain the manner in which Speedy had retreated with such apparent blindness to the very edge of the fire. The final flurry in which Joe had been cast into the embers of the fire was merely a part of that plan.

Cliff Derrick sat helplessly on the mare, bound hand and foot, gagged, incapable of sound or of motion! He could endure the rope that would hang him by the neck until he was dead; he could not endure the laughter with which the world would greet his capture in this fashion by a man who did not even carry a gun!

The music continued, and again the boy was singing:

> "Julia,
> You are peculiar;
> Julia,
> You are queer."

They came, in this fashion, around the shoulder of a hill, and there a solitary horseman hove in view.

He waved a hand. "Hello, stranger," he said.

"Hello," said Speedy.

"Ain't you Speedy of the Best Chance?" asked the stranger.

"That's my name. I've been in the Best Chance," said Speedy.

"I'm glad to see you," said the other. "I was driftin' on back to camp. My name's Clevenger, if you wanta know it. I was hearing today that there was a— Hello, who's this here with you?"

He had discovered the condition in which Cliff Derrick was riding, and the face of the outlaw became hot with shame and with rage. Close up to him came Clevenger, gaping more and more, and then, with a shout: "It's Derrick! Dog-gone, it's Derrick! How did you—where—what— Great Scott, this'll drive Sunday Slough crazy! You went out and got Derrick, did you? By thunder, the boys'll plate you with gold and set you in diamonds."

To this outbreak Speedy merely said something about "good luck" and happening to be "at the right place at the right time."

Derrick ground his teeth in a hopeless fury.

"Well," said Clevenger, "there's one thing that we can thank a seven-day man for. And Buck Masters, too. I was kind of losing all faith in that gent. I thought that he was a crook plain and simple."

He was still talking in this vein as they came around the shoulder of the hill and entered a narrow defile, the farther end of which was bright with the light of the town. When they were halfway down the shallow little ravine, there was a sudden rush of dark horsemen from the trees. They came upon them inescapably close.

Speedy abode his ground with his prisoner, but Clevenger did not wait. He had a glimpse of the lot as they spurred ahead, their faces illumined by the moon, and now he turned his horse about and galloped it with all its might for freedom.

There was no pleasure in the heart of Derrick as these strangers swept about him. He could guess why they were come. He could imagine that a mob and a lynch scene would now quickly end his career. But was not that better than the prolonged wretchedness of a trial?

He heard the voice of a big man saying: "Hello, Speedy. Dog-gone my ribs if you ain't gone and done it. Pretty slick, my boy. This is gunna go and get you famous. Here's the man. Here's the old slickster! Derrick himself!"

"Glad to turn him over to you," said Speedy. "It's not too comfortable, having a red-hot piece of iron in your hands—a fellow like this, I mean. You watch him, will you? I'll jog on up to town and get them ready for him at the jail. Watch him, sheriff, because he's a slippery one."

"Go ahead, Speedy," said the sheriff. "You're gunna get a lot of fame and credit for this!"

"Thanks!" called Speedy, and hurried the mule down the trail.

CHAPTER 15

When the captor had left, there was a sudden change in the demeanor of the big sheriff. He said: "We got you pretty easy, Derrick. We thought that we might have to fight for you."

He removed the gag as he spoke. As the outlaw pulled the sweet night air into his lungs, he heard the sheriff continue: "I didn't know that Speedy had tricks like this up his sleeve. He's a pretty smart boy. But we can't do business with him. He's too smooth for us. We might as well do a little introducing. This here is Sid Levine, that has Sunday Slough in his pocket. And this here is Mike Doloroso, that only has one eye, and that's maybe why his last name is Doloroso. And me, I'm Buck Masters, that happens to be sheriff of this county just now."

Derrick could sense that something was in the air. He

71

could not tell exactly what, but he found himself at ease among these men.

"I'm glad to meet you, boys," he said. "I'd like to shake hands all around, but you see how it is. My hands are not exactly at my disposal just now."

"We'll be fixin' that, too, in another minute," said Sid Levine. "What we wanta do is just talk a little minute with you, Derrick."

"I'm glad to talk," said Derrick, "as soon as I can get the ache of the gag out of my jaws."

"That's too bad," said Levine, "but that little rat, Speedy, he's gunna get his own share of poison some of these days. I may not be a wise guy, but I can guess that."

"Yeah, so can I," said Doloroso.

It was music to Derrick to hear these words. Sudden hope flowed in upon him.

"Business is what I wanta talk, Derrick," said Levine.

"All right," said Derrick.

"Tell him, am I the guy to talk business?" said Levine. "You tell him, Mike."

"He ain't the guy to talk nothing else," said Mike.

"You can trust Levine," said the sheriff. "He's never let anybody down. Nobody that was right."

"I'll hope to be right," said Derrick.

"I know some of the things that you've done for yourself," said Levine, "and you'll be all right. I can say that to begin with."

"That ought to make things easier, then," said Derrick.

He knew that at least a part of the game was in his hands. He no longer thought about public shame and the hangman's rope, but about what vengeance he should pour out upon the head of Speedy when the day came for him to turn the tables on that youth.

Said Levine: "You see how it is, Derrick! I wouldn't wanta see a fellow like you, that's got brains—I wouldn't wanta see him go to jail, would I?"

"I hope not," said Derrick.

"Nor under ground, I wouldn't wanta see him, would I?" said Levine, pressing the happy point.

"Thanks," said Derrick again, but rather more shortly. He warmed up this word by adding: "Why shouldn't you and I do business together, Levine?"

The latter made a gesture, swinging both hands out and shoulder-high.

"What would I be talking for here," he said, "except I had an idea like that, I ask you?"

"Go ahead," said Derrick. "I imagine that you have some ideas of how we could club together."

"Ideas?" laughed Mike Doloroso. "He ain't got nothing else but. Ideas is what he's made of."

"Shut up, Mike," said Levine. "Mike, he's always gotta be butting in. Lookit here; what I wanta say is: I got Sunday Slough in my pocket. I take it out and polish it once a week, that's all. I got my initials carved into it. You know what I mean?"

"I know," said Derrick gravely. "There's a lot in Sunday Slough."

"Gravy. That's what there is," said Levine. "It's all full of nothing but gravy, is what I mean to say. Am I wrong, Buck?"

"You're never wrong," said Buck Masters. "Is he ever wrong at all, Mike?"

"He can smell a dollar ten miles off and upwind," said Mike.

"Shut up, Mike," said Levine, more good-humoredly than ever. "Don't you mind him, Derrick.' '

"All right. I won't mind him," said Derrick, with a broad wink.

"I say that I got Sunday Slough in my pocket," said Levine, "and here's the sheriff to make everything safe, and Mike Doloroso, that can break iron bars in his teeth.

73

"Now I say, ain't the three of us enough? Sure, and we oughta get all there is in Sunday Slough. But the trouble is that we own that town so deep down that it don't know that it's owned. And there had oughta be somebody that could step in from the outside and know the right places to step. We know the right places to step, but we're too far inside, if you know what I mean."

"I know," said Derrick. "You want an outside man, somebody you can trust, eh?"

"Derrick, there's a clean million in that town," said the other, answering indirectly. "There's a clean million, and only about three jobs to get the whole caboodle."

Derrick narrowed his eyes.

"That's a lot of money," he said slowly. He repeated: "A million is a whole lot of money

"I ain't no piker," said Levine. "Either I bust everything open wide or else I let everything go. What should I wanta go and be a piker for? I got money. So have my friends. I see that they have money. Don't I, Buck?"

"You never gotta worry if Levine's your friend," said One-eyed Mike.

"Shut up, will you, you big Irish bum," said Levine tenderly. "Now you go on and tell me how the idea sort of strikes you, Mr. Derrick. I wanta hear from your side of the case."

Derrick paused. His words, when he spoke, were clear and coldly precise.

"I play on my own, usually," he said. "I have my own schemes, and I make no splits outside of my own men. But, except for you boys, I'd be the laughing stock of the world inside of another half hour. I'd be buried in another day, with not even a shingle to mark the spot. Now I say, you name the jobs and give me the frame, and I'll do the work for you, and turn over the whole loot, without a penny for myself. I'd be glad to."

The eye of Levine kindled with a deadly fire of joy. But this first thought he mastered. The next instant he was blinded by a rush of Christian kindness.

"I wouldn't do it," he said. "No, sir; all I want is my fair split, and I never wanted no more."

"That's all he ever wanted," said One-eyed Mike.

"Shut up, Mike," said Levine, "and get those ropes off Mr. Derrick. Why don't you do something to make yourself useful instead of always shooting off your face?"

Said Buck Masters: "Levine, you fix a date to meet up with Derrick and frame the whole job. We gotta get back into town or there'll be trouble in there waiting for us. We gotta let the boys know how we had this Derrick in our hands —because we were seen with him—and then he outslicked us and beat it away. I gotta raise a posse and start some trouble! We gotta go in on the gallop, because we was seen to take him over. One was Speedy, but the other—who was the other bird, Derrick?"

"A fellow named Clevenger. Picked him up on the road. That's all," said Derrick. "Outside of you fellows and Speedy, he's the only one who saw me in ropes."

"I'll fix Clevenger," said Levine. "I'll fix anything in the town, what I mean! Only Speedy—I wish that you'd batted him one over the head like you said you was going to do."

"I would've," said Buck. "But you know how quick he cleaned out. And the way he handed over Derrick and didn't make no fuss, I didn't hardly have no excuse for slamming him. You seen how it was. But now we gotta get back into town and get fast. You frame it with Derrick."

"Tomorrow night, right here, and right at this time. I'll bring plans and all the details. You'll need some soup, though. Want me to bring it?" said Levine.

"I've got the soup and the makings," said Derrick. "Good-by, boys. We're going to do business together!"

He turned his horse, the lovely mare of Joe Dale, up the

75

ravine and rode on, very slowly.

The other three wheeled about and galloped at full speed toward Sunday Slough, Levine grunting and protesting, his fat bulk reeling in the saddle.

They came into Sunday Slough with a rush, and there they found that everything in the town that was "in Levine's pocket" was oddly changed. The saloons, the dance halls, the gaming establishments, even the Grand Palace, appeared deserted, and instead, on the street about the entrances to these places, stood grim-faced men, silent and still, with guns in their hands and eyes that followed gloomily the galloping trio!

CHAPTER 16

The sheriff strove vainly to rouse any enthusiasm. He dashed up to a group and yelled: "Boys, get your horses! I want twenty picked men. We've had Cliff Derrick in our mitts, and the dog-gone fox slipped away from us. Meet me at my office in five minutes. I'm gunna get him again if I have to pull up the mountains and juggle 'em around!"

But no one answered. The silent, staring faces regarded him and made no response.

At the office, the three stood panting around the sheriff's desk, with the light of the single lamp in their faces.

"What's up?" said Levine, green-gray with fear. "They don't seem like they used to be. What's happened?"

"Something's busted," said the sheriff, scowling. "This town don't look good to me no more. Go on, Levine. You own it. Now make it up and make it dance like you used to!"

"I need a little time," said Levine, loosening his collar.

"What could've happened? Why didn't they pile on their horses and come chasing?"

"I dunno," said the sheriff, "but if—"

"Cheese it! Back up! Hold everything!" gasped One-eyed Mike.

And he himself backed into the room, making warning gestures behind him.

And through the doorway now, with a slow and relentless movement, poured many men, those same armed men who had gathered in the street. Their grim eyes surveyed the three. A big man, whose face was covered with a red stubble, was the first and the foremost.

And Sid Levine backed up before them until his fat, loose shoulders were pressed against the wall. He was accustomed to smiles and cheers. Explosions of wild rage he also understood. But this purposeful advance unnerved him.

Where were his men, his hired men, his bouncers and advocates of all sorts, who always percolated through every gathering in Sunday Slough, ready to swing the mob according to the dictates of the master?

Not a single familiar face did he see. These were men lean and hard with labor. He had not dreamed that there were so many of them in the town. They looked ready for anything. And what did they want here?

The man of the red beard said:

"You wanta know why we're here. I'm gunna tell you. My name's Clevenger. I met up with Speedy and Derrick on the trail outside of town. I seen you three come busting down on them. I guessed what was up right then. You'd make a deal with Derrick. You'd slam Speedy and roll him under the leaves, or put a bullet through him and say that Derrick done it. But Derrick didn't do it. You did it. Speedy's a dead man; and you're dead, too, all three of you!"

A stern murmur ran through the crowd.

"Mike, say something!" gasped Levine, putting out his

fat, helpless hands.

And Mike, though gray of face, said: "You boys are all wrong crowding Levine like this. He never done a crooked turn in his life. He's the best friend that most of you ever had."

"He may be to some," said one blunt-jawed man of middle age, "but he looks to me like a crooked gambler and hound. Boys, I think we wouldn't be wasting rope if we stretched the necks of these three—unless we find out where the boy is— Speedy, I mean, who went out by himself and got Derrick. It's a thing I would have sworn that no man in the world could do!"

Said Clevenger: "What did you do with Speedy?"

"Do with him?" said the sheriff. "We didn't do nothin'. We didn't touch him. Nacherally, he turned his prisoner over to us and rode on in to get the jail ready—"

Loud, derisive laughter closed over that protesting voice. And with a sudden movement, like the sway of a wave, a hundred hands mastered the three. The strength ebbed out of Levine. His loose body sank to the floor.

But now, from the street, a sudden uproar, a wild and riotous cheering broke out, rose and filled the air, rang and re-rang. It was a name that they cheered, and it was as life to the three captives. It was also a complete shock to the vigilantes. For that name, many times repeated, was "Speedy!"

The sound came closer.

Pressing to the door of the office and to the windows, then back again into the street, they saw an old gray mule and Speedy himself on the back of it. Beside him followed a magnificent mare on which, gagged, feet and hands tied, was none other than the great Derrick!

"Sheriff," said Clevenger, "I've done you all wrong. There's Speedy, and he's still got his man. I didn't understand. We're all in the soup for this. Let's get out, boys!"

Speedy, the next morning, sat with Marshal Tom Gray in a hotel room, writing on a scrap of paper and yawning as he wrote.

"But after that, how did you know that you'd get him again?" asked the marshal.

"I didn't know," said Speedy. "I simply played a pretty fair chance; not a very long one. I went up to the ravine and waited with a noose in a rope, and pretty soon, up came Derrick, riding with his head down, like a fellow who has something to think about. I'm no expert with a rope, but it was no trick at all to drop the noose over him and bind his elbows to his ribs. No man can put up a fight in that shape."

"Well," said the marshal, "he's in jail, and watched by my men. I'll have his neck in another sort of a noose for another purpose before long. I think that you've broken the back of a very big gang, Speedy. But if you had waited a little longer before coming in, all three of the thugs would have been wiped out."

Speedy sighed. "If I'd guessed that," he said, "I would have waited, of course. As it is, I have to go and report to the sheriff and have a drink with him and let Levine slap me on the back. They don't know where I stand, now. And before I'm through, I'll surely spring the trap under them good and proper."

"You may," said the marshal, "but I'd rather make down my bed in a rattlesnake cave than be in your skin in this town from now on. What are you writing?"

"A note. Got a boy who'll do what he's told?"

"In the next room," said the marshal. He called, and a lad of fifteen came to them.

"Partner," said Speedy, "take this note and go down to the stable and put the saddle on the mare that Derrick rode into town last night, and lead that mare straight up the valley toward Castle Ford. Lead her, mind you, and don't ride,

or you're likely to get a terrible fall! When a man comes out and claims her, give her to him and come back. That's all."
He reread the note, which ran:

Dear Joe: The Japanese tricks are the very mischief to stand against until a man knows them. I hope you'll find Betsy safe and sound, and that we'll meet again.
                                                    Yours, Speedy

PART TWO

CHAPTER 17

Just outside the shack, Pier Morgan lay beneath the pine tree. It was his first day outdoors. The boy had carried him by the head, and Anna, the old Mexican woman, had carried him by the feet. There had been some pain, just enough to make him taste the first pleasure longer and deeper as he lay now, looking up through the deep green heaven of the pine tree boughs.

Juan, his arms filled with branches of dead shrubbery which he was bringing in for the cooking, paused beside Pier Morgan and looked down with smiling eyes, his white teeth brightly flashing.

"Pretty good, eh?" said Juan.

"Pretty good," whispered Pier. He could speak out loud now. But the habit of whispering held strongly over from the days when he was supposed to die, when only the grim face of Speedy beside him forced him to live.

"Yellow dog, quitter, now turn up your toes and cash in," Speedy would say. "You're only scratched, you're not hurt. But you're a quitter. You're going to die because you're afraid."

"I'm Welsh," Pier Morgan had said one day. "Welshmen, they don't quit. They fight till they die."

"Then keep on fighting," Speedy said. "You're only quitting, and I want to tell you why I'm staying on here. It's only because I want to see a dirty Welshman die because he's scared."

Pier had gritted his teeth and rolled his eyes aslant with fury; he had not strength to turn his head. "If I get well, I'm gonna wring your neck," he had said.

Now, as he lay beneath the tree, he smiled a little, remembering this.

He could see, with perfect clarity, that Speedy had tormented him merely to keep some hot spark of life in his breast. Pier Morgan had held on because of the savage hatred he felt for his tormentor. He used to whisper his curses against Speedy until he fell into a deep sleep. Every time, when he awoke, there was a slightly brighter spark of life in him. But he understood, now.

Juan and old Anna, his mother, had helped him to a right understanding of Speedy. For they worshipped the careless tramp. He was their hero.

"Juan," said Pier, "tell me how I got here."

"Speedy found you in Sunday Slough. That's all what I know," said Juan. "He brung you out here."

"Yeah, Sunday Slough. That was the place, all right," said Pier Morgan. "I wouldn't forget that. I thought I was gonna live to kill Speedy. Instead, I gotta live long enough to get Buck Masters and One-eyed Mike and Sid Levine. That's what I gotta live for."

"Maybe, better you go and get well for your own sake," said Juan, shaking his head. "My mother Anna, she say you got no right to live, anyhow. She say you been no more'n dead."

He went off to the house; Pier Morgan could hear the wood falling with a crash, and his eyes returned to the consideration of the green heaven of branches above his head.

It was very true. He had no right to live. He wondered how Speedy had managed to find him, how he had managed to bring him out here. Juan and Anna said that the shack was three whole miles from Sunday Slough.

Then he returned to his first memory of Speedy, the singing tramp. He had met him first in a jungle near Denver, where the thunder of a railroad bridge was shaken out over a forested ravine. There, the hobos used to rest and refresh themselves, eating stolen mulligan stew, boiling their clothes, drinking black coffee, telling tales of all the world, from Shanghai to New Orleans.

It was in that jungle that he had grown sick of the life of a tramp. It was there that he had resolved that he must go back to the world of honest, hard-working people. Only chance had thrown him out on the road. And it was while he listened to Speedy, singing sentimental ballads, that he realized that he had a place, somewhere, in the working world.

Before he turned in, that night, he went over and shook hands with Speedy.

"Thanks, kid," said he.

"Yeah. You go straight, boy," said Speedy sleepily.

He had been surprised by that remark. It was as though Speedy, all the evenings, had been singing straight at him and understanding him.

The next day he talked again. He was going West, going to join the gold rush to Sunday Slough.

"Don't go there," said Speedy. "Any other place but not a mining camp. You believe in your hands, but a mining camp believes in knives and guns."

Morgan had laughed. "I can always take care of myself," he had said.

And so he had, at first. And he had found his claim, and dug out ten thousand dollars in a few weeks, and he had taken his gold dust into town for a little party, and then a big investment which would enable him to open up the claim and work it to good purpose.

Then everything crashed. His claim was jumped. He had appealed for justice. The kind of justice that emanates from a crooked judge, had been done him. Bertram Daly had sentenced him for vagrancy and, while he was in jail, fury had boiled up and overmastered him. They were looting his claim in the meantime!

So he had tried to break out of jail and, as a result, Sheriff Buck Masters and One-eyed Mike had managed to shoot him to bits.

Oh, how well he could remember it all! No, it was Speedy who had saved him, shining into his life again like a lucky star.

So the thoughts of Pier Morgan dipped into the past and then, into the present until, down the mountain trail, he heard a clear, familiar voice singing a Spanish song in the distance.

It was the voice, he finally realized, of Speedy himself, and the words of the song might be translated into English somewhat as follows:

Like a golden apple in a golden snood,
Oh, lovely Anna, fair and good!

He knew that the words and the song were meant for the ears of that withered, bent, half-toothless old dame, Anna. A golden apple, indeed! And here she came, running out of the house.

"Juan," she screamed. "Juan, Juan! He has come. Señor Speedy is here!"

She was like a tired old bird with a cracked voice, hailing the rising of the sun. Pier Morgan turned his head and presently, down the trail, he saw Speedy coming. He was riding an old, slow, wise-footed gray mule. His guitar was slung by a strap across his shoulders, and he was singing in a clear tenor voice.

He was in no haste. Sometimes the mule paused to crop the mountain grass. A worm's way was the way of that mule, it appeared, and yet Speedy was not troubled by this slow procedure.

Time did not seem to exist for him. For that matter, it never had appeared to exist. It was as though he had an eternity of youth before him.

"Well," said Pier Morgan to himself, "he don't have to worry. He's not the kind that could worry."

Speedy came nearer. The sun gleamed on the golden brown of his tanned face, glistened on his dark hair and eyes. He was smiling as he sang.

Gratitude and wonder blended in the stern heart of Pier Morgan as he looked at Speedy.

He saw the gray mule stop in front of the shack. There Anna and Juan were pulling the rider from the saddle. One of them was taking his guitar, and the other was holding his hat, and then Juan was leading away the recalcitrant mule toward the hay shed, while Anna, holding the guitar with one hand, with the other urged her guest forward, half embracing him, laughing, crying out, with tears of happiness in her voice.

They were gone some minutes inside the house, and at last Speedy came out, still eating. He had tasted the hospitality of Anna before he hurried to see the sick man. And Pier Morgan grinned.

The nurse must be flattered before the patient was seen. That was the scheming way of Speedy; the hobo.

Yes, he was finishing a mouthful and also puffing away at a long-stemmed pipe, a household treasure of the Mexican woman.

Well, perhaps Speedy had done for some member of her family what he had recently done for Pier Morgan.

CHAPTER 18

Speedy came up the path and paused beneath the pine tree, looking down and smiling at the boy stretched out in the hammock. Then he said:

"Well, Pier, I see you're up, kicking the world in the face this morning, eh?"

"Not this morning, but it won't be long now," said the wounded man, his voice beginning in a whisper and strengthening toward the end.

He held out his hand. His arm was so weak that his hand shook. Speedy took the hand and held it a moment, looking him over with a critical eye.

"You're a good nurse, Anna," said he. "You could make extra legs grow on grasshoppers. I thought that he'd never be able to handle a soup spoon with that arm; I tell you, Anna, you're wonderful. Go back to the house and lie down and take a rest. I'll look after him for a while."

She went back, chuckling with pleasure, like a child, and wagging her head from side to side, as though to say that she knew very well that there was talent in those old hands of hers.

Speedy sat down on a stump near by, a high one, from which he could easily look down on the patient.

"What have you been doing, Speedy?" asked Pier Morgan.

"Looking things over in Sunday Slough," answered the youth. "I looked the mine over, too, your mine."

"They've looted it," said Morgan.

"It was only a pocket, but it was a deep pocket," said Speedy. "Before it pinched out, they took away ninety-five thousand dollars."

A bitter exclamation burst from Morgan.

Speedy said nothing and presently, opening the eyes which he had winked shut, Morgan said: "With the ten grand that they picked out of my pockets before, that makes over a hundred thousand that I've been done out of, Speedy."

Still Speedy said nothing, and presently Morgan grinned.

"Yeah, I know," he said. "I'm still alive, and that's something, thanks to you."

"I'll thank you a lot more for something else," said Speedy.

"What's that, partner?"

"For getting well enough to do some practicing with a gun. I'm going to need help."

"Where?"

"In Sunday Slough, of course."

"What's happened there? What's wrong there—except everything?"

"I'm in the middle of everything, now," said Speedy, yawning widely and stretching.

He relaxed from the stretching and smiled sleepily at Pier Morgan.

"I'm the deputy sheriff. I'm a hired hero," said he.

"Deputy sheriff?" muttered Morgan.

"Yes. I'm working under your friend, Buck Masters."

"What's this all about?" asked the sick man.

"It was a three-headed monster that put its teeth in you, Pier," said the tramp. "The main head was Sid Levine, of the Grand Palace. The number two is Buck Masters. Number three is important, too. One-eyed Mike, I mean. I went down to Sunday Slough to look things over, but I soon saw that that nut would have to be cracked from the inside."

"Whatcha mean by that?" asked Morgan.

"I'd have to be inside the ring to do them up," said Speedy calmly. "So I decided to get in with the thugs. Not as a real friend, you understand, but force myself into a position where they'd have to accept me on my own terms. I mean, I wanted to make myself important in the town's eyes. So I managed to get their guns, and left them in the window of a gunsmith to be claimed by the owners. Pretty soon the town was talking a bit about the thing. A Greek never left his shield on the battlefield. A Westerner doesn't leave his gun. In the middle of the chatter, I dropped around to the sheriff's office and applied for a job as deputy. You know."

"I know they call the deputies in that town the seven-day men, because that's the average length of their lives after they become deputies," said the wounded man. "Why did you want that job?"

"To get on the inside. The sheriff gave me the little job of capturing Cliff Derrick—"

"Derrick eats a tiger a day!" said Morgan.

"He slipped this time," said Speedy. "I had him almost back to town when Mike and the sheriff jumped me and took him away. They made a deal with him and took him away, but I'd been expecting that and slipped back up the trail to wait. When Derrick came by, I dropped a rope over him, and brought him back to Sunday Slough just as a handy little mob was getting ready to lynch Levine and Mike and Masters for letting Derrick go. If I had known what was happening, I would have come in slower. As it was, they were turned loose; and I handed Derrick over to Marshal Tom Gray. Derrick's in prison, now; he'll hang before long, I suppose.

"And there I am like a cat walking a fence, with public opinion holding me up and the sheriff and Levine's gang trying to pull me down. But everything's polite and good feeling, if you know what I mean. The Sunday Slough *News* makes a feature of me. When I go to bed, when I get up, what I eat for dinner. You know. A lot of bunk. But it makes Levine's thugs go slow. They know that the crowd in Sunday Slough has teeth now. And they're rather afraid to tackle me. When they do, it will be at about the same time that they loot Sunday Slough of everything down to its gold fillings in the eyeteeth. That's the picture for you to look at, Pier."

The latter considered.

"You're in hot water," he said.

"Boiling," said Speedy.

"And you like it, I guess?"

"It's interesting. I like thugs. I like to see the way they jump," confessed Speedy. "Levine is as smooth as oil with me now. Oh, he's a bright boy, is Levine. And he wants to cook me. He wants to roast me in butter and serve me with capers."

"He'll do it, too," said Morgan, "some day when you're not looking."

"Anyway," said Speedy, "as I was saying before, it's rather lonely down there in Sunday Slough—what with being the town hero on the one hand and the deputy sheriff on the other."

"I know," said Morgan, nodding. "I suppose every time a tough mug comes to town, Masters sends you down to pinch him and throw him in the hoosegow."

"It's that way," sighed Speedy. "I don't mind excitement. But before long, I'm likely to use up my welcome, and then I'll be needing a friend at my back. A friend like you, Pier."

"I'm getting better every day," said Morgan. "I'm hurrying to get well, because I remember the way you used to abuse me, when I was lying flat on my back in the shack, there. I have to lick you for that, one day."

Speedy considered him; they smiled at one another.

"You're a hardy lad, Pier," said the tramp. "But you have to learn to use a gun. You'll need a gun before you're through with Sunday Slough."

"I'm sitting up tomorrow," said the other. "And every day after that, I intend to do a little shooting at a mark—until I peg out. I'll get my hand in, before long. I have a pretty good eye."

"Good!" said Speedy.

"But, look here, Speedy," he went on, "you talk about me learning to shoot, and you never will use a gun yourself!"

"Last thing my old mother asked me," said Speedy, yawning again. "Never to drink more than a quart at a time, and never to use a Colt. She preferred Smith and Wessons. But, talking about getting well, I expect to see you in the saddle inside of ten days."

"In five days," said Pier Morgan. "I've been lying here daydreamin' about the time when I'd get my teeth into that gang in Sunday Slough. And there you are on the spot, breaking the ground and getting ready for the harvest."

He wriggled a little. "I'd crawl a hundred miles on my hands and knees just to get at Sid Levine," he said.

"All right," said Speedy. "I've just come up to see that your appetite is good. Now that I know it is, I feel better. I'm going to need you, Pier. I'm going to need you pretty badly. Don't hurry too fast, don't take chances. But the sooner you can manage to get on your feet, the better it will be for me. I need you!"

"Then why not use me?" said a voice half deep and half nasal.

"Don't move!" whispered Pier Morgan to his friend.

Over the shoulder of Speedy, he saw a young man of not more than twenty years, with broad shoulders and long arms —a youth whose face would have been handsome, had it not been so muscular. Beside, it was marked in three places with large red scars, which looked as though they were the result of burns.

Most interesting of all, however, was the .45-caliber Colt which he balanced with familiar and affectionate ease, just above the level of his hip. The muzzle pointed at Speedy.

The latter, without turning, caught a glimpse of the youth out of the corner of his eye.

"Hello," he said. "Pier, this is a friend of mine, Joe Dale."

"Derrick's man?" said Morgan, in a whisper, his face covered with prickling goose flesh.

"What makes you think that I'm your friend?" asked the voice of Joe Dale, pitched higher and in a more nasal strain than before.

"That was just my little joke," said Speedy. "Have you come to drill me, Joe?"

"I've come to learn Japanese wrestling or whatever the heathenish tricks are that you use," said Joe Dale. "And I've brought Betsy along to thank you for sending her back to me. Come here, Betsy. Come here, you old fool, and thank the gentleman!"

CHAPTER 19

From behind a big, weather-grayed rock stepped the loveliest bay mare that Pier Morgan had ever seen. With her ears pricked and a red forelock blowing across the white star on her forehead, she stepped daintily down the hillside.

"Maybe I can stow this cannon away?" said Dale.

"It's the only one on deck, just now," said Speedy.

"Well," muttered Joe, "I didn't hardly know how things would be around here. I had to sort of take a care, d'ye see?"

He was rather shamefaced as he put up his weapon.

"Betsy, here," said Joe Dale, "she said that she wanted to come back and say hello to you, if you know what I mean. Betsy, go and say howdy to the gent."

He waved his hand, and Betsy, approaching Speedy, swayed her head up and down three times. The last time, she bent her knees a little, with the effect of a curtsey.

Pier Morgan laughed at the pleasant sight, and Betsy,

having finished her trick, advanced her velvety muzzle and nibbled at the shoulder of Speedy's coat. Mischief was bright in her eyes.

"Come here, Betsy, you onery old gal," said Joe Dale, filled with pride. "You look out, Speedy. She's likely to pinch you black and blue, when she gets to fooling around. She's an imp, is what she is. Come here, Betsy."

She shook her head angrily and went back to her master with a sudden gallop. Now she threatened Joe Dale with her teeth, now with her hoofs.

"Aw, go on and shut up and lie down, will you?" said he, pretending to be bored.

She lay down at his feet. He took her head on his knee and ran his fingers through the bright flowing of her mane.

"You see the kind of a nuisance she is," said Joe Dale. "Just kind of always flying around and making trouble. Go on and get out of here, then, you rattle-head."

Betsy sprang to her feet, as though released from a prison, and made a furious run, around and around the pine tree, flashing like red metal in the sunshine.

"Aw, quit it, will yuh?" said Joe.

She stood still and looked at him expectantly, and Dale, rather sheepishly, took from his pocket a piece of lump sugar.

"She's wonderful," broke out Pier Morgan. "I never seen a horse like her. She's the finest thing that I ever laid eyes on."

"Yeah," said Joe Dale. "That's what gents say that ain't been at the raising of her. Some mighty dog-gone mean times she's give me, and a lot of worry and trouble, too. She got a cold once, that pretty near turned into pneumonia. I was up with her for eight nights in a row. I had to go and sleep right under her feet, you might say, and hear the groanin' of her breathing. Them was bad days. I thought that she was a goner."

He looked at her with a fond eye; and Speedy smiled at him.

"Look here, Joe," said he, "how would you sell that mare?"

"Sell her?" said Joe Dale. "I dunno that I'd sell her."

"You don't like her much. What's the price on her?"

"I'm kind of used to her. I don't guess that I'd sell her," said Joe Dale. "I'm kind of used to her, like to a scolding wife, or my pipe, or something like that. You know it ain't much use, but it's a habit that you can't get along without!"

He fixed his keen eye upon the face of Speedy.

Then he said: "Speedy, I reckon that you're kind of a bright fellow."

"Thanks," said the youth.

"But you ain't a bird that flies through the air. You can't move without leavin' some kind of a trail behind you, I guess?"

"I suppose not," said Speedy.

"The kind of a trail that I could follow it up here to the shack, for instance," argued Dale.

"That's true."

"Now, suppose that I'd been as mean as I might've been, why shouldn't I 'ave laid low and socked a bullet through you, from there behind them rocks?"

"I knew that you'd been trailing me up here," said Speedy.

"Hold on! You knew it after I showed up with a gun!"

"No, I knew it long ago. Three days ago when I came up this way you were trailing me. You know, I'd ridden Betsy. I knew her. I know the sign of her hoofs and the length of her step. Going back, I looked the trail over, and I knew that you'd been up here."

"And you didn't keep no better lookout, in spite of that?" asked Dale.

"No, I wasn't afraid of you. That is, I knew that you'd play in the open, partly because I might still be riding Betsy. Besides, I took a liking to you. I trusted you to be white, Joe."

The boy listened with wide-spread eyes.

"You took me to be white, did you?" he asked huskily.

He cleared his throat. Then he said to Pier Morgan: "This gent stands up to fight me and he paralyzes me with a lot of his—"

"I know," said Morgan. "He's a jujitsu fiend, is what he is."

"He ain't nothing but," replied Joe Dale. "And he takes and throws me into a burning fire at the windup, and I get burned fifty places. That's what he done to me."

His eyes narrowed at the recollection.

Said Pier Morgan: "I recollect a big half-ton truck of a no-good, slab-jaw Canuck, is what I recollect. And this here lumberjack, he decides to bust up Speedy smaller—kindling wood size. And he crowded the kid, here. And the kid had to defend himself.

"But the way he defended himself, it was a terrible thing. Because he took hold of that Canuck and handled him like he was putty. It took four men pulling different ways to straighten the kinks out of the Canuck after that fight. Then he laid down in a corner and cried for a whole day and a night. He left camp and never was seen no more. That was what happened to the Canuck. You was lucky that he didn't throw you into the fire and hold you there."

Some of the hardness left the eyes of Joe Dale.

He actually heaved a sigh of relief, and then he said: "Well, I'm glad it's that way. I was kind of a champeen!"

He added, to Speedy: "What I wanted to tell you was something that maybe you'd like to know."

"Go on," said Speedy. "I'd be glad to hear it."

"You wouldn't believe it, what a skunk a man can be!" said Joe Dale. "And him laying himself out to be a friend of yours, too, and always patting you on the back. I mean, that greasy-faced, pig-eyed lump of a no-good Levine; and the sheriff, too. Your own sheriff, what you're the deputy under! Your own sheriff, that got himself so dog-gone famous because you caught Cliff Derrick!"

"What's the matter?" asked Speedy.

"They're out for you."

"They're out to get me. Yes, I knew that, Joe."

"You—knew—that? Then, why have you been herding with 'em?" asked Joe Dale, wide-eyed with amazement.

"Because," said Speedy calmly, "I'm out to get them!"

"Hold on," said Joe. "I don't foller this very clear."

Speedy hooked a thumb at Pier Morgan.

"They did that to him," said he.

"I see," murmured Dale. "And him a friend of yours, eh? So you're gonna trim the whole bunch of 'em. Is that it?"

"That's the main idea," declared Speedy. "I want to stick one hook through that whole row of three faces, including One-eyed Mike. Catching them one at a time wouldn't make the same pretty picture. I want to fry them all in one pan afterwards."

"Well," said Dale, "it's a bright idea. But lemme tell you something. They're likely to fry you before you fry them. That's what I come up here to tell you."

"Thanks," said Speedy. "Have they got some plans?"

"Yeah. Murder is their plan. Murder that you hire. That's the way they're thinking."

"That's bad," said Speedy. "It's bad, because it's so simple, and murder is so extremely cheap in Sunday Slough."

"They ain't trying to make it cheap, though," said the other. "Will you listen?"

"I'm listening, Joe."

"If I'd pulled the trigger a minute ago and clipped your backbone into two parts, I could've collected ten thousand bucks from Sid Levine!"

He took a breath.

"I ain't flush," he said. "But that kind of a skunk I ain't."

CHAPTER 20

Speedy, when he heard this, began to whistle softly to the green heaven of the pine tree above. The woodpecker stopped those rapid, accurate strokes, and the last chips floated softly down to the ground and lay unseen in the grass.

"Well," said Pier Morgan, "nobody in the world is alive when there's ten thousand dollars on his head. That's all I know about it."

"You know enough," answered Joe Dale. "That's the price they offered me. I went and I seen One-eyed Mike. No, I mean he come and he seen me. That's the price that he offered. Ten thousand bucks flat, and no lying about it. They're plumb loose with money. He wanted me to take five thousand down."

"Why didn't you take the five thousand?" asked Pier Morgan curiously.

"Well," said Joe Dale, with a singular honesty, "I thought maybe that I would knock you off, Speedy. And then, ag'in, I thought maybe that I wouldn't. So I didn't go and take the five thousand. You know. I didn't wanta be tempted too dog-gone much. That's why. Five thousand is all right to talk about, but it's a lot of money to have in the hand. It's a ticket to the Solomon Isles and soft days the rest of your life, is what five thousand dollars is. You know what I mean, Speedy."

"Yeah, I know what you mean," said Speedy.

He stood up and stretched himself.

"Something had oughta be done about this," said Pier Morgan, with a frown.

96

"Look at how he likes to walk a tight wire," suggested Joe Dale. "He wouldn't be happy, if he wasn't walking a tight wire, like that. Say, Speedy, you little woolly, asbestos lamb, you, what are you gonna do about this here job?"

"I've got to get somebody," said Speedy. "Maybe I've got to get all three of them, and get them quick. I wonder what makes them so anxious to have my scalp, Joe?"

"I dunno," said Joe. "It makes Levine nervous that way that you're always around, and ain't dead yet. You're spoiling the landscape for him and old Buck Masters. They got some big jobs on hand. You see, after I've bumped you off, I'm to go and take a whack at some of the easy money here in the town. I'm to crack things wide open. You know what I mean. They're gonna loot Sunday Slough. They're gonna clean it like a fish, is what they're gonna do."

"I suppose they are," said Speedy. "I'm a lazy beast, and I've taken too much time. Now I need to jump like a cat on a hot stove and I've no ideas. Say, Pier, you hurry up and get well, will you?"

"You bet I'll hurry," said Pier Morgan softly. "Oh, how I wish that I was riding down along the trail to Sunday Slough with you, right now!"

"You've got enough to worry about," said Joe Dale. "I tell you what, Morgan, I wouldn't cry about not having nothing to think about, if I was you. Because they know, now, why Speedy rides up this way. And they wanta get you plenty. They got some money out of you, and they want you dead. They don't like you alive and getting well up here. They want you, Morgan. Not like they want Speedy, but they want you."

"I'd better be moving, then, Speedy," said Morgan.

"Old Anna and Juan will take care of that," said Speedy. "They know how to fade you out of the picture. Don't worry about that."

"I heard them talking about Juan and Anna," said Joe

97

Dale. "They couldn't make out how you had 'em both under your thumb. Ain't old Anna the girl that's wanted in Mexico for poisoning, and ain't Juan the fellow that knifed a coupla gents in the back in Chihuahua?"

"I don't know anything about that," said Speedy, with iron suddenly in his back. "I don't think that you know anything about it, either."

Joe Dale blinked.

"Sure I don't know anything about it at all," said he. "I didn't know that you always played that close with fire, though."

"Speedy," said Pier Morgan, "are they—"

But Speedy interrupted him to say, pleasantly enough, to Joe Dale: "I didn't know that you were such a merry little chatterbox, Joe. I say, Pier, that Anna and Juan will take care of you and keep on taking care of you until the sky falls down and drowns them with blue. D'you believe me?"

"I'd be a fool not to believe you," said the sick man.

"I say," went on Speedy softly, but thoughtfully, like a man who strives not to be inaccurate, "that either or both of them would walk a thousand miles up a glass cliff to keep you from losing a hair from your head."

"Man," said Pier Morgan, "what did you do for them, then?"

"One wet day I asked them in out of the rain, and they came," said Speedy, more gently than ever. "Joe, are you playing this game with me?"

"To the limit," said Joe Dale. "I'm young enough to stay in school for a while. I used to think that Cliff Derrick was the whole show as a teacher, but he's all in the rough, compared with you, Speedy."

"You come down and see me at the hotel," said Speedy. "See me today. When you come to my room, knock twice, count twice, and knock again. That's all."

"You know, Speedy," said the outlaw, "that if I show my

98

face around, I'm gonna get rapped over the head. Likely with a half-inch slug of lead that will go right through the brain."

"I mean after dark," said Speedy.

Joe Dale rose.

He shook hands solemnly with Speedy and with Pier Morgan.

"I'm supposed to be on my way, I guess," said he. "I'm glad to know you, boys. You're gonna see me play up, Speedy."

He called his mare. "Come here, Betsy. You can't eat all the grass in the world every day. Come here and sit down." She came to him and sank on her haunches. He stepped into the stirrups and said: "All right, beautiful."

She rose gently, seating him comfortably in the saddle.

"Terrible lot of trouble, she is," said Joe Dale. "Always gotta be watched, all the time. Look at the way she stood up crooked! I never seen such a horse."

He waved his hand. "This evening, Speedy!" said he.

Instantly the mare, though she had received no visible sign, floated away up the trail at a gallop like the blowing of a cloud on the wind.

"The neatest thing I ever saw on four legs," said Pier Morgan.

Speedy was looking after the outlaw with a squint, as of one seeing distant mountains.

"That cost blood," he said.

"The horse?" asked Morgan.

"No, the coming here of Joe Dale. He's not such a woolly lamb, Pier. He's as mean as they make 'em. He'd murder, that lad."

"He eats out of your hand," said Pier.

"Just now, perhaps," said Speedy. "But it worries me."

"What does?"

"Seeing him so good—so like a lamb."

"Look, Speedy," said Morgan. "He was all in position. He

could have split your wishbone, from behind, and then mine, and nobody would have known anything about it."

"Oh, yes, they would," said Speedy. "He wasn't all alone, and perhaps he knew it."

"How do you mean?" asked Pier Morgan.

"Look up there toward the berry patch," said Speedy.

"I'm looking. There's nothing there."

"Nothing but Juan and his rifle," said Speedy. "And maybe Dale got the idea just as he started to drill me. I don't know. I'm only supposing!"

Just then, Pier Morgan saw Juan, the half-breed, walk out from the berry patch and saunter slowly down the hillside, half-carrying, half-dragging a rifle behind him. Every day, Juan spent a full hour with that rifle, shooting at targets; and no targets under five hundred yards were of interest to Juan. Scores under nine out of ten were to him a deadly sin.

Pier Morgan stared, remembering these things. He began to feel that Speedy was more and more complicated.

"Did you tell Juan to go up there and look things over?" asked Pier Morgan.

"Yes," said Speedy. "I told you that I saw Betsy's trail the other day. I like Joe Dale. Still, one can never tell. A good rifle at hand is never wasted in a country like this. But you stick to the revolver, when you begin to practice. I know your nature, Pier. You're going to be close to trouble before you open up. It takes a nerve of cast steel to do your killing at half a mile."

He went back to the shack and stood before the door, softly thrumming on his guitar. Old Anna, scrubbing wet cornmeal to a mash on a roughened stone, continued her motion, but looked up at him with a half-toothless smile.

Continuing to thrum, he said: "They're after my friend, Anna. So take him away. Fade out, into the mountains, you and him, and open your eyes and keep them open, night and day. How is Juan?"

"Juan will be good for another week, perhaps," said Anna, without emotion. "Life is just a little quiet, for him."

The thrumming ended.

Speedy, speaking in the same purring Spanish, said: "That may be enough. Get my friend to his feet every day, and let him walk a few steps, leaning on Juan. A helpless man makes crooks go straight."

"Father," said the old woman, "your wisdom is out of the central blue of the sky! I shall do as you say. Is there much danger?"

"Yes," said Speedy. "There's throat-cutting in the air you breathe, all around here."

Then, he went to the gray mule, climbed onto the rickety saddle, and, having waved a good-by, steered the old animal back up the trail, singing cheerfully to his guitar as he went.

CHAPTER 21

In the meantime, the swinging gallop of the bay mare had carried Joe Dale up the slope, over the crest of the divide, and down the slope from which he saw the long ravine of Sunday Slough, with its ragged cliffs gleaming on either side.

Now bare rocks cropped up on either side, and he scanned them with a rapid eye. Now a grove of pines on one side and of poplars, beside swiftly running water, on the other screened him. As he galloped by this double screen, on either hand, suddenly he pulled the mare to a halt and brought a heavy revolver into either hand.

At the same time, a heavy bass voice exclaimed: "Aw, quit it, kid. If I'd wanted your scalp, wouldn't I 'ave gone and got it before you seen me?"

And One-eyed Mike Doloroso, adjusting the patch upon his face, rode out of the screen of the poplars into the trail.

The muzzle of the gun in Joe Dale's right hand slowly tipped down.

"What's all this about, anyway?" he asked, in none too pleasant a voice.

"What's all that about, yonder?" asked Mike Doloroso, with a scowl. "You go out to get Speedy and ten grand, and you come back without doin' nothin'. I seen you down there behind his back, with a gun in your hand."

"Yeah, and you wondered why I didn't do nothing?" asked Joe Dale, as they rode their horses side by side down the trail.

"That's what I was asking myself," said Mike.

"Because there was somebody behind me," said Dale.

"Like what?"

"Like a no-good half-breed, sitting in a berry patch with a rifle glued to his shoulder, and me for a target, a hound that splits your head at five hundred yards and don't ask no questions who his name might be."

"That Juan, maybe," said Mike.

"Maybe it was," said Joe Dale.

"That was a bad pinch," said Mike. "I know that Juan. He can shoot till the cows come home, too."

"He can't miss," said Joe Dale. "I know about him, too. He shoots a man as slick as a deer, too. He don't get no buck fever when there's a man in front of his rifle sights. He gets a dead center, and away you go."

"I recollect something like that," said One-eyed Mike, nodding his massive head. "Yeah, that was a bad break."

"You're right," said Joe Dale. "Did Sid Levine send you out to police me?"

"You know," remarked Mike Doloroso, "when a job like this has to be done, it's better to have a man on hand to check up. I mean, what with a slick talker like Speedy on deck, how was we to know that you wouldn't play double-cross as well as the next man?"

"Look at them scars."

"I can see 'em."

"That's where he rolled me in a living fire. How would you feel about a gent that had rolled you in a fire? And the rest of me is a match for my face. I'm all over scars."

"The way I heard the story," said Mike, "you didn't let nobody roll you."

Growing redder than his scars, so that they disappeared, Joe Dale said: "You know how it is. This here Speedy, he's a streak of greased lightning with his hands and he can talk seven languages with them. By the way, how come that he got the guns of yourself and Buck Masters, all in one day? Was that an accident?"

"The way that happened—" began One-eyed Mike.

Then he paused and looked dourly at his companion.

"Yeah, and I can guess how it happened," said Joe Dale.

"All right, you guess and maybe you won't be so far wrong," admitted Mike Doloroso. "He kind of has an extra set of brains in each hand, I guess."

"That's what he kind of has," agreed Joe Dale. "We both been stung, and so that makes us even, with him, so far as that goes."

"Yeah, maybe it does, all right," said Mike and added: "You seemed to be pretty good friends. I seen Betsy doing her tricks down there."

"Sure you did," said Joe Dale. "We got to an agreement."

"Like what?"

"I'm gonna double-cross you boys," said Joe Dale.

"Hold on!" said Mike.

"That's what I mean."

"You told him that you was playing with us, you fool?"

"Aw, he knew that already," said Dale.

"Did he?"

"Yeah. And now I like him so good that I'm gonna double-cross you, all three. You and Levine and Masters."

"How?"

"The details, they ain't fixed. I'm gonna see him later on."

"When?"

"That ain't settled, either, but if that hound hadn't been sitting in the berry patch, I would've settled Mr. Speedy today."

"There's been a lot of guys," said Mike, "that would've settled Speedy if things had been different."

"Yeah. Guys like you, maybe?" said Dale.

Mike suddenly laughed. "I guess that you're all right," he said. "Come on. Let's get down to town. Levine, he'll wanta know what's been happening."

"How can I get into Sunday Slough in the daylight?" asked Joe Dale. "There's too much money on my scalp, dead or alive."

"I'll show you the back way in," answered Mike. "Don't you worry about that."

It was midday, heavy with sunshine, thick with sleep, when they came in, rounding behind Sunday Slough, and One-eyed Mike Doloroso showed the way through the rocks, through the trees and tall shrubbery, until they were close to the Grand Palace.

In a patch of tall bushes, they dismounted.

"I don't like this, much," said Joe Dale. "I tell you this, sucker. If there's a bad break, my first bullet is for you, Mike, and no questions asked."

"Aw, I know that," said Mike. "But there ain't gonna be no trouble. When the boys in the Grand Palace see me, they stop looking. You pull your hat down over your eyes. That's all that you gotta do. The boys don't try to look through the shadows, when they see me. They know a friend, and a friend's friend."

They came in through the back door. A double-barreled,

sawed-off shotgun confronted them, along with a burly man who looked like a pirate behind the gun.

"Who you got there, Mike?" he asked.

"Your mother-in-law," said One-eyed Mike.

The guard laughed. "That's all right, too," said he, "Come in, brother."

They passed on to an inside room. Mike banged on the door, according to a certain well-memorized rhythm.

It opened. Buck Masters, the sheriff, big, powerful, magnificent, in a new checkered-flannel shirt, stood before them.

"All right, Mike," he said. "Come in. Bring your kid friend in with you, if you want."

"If I'm a kid, you're a goat," was all that Joe Dale could think to say.

Afterwards, he felt under the sneer of the sheriff that he had talked like a fool.

"Come on in, anyway. We all gotta be young, sometimes," said the sheriff. "Only some of us don't have to be so awful young as all of that!"

They passed into an inner chamber, and Joe Dale was uneasily aware that he was walking first and that Mike Doloroso and the sheriff were behind him. He was aware, through the back of his head, that they were exchanging looks, or whispers, or signs, or all three. In fact, he was distinctly uncomfortable.

In the inner room, he saw the small, bald head and the bulging red cheeks of Sid Levine, bent over a large ledger, in which the boss of Sunday Slough was writing slowly, with a most delicate and clerkly hand, finishing off each word with a little flourish. He wrote with one pen; he held another between his teeth.

He said thickly, his tongue rubbing against the pen between his teeth: "What's the matter, boys?"

No one answered.

Sid Levine blotted the last words he had written. Then he

put down pens number one and two, and raised his head to look at the trio.

He nodded.

He took a cigar from a silver box before him, examined it, laid it aside, chose another, and lighted it.

"Now what's anybody got on anybody else?" he asked, through a cloud of thick, rich smoke.

Said Mike Doloroso: "I dunno. I reckon that Joe Dale here has double-crossed us, but I ain't so sure. I leave it to you brainy guys to find out. I can only tell you what I seen."

CHAPTER 22

Joe Dale grew uneasy. He had not expected a reception exactly like this. Then Mike Doloroso spoke again: "This bird may be all right. I dunno."

"We ain't asking you for your brains," said Sid Levine. "We know what kind of brains you got. All we want to ask you is: what did you see and hear? What about our young friend, here?"

Joe Dale did not turn his head. He did not have to, to understand that the sheriff had shifted a revolver to a coat pocket, and that through the cloth he was leveling the revolver at the guest.

A thrill passed through the outlaw, not of fear, but like the touch of cold steel that gores the side of the thoroughbred and makes it put forth the ultimate effort in the home stretch. He grew calm, clear-minded, clear-eyed, ready for a death struggle.

"I trailed him up there to the place where Pier Morgan is hanging out," said One-eyed Mike, "and there was our friend, Speedy, all right, just as bright as ever, and setting out under a tree talking to his sick partner. And I seen Joe Dale go and soft-foot it down and come up behind the tree, then pull his gun and have the game in his hands."

"You plugged him, Joe?" asked Levine comfortably.

"No, that's what he didn't do," said One-eyed Mike.

Levine removed the cigar from the pale purple of his lips. "Uh!" said he. "Go on, Mike."

He looked not at Mike, but at the accused man.

Said Mike: "Instead of pluggin' Speedy, he got to talkin' to him. They talked real cheerful. He called Betsy over, and the mare done some tricks. Then he rode away, and I met him on the trail. He said that he hadn't shot Speedy because Juan was setting out in a brush patch up the hill, with a rifle ready."

He finished his narrative with a shrug of his heavy shoulders. "I got nothin' against Joe," he said. "I like him, in fact. But I like my boss better. That's all."

"Thanks, Mike," said Levine. "You know what it is—I got friends, and I got a lot of people workin' for me, but I appreciate what you just said. Enough things like that ain't said in the world. Guys get too hard."

"That's right," said the sheriff. He added, to Joe Dale: "What about it, Joe?"

"The greaser was up there in the berry patch," said Joe Dale. "That boy can crack nuts with his rifle at five hundred yards. I wasn't gonna go and make a fool out of myself."

"Can that dago shoot like that?" asked Levine, of the sheriff.

"He's pretty good," said the sheriff.

"He's pretty good," said One-eyed Mike. "He's too good, if you ask me."

"Speedy was setting under a tree, was he?" asked Levine.

"Yeah."

"And the kid, here, got up close to the tree?"

"Yeah, right beside it."

"You could've shot Mr. Speedy and hopped around the tree away from the greaser," said Levine.

"How would I 'ave got away, though?" asked Joe Dale.

"What I mean," said Levine, spitting another shred of tobacco toward the ceiling, "is that a real go-getter like you, he don't waste no time. He just steps out and takes his chance. You wasn't taking no chances. Why not?"

"I told you why not. Mike saw why I didn't, if he had an eye in his head," said Joe Dale. But he felt that he was being cornered.

"Ten thousand dollars is a lot of money," said Levine.

"Yeah. Sure it is," said Joe Dale. "And a lump of lead to fit a rifle barrel ain't such a load, either. But it's pretty heavy when it sits in the brain."

Levine shook his head.

"We oughta be reasonable," he said.

"I'm reasonable," said Joe Dale.

"You cooked us with Speedy," said Levine.

"I dunno what you mean."

"You went up there to kill Speedy. But the price didn't look good. He bid over us. You're playing with him right now."

"You're crazy," said Dale.

"I ain't as crazy as you'd wish," said Levine. "I'm smart, Joe. You can't pull the wool over my eyes."

"You can't make a fool of Mr. Levine, Joe," said One-eyed Mike.

"Oh, shut up, Mike, will you?" said Levine gently.

He put the cigar back into his mouth and puffed it carefully, until the coal glowed in a bright circle again. He said around the tobacco: "You went and double-crossed us, Joe."

"Speedy chucked me in a fire," said Joe Dale. "He made a fool of me. Why should I double-cross you boys for him?"

"He sent back your horse to you," said Levine. "Not that

a horse is much. It's only so much money on the hoof. But he sent your horse back. I know how it is. I know what sentiment is, all right. I wouldn't wanta see a gent without no sentiment in his make-up. Would I?"

"You was always kind of soft," said One-eyed Mike.

"Shut up, Mike," said Levine. "What I mean is, ten thousand wasn't enough for you, Joe."

"I didn't say that," said Dale. "You're stringin' your own story together out of this here."

"Ten thousand ain't so much, either," said Levine. "Maybe you could use more."

"Say, what are you driving at, Sid?" asked Buck Masters.

Levine said: "I like the kid. I could use him. He could use me, too, only he don't know it. I could be a friend to you, Joe, know that?"

"Thanks," said Joe Dale.

Levine went on: "You want enough coin to do something big, something pretty. When you left home, you was never coming back till you could buy the farm next to the place where your old man lives. You were gonna show him that you're as big a man as he is. Ain't that so?"

The mouth of Joe Dale fell open. "Who told you that?" he asked.

"A little bird," said Levine. "I got a lot of little birds working for me. I know the language."

He winked, without smiling.

Dale said: "Well, what about it?"

"How much is that ranch worth?"

"Twenty, thirty thousand," said Dale. "What about it?"

"Suppose," said Levine, "that you ride home, one night, and rap on the front door. The old man comes and opens it. 'Who's there?' says he. 'It's Joe,' says you. 'Maybe you think you're good news?' says he. 'I don't think nothin',' says you. 'Here's twenty-five thousand bucks. Take this here coin and buy the Smith place, and run it for me till I can run it for myself. Just now, I'm too busy doin' things more important than that.' Well, suppose that you could talk to the old man like that, Joe?"

Joe Dale considered. His eyes began to burn.

"They always called me a worthless bum!" he said through his teeth.

"That was because they didn't know a man when they seen one," said Levine. "But I'm different. I know a man when I see one! I know a man's price, too, usually. I thought that ten thousand was your price—I was wrong. Twenty-five thousand dollars is your price. Wait a minute."

He went to a safe in the corner of the room. Most of the paint and gilding was battered from the face of it. He unlocked the doors, spinning the combination deftly in his big, soft fingers. Then he took out three packages wrapped in brown paper. These he brought back and gave into the hands of Joe Dale.

"What's this?" asked Joe Dale.

He was gray-green and trembling a little.

"That's twenty-five thousand, paid in advance," said Levine. "You can count it over, if you want to."

Joe Dale closed his eyes. He felt helpless and hemmed in on every side by stronger wills and superior brain power. If he avoided this lure, he would be taken in another way. Or, else, very likely the revolver in the pocket of Buck Masters would drive a bullet through his back.

But, as he closed his eyes, what he chiefly saw with his mind's eye was the picture which had been so skillfully painted for him by Sid Levine.

Levine knew everything, or else he could not have known this much! It was exactly what would happen. Afterward, he could see his bearded father slap the money down on the kitchen table and hear him say: "Ma, you was right all along. The kid had something in him!"

For some reason, that seemed to Joe Dale the greatest

reward that he could ever hope to find upon this earth.

He gripped the three brown-paper packets. He thrust them into an inside pocket. It made the breast of his coat bulge.

"It's twenty-five thousand, eh?" he said dreamily.

"Count it. Be business like," said Sid Levine.

Joe shook his head.

"You're right," he said. "I was gonna double-cross you. Speedy, he kind of hypnotizes me."

"Yeah, he's a fox," said Sid Levine.

"I was gonna rig up a play with Speedy, tonight," said the boy.

The other three exchanged looks.

"What sort of a play?" asked Levine.

"I dunno. I was to meet him at his room in the hotel," said Joe Dale.

"I see," said Levine. "No real plans laid out yet?"

"No. And I see what the real plans are gonna be," said the boy. "You have some men waiting in the hall outside the door. When the right times comes, I'll see that they get in. We'll all work together to finish off Speedy!"

CHAPTER 23

Later, when the boy had left the place, One-eyed Mike said: "You never threw twenty-five thousand at my head like that, did you, Levine?"

"You wouldn't want it," said Levine.

"No? I wouldn't want it?" exclaimed Mike.

"What would you want with twenty-five thousand of the queer?" asked Levine.

"Hey! Was that queer?" asked Mike.

"Sure it was. What kind of a fish d'you think I am?"

"He'll spot it," said Buck Masters. "The kid has an eye in his head!"

"He won't spot it, not for a long time," said Levine. "The point is that he's outlawed. He don't dare come close enough to a place where he can spend money. Besides, Speedy's to die tonight. And I'm thinking that it's worth twenty-five thousand to have him out of the way."

"Yeah, or a hundred thousand," said the sheriff, "if you come right down to that!"

"Yeah, if we can get him out of the way. I'm sorry about Speedy, though."

"I'll bet you're sorry," said Buck Masters.

Then he began to laugh.

"The way you done it was pretty slick, Sid. I mean, the way you handed him that package like it was diamonds."

"Yeah, it's the way you do thing that counts," said One-eyed Mike, leering with admiration. "It ain't the words. It's the way you speak 'em."

Sid Levine let his tongue loll, then licked the cigar into his mouth and stowed it comfortably. There was plenty of mouth left for smiling, and he smiled.

"It's good stuff," he declared. "Those green goods are worth twenty per cent of anybody's money, if they're handled right. The kid ain't beat so bad, if he uses his brains, but his brains ain't much good, except for handling a gun."

"You're the brain, Sid," said Buck Masters. "You always know what to do when the pinch comes."

"I got some ideas, that's all," said Sid Levine. "This brat of a Speedy, he's been getting on my nerves, what I mean. I got tired of him, is all. And tonight I'm gonna have him out of the way. Who'll we send to the hotel tonight? Mike, you'll go along?"

"I wouldn't be nowhere else," said Mike. "How about you, Buck?"

"Don't be a fool," said the great Levine. "Sometimes you ain't got any sense, Mike. We gotta have the sheriff safe. He's the front of the store. He's half the business. We can't mix him into gun plays. Not before the final clean-up starts anyway. We gotta be careful of each other."

"Sure," said Mike. "Careful of everybody except me. I don't count."

"Aw, shut up, Mike. I'm thinkin' about you all the time," said Levine. "You're proud; that's the trouble with you. You're proud and you're always afraid that people ain't paying enough attention to you. I tell you what—I'm paying attention and I'm paying you cash, too. Something better'n cash. You see this here diamond in this scarf?"

"I can see a headlight on a train, too," said One-eyed Mike, "if the night's dark enough."

"This is gonna be yours," said Levine. "If it ain't worth five grand, I'm a sucker. It's gonna be yours the minute I read in the papers about how poor Speedy was shot up and laid out. I'd give you money, instead, but I wouldn't wanta pass money between friends like you and me are. I got an affection for you, Mike. I want you to have something of mine. Now you go out and rustle up three more good boys. You'll know where to find 'em. Boys that wear a padlock on their jaws and that know how to shoot. Sunday Slough is full of 'em now. They may not all be Joe Dales, but they're tough enough to finish the job if he breaks the ice."

One-eyed Mike left the room.

"You done that pretty good, too," said the sheriff.

"Aw, Mike's easy," said Levine. "You gotta give him both sides of your tongue, is all. The rough side and then the smooth side. You know how it is! Like stropping a razor."

"Is there a flaw in that rock?" said the sheriff.

"Yeah, there's a flaw, all right," said Sid Levine, grinning. "There's a flaw, but the setting covers it up, pretty good. And Mike, he won't never look at it except to admire it."

"Except when he's broke and goes to pawn it," said the sheriff.

"He won't be broke while he's with me," argued Levine, "and when he ain't with me, what do I care?"

He then leaned over toward Buck Masters.

"You know how it is, Buck. A man has gotta have tools to work with. And you can't always choose. You gotta take the handiest thing. Ain't I right?"

"You ain't never very far wrong, maybe," said Buck Masters. "That's why you get along in the world, partner."

"But now and then," went on Sid Levine, "I find a man after my own heart, a man that I can talk to. I mean, a coupla times in my life I've found a man like you, Buck!"

"Aw, that's all right," said the sheriff lamely.

"I ain't a man that talk comes easy to," said Sid Levine. "Not when I wanta say what's in my heart. Only, I had to say a coupla words to you, Buck. That's all. Just between you and me. I wouldn't let the rest of the world in on it. I wouldn't let Mike know. Mike's all right, but he's small-time. You know what I mean?"

"Well, he's small-time," said the sheriff, clearing his throat. "Yeah, he's useful, though."

"He's paid for being useful, too," said Levine. "But when it comes to cutting the big melon—you know what I mean—you and me, we sit right here and split everything fifty-fifty. When we're through doing that, we pay off the small fry. Am I right?"

"It sounds like you're right," said the sheriff.

He felt enlarged with importance. He was glad that Levine had been able to look through the roughness of his exterior and find in him qualities which he was conscious that he possessed, judgment, tact, real weight of mind.

He stood up and helped himself to one of Levine's cigars.

He lighted it, dropped the match thoughtfully upon the floor, and watched it burn out, leaving a straight, black mark.

"Yeah," said the sheriff, "you and me could do some big business together, Sid. No mistake about that. We could get along very well together, because we know one another."

"We know one another, all right," said Sid Levine, his glance resting upon the plundered cigar box.

"I gotta buzz along," said Buck Masters. "I got an idea about Chambers' place across the street. They're pulling in too much trade, and I got an idea for queering that joint. So long, Sid."

He went out, and Sid Levine, gloomily, for a moment eyed the cigar box. Then he jerked the lid shut with a snap.

He took the half-consumed cigar from his own mouth, looked at it, and sighed. He was beginning to wonder how he could skid Buck Masters out of the way when the moment for the cutting of the big melon finally arrived.

Time would take care of that. He always found, when the pinch of the crisis came, ideas leaped, full-armed, from his Jovelike brain.

It was an odd world, he reflected, and one of the greatest of oddities in it was the manner in which the nameless, worthless tramp, Speedy, had grown large upon the horizon of Sunday Slough and his own mind. However, the last day of Speedy had apparently come.

Gradually, Sid Levine began to smile. His face softened and grew younger. For he was, as he himself confessed, a man who had some deep sentiments.

CHAPTER 24

Speedy lingered on the way into town, not because of the slow pace of the gray mule, particularly, but because he disliked towns of all kinds and, of all the places he knew, Sunday Slough was the town most peculiarly distasteful to him.

However, it held a certain amount of excitement. For he told himself that he was approaching the end of the trail leading to the downfall of the great Levine and his cohorts.

He had needed, from the beginning, a man in whom he could trust, a man to guard his back, as it were. Pier Morgan would have done, but Pier was long in recuperating. Now, however, chance had put a more valuable ally in his place, young Joe Dale.

Joe was exactly the fellow for him. In the first place, the opposition would not be likely to guess that he had recruited as a friend a man who had so many reasons for hating him. In the second place, Joe Dale was a man without fear, a man, too, who wielded a most accurate revolver. He would be ideal for almost any situation that could arise. And before the end, Speedy was sure that guns would start barking and smoking.

His peace of mind was almost perfect, therefore, as he finally rode into Sunday Slough that evening.

A galloping party of punchers from the range land beyond the valley, overtook him at the edge of town, recognized him, and swept him into Sunday Slough in the midst of cheers and the shooting of guns.

When he came near the sheriff's office, he saw big Buck Masters in the act of locking the front door and reined in the stumbling, trotting mule. He waved the cowpunchers ahead, and they went, still roaring like a great wave on a rocky beach.

Speedy waited until the sheriff stepped onto the wooden sidewalk. Then he said: "What's doing, Buck?"

"Nothing much," said the sheriff, looking at him with a calm and considering eye. "You oughta go home and rest yourself, Speedy. You're always on the move."

"It's hard to shoot a bird on the wing," said Speedy carelessly.

"Yeah, that's true, too," said the sheriff. "It's better to wait till they're sitting down, if you're shooting for the pot. It's better to wait till they're on their own roost and going to sleep for the night, as a matter of fact."

He nodded his head. He seemed to attach a good deal of importance to his own words and the thought behind them.

"You won't be needing me this evening, then?" Speedy said.

"You might make an eight o'clock round, maybe," said the Sheriff. "That's when things begin to warm up a little. Look in at Chambers' joint. He's running crooked games, too, I guess. Gonna be trouble in that place, one of these days."

Speedy agreed, and so turned off towards the hotel. When he reached it, he said: "Anything for me to do, Sammy?" The clerk shook his head.

"We're pretty peaceful today, Speedy," said he. "Been some boys here looking for you, and Bill Turner of the *News* was in here, wanting to get some new copy for his paper."

"You tell him that I'm tired of being copy," said Speedy. As he turned from the desk, Bill Turner, editor, reporter and printer, and most other things to the Sunday Slough *News*, came running in. He wanted a new story, and he knew that Speedy could furnish him with one.

Speedy, on second thought, took him up to his room. It was a corner room, with two windows. The hotel refused to charge a price for it to the benefactor of the town.

In the room, he said: "Bill, I have no news for you. Nothing that I can give out today. Suppose that you give me some news?"

"Me?" said Turner, blinking. "Why, Speedy, I'm a reporter, and I go around and collect what I hear, and—"

"Tell me what you hear," said Speedy.

"About what?" asked Turner, gaping.

"I'm a seven-day man," said Speedy. "That's as long as a deputy sheriff is supposed to last in Sunday Slough. I've lasted longer than that already. Now open up and tell me

117

something, like a good fellow. What gangs are after my scalp?"

"Levine is the main gang, and you're in with him," said Turner. "You ain't got anything to worry about."

Speedy shook his head. "Come clean for me, Bill," he urged.

Turner began to sweat. He went to a window, looked out on the street, and then turned suddenly around, with his jaw set.

"This town don't like law and order, Speedy," said he. "It's always been wide open. There's a lot of boys that like to turn loose with their guns and settle their troubles offhand. But Boot Hill Cemetery hasn't been growing very fast since you started in Sunday Slough."

"They're tired of me, are they?" asked Speedy.

"You know," explained the reporter feverishly, "the minute that there's any trouble anywhere, in a bar or a dance hall or a gambling house, there's a hurry call for you, and you always get there in time. Look at the number of fellows you've thrown into jail, since you came to town. It makes the nights quieter, but it kind of takes away some of the life. About the only way I can find a story, nowadays," he finished plaintively, "is to go and ask you what you've been doing lately. And Sunday Slough isn't satisfied with a one-ring circus. It wants three rings, and all of them filled all the time!"

He mopped his brow.

"You wanted to know, and I had to tell you," said he. "You know how it is. A lot of the workers in town, the miners and such, they'd pay you your weight in gold to keep you on here. But a lot of the other boys want more elbowroom. That's all I can say, except—"

He paused.

"Go on," said Speedy.

"If I was you, I'd move on," said Bill Turner softly. "Don't say that I said so. But if I was you, I'd move on. You've lived several times seven days here in Sunday Slough, but seven times seven, you ain't gonna live. That's the fact!"

Now that he had spoken, he turned and hurried from the room, and Speedy saw a shudder go through the body of the reporter as he opened the door and looked up and down the hall. Then Bill Turner closed the door behind him and was gone.

Left alone, Speedy sat quietly in a corner of his room, and for a moment he added up the facts.

It was true that he was each day nearer to a gun play that might end his life. On the one hand, he had built up a reputation that was a fortress. On the other hand, his very reputation was a lure to the gunmen. Any lad on the loose, desiring to make a reputation for himself, could establish a very great reputation, even though it led to outlawry, by putting a bullet through the heart of the deputy sheriff of Sunday Slough.

And he, Speedy, went unarmed!

He shivered at the thought. He felt naked in a winter wind.

However, now that he had Joe Dale on his side, it was worth lingering out his time and spending a few more days to settle the hash of Levine and company before slipping away from Sunday Slough forever.

He went down to supper.

There was a general squeaking of chair feet on the floor, as the men turned in the dining room to stare at him. In the corner next to the wall, there was a comfortable armchair placed at the table, with plenty of space left on either side of it. That chair was his chair. It was always reserved for him.

Now, as he approached it, a tall, big-boned young fellow as brown as a nut stepped in before him, dragged back the chair and slipped into the vacant place.

He stretched forth a great hand toward the bread plate and

took off a stack of slices. He hurriedly began to devour one of them, without butter.

Speedy stood still. He was not deceived. The intentness of the youth on the bread was a mask to cover his real interest —which was the result that would follow his usurpation of the privileged chair.

The very thing that Bill Turner had warned Speedy about was to happen here, perhaps in the hotel dining room. For his own part, however, he would by no means fight about so trivial a matter as a seat at a table.

But a rough voice beside the stranger exclaimed: "Kid, you're in the wrong place."

"Am I?" said the big lad. "Where ought I be, then?"

"I dunno. In the street, maybe," said the unshaven miner who had made the remark. "That chair belongs to Speedy, and you had oughta know it."

"If I belong in the street, you put me there," said the stranger.

"You're askin' the right man for a free ride as far as the street," said the miner. And, half rising, he lashed with his fist at the head of the big fellow. The latter put the blow aside with ease. Then, from the thin air, he produced a gun and laid the muzzle against the breast of the other.

"Back up, brother," said he.

CHAPTER 25

The flash of that gun scattered people from the table. Speedy came as fast as he could, now that he saw a friend in mortal danger, but with all of his speed, he knew that he would never be in time to save the miner of the unshaven face from a bullet wound.

Moreover, people got in his way. In their haste to get out of the probable path of flying bullets, they dived here and there.

"It's Dick Cleveland!" somebody yelled. "Gimme room! It's Crazy Dick Cleveland!"

The name definitely registered upon the ear of Speedy, but he could not place it in his memory. However, it was plain that this youth was formidable.

The big miner was a strong man, well developed by manual labor and apparently familiar with rough-house fighting. He merely snarled at the sight of the revolver and, clubbing a fist, he smashed it into the face of the big boy.

The head of "Crazy Dick" bobbed. But he was not stunned. He was a giant of strength, it appeared at once. With his left hand, he took the left fist of the miner, a left-handed man. With a jerk, he turned him halfway around. Then he slammed the length of cold gun barrel along the skull of Speedy's champion, and the latter slipped in a loose heap to the floor, completely out.

Speedy was only glad, as he came darting in, that it had been a blow rather than a bullet that had ended that preliminary fray. In the split second that remained, he estimated his foe more carefully and intelligently.

The lad was older, perhaps, than he had at first appeared. He was twenty-one or two, in the first strength of manhood, when strength is most dangerously supple. His three or four inches over six feet might weigh two hundred and twenty pounds; yes, even a shade more than that. And he was all of a piece, in spite of his inches.

Speedy came in like a flash. He was not wasting time, no matter how many judgments he was summing up. His friend, the unknown miner, was already disposed of and lying limply upon the floor. That was something to charge against the supposedly invulnerable Speedy at the start.

Now, coming in with a final leap, he saw that he would not have time to reach the man, only the gun hand of Crazy Dick. That hand he reached with his best weapon—the edge of his palm with which he gave the cleaver stroke of his hand, the edge serving as the cleaver's rim. He aimed with accuracy and smote the wrist of the big fellow just across the tendons, where they stood out like a whipcord.

His own hand rebounded. It was as if his own flesh were frangible and had been brought into sharp contact with wrought iron. At the same time he saw the gun hand of the other relax slowly, and the heavy Colt slid to the floor.

It exploded as it struck. The bullet skidded across the flooring, raising a great furrow of splinters. Somebody with high-strung nerves seemed to think that he had been hit, and yelled in terror.

The loss of the gun did not seem to dishearten the big youth. He turned on Speedy with a flaring sneer on his mouth, and the wild delight of battle in his pale blue eyes.

Speedy was suddenly swallowed in a powerful embrace. By sheer luck he managed to have his right arm free. The palm of it was bruised from the first blow. But he nerved himself to deliver another. The arms of the other were around him like two tightening coils of steel cable.

The breath went out of him with one husky gasp. Then, desperately, he smote with the cleaverlike edge of his palm, high up on the deltoid muscle just where it sprang from the shoulder, just where the tendons took hold of the bone. But his bruised hand simply rebounded as though he had struck down on a tangled mass of India rubber.

He could feel a roar and hear it in his ears. It was partly his own blood and partly the thunder of the crowd. From the corners of his blurring eyes, he could see men standing on chairs, on the table, yelling and whooping, some in delight, some in sheer amazement.

For here was an almost nameless man literally swallowing

the firebrand of Sunday Slough. Here was the conqueror of Cliff Derrick being treated like a novice!

Speedy tried his cleaver stroke again, this time lower down, where the deltoid muscle sloped away, close to the bone of the upper arm and almost halfway down to the elbow. It was a cruel stroke. It made a leaping pain run up his own arm to the heart, but it brought a grunt from Big Dick. His left arm was suddenly, for the moment, almost helpless. And a twisting whirl brought Speedy into the clear.

A great thunder of applause greeted him. He heard men fairly screaming with pleasure. But he could feel the effects of that bear hug still. Altogether, he had been in that terrific embrace not more than a second or two; but, if it got him again, he felt that he was fairly beaten.

And now Crazy Dick, with flaring, dancing eyes that lived up to his name, was after him as a hound is after a rabbit.

Speedy tried out his man with plain fists. He had his doubts, but, after all, he had felled men of much greater bulk than Crazy Dick with simple fisticuffs.

Under the big paws of Cleveland, he ducked and, rising, he struck four times without a return. Every blow had all his might behind it and every blow was on the jaw of Crazy Dick, close to the button.

But Dick did not fall. Instead, he made a long, gliding pace forward, feinted with his left hand for the face, and then drove a steam-piston right, full at the body of Speedy.

Speedy was taken by surprise; nevertheless, he blocked that blow. He blocked it and felt as though he had put his arm in front of the stroke of a walking-beam.

The punch was thrown a little out of line. It merely grazed the ribs of Speedy, but he thought the flesh had been ripped away. The glancing force of that stroke spun him around like a top and sent him staggering backward.

The lights blurred before him. The room dropped into silence. He could fairly feel the sinking pulse of those who had felt that he was the sure winner of any contest.

Then a snaky arm of iron, clad in a rubber-hosing of hard muscles, caught him around the neck.

That strangle hold shut off his wind, crushed his windpipe and sent red-hot splinterings of metal shooting up through his brain. He was lifted from the floor and swept about as a hammer thrower lifts the hammer and spins before he hurls it.

Where would he be hurled? How hard would he hit the wall? Or would his neck break before he was flung away?

Then the support that held him up staggered, went down.

Crazy Dick, in the excess of his joy at getting this unfair but certainly victorious hold, had overdone the thing and lost his balance.

Speedy was flung away, to be sure, and spun over and over along the boards of the floor; but Crazy Dick had dropped, at the same time, and given the back of his head a promising thump against the same flooring.

He was still rolling as Speedy scrambled to his hands and feet. He was sick, very sick. The sparks were still shooting, in diminished showers, across his eyes. His knees were weak. His jaws seemed to lack hinges but, as the formidable length of Crazy Dick rose from the floor, Speedy forced himself to run in toward the other. He knew that, as fighting tactics, this was wrong. He merely hoped that his charge might break the morale of the other. But he saw at once that this was a mistake, for Crazy Dick did not even wait to receive the charge. He rushed forward with immense strides to meet the attack.

As he came, he made only one trifling mistake; he drew his right hand back as a fist, halfway to his shoulder.

It was not a big mistake; it was merely telegraphing a punch; but Speedy needed only a chance, even though that chance was a small one.

Now, at the very moment of impact, he checked his own

124

rush short and stood to receive that of the tall man.

Sure enough, the terrible right hand launched forth, straight and swift as a piston stroke, a piston whose head was finished off with knuckles of brass and steel.

As it came, Speedy swerved and spun. It was a very good trick. It could only be used against a big man, a confident man. And Crazy Dick was both of those things.

So he thrust the whole length of his right arm into space over Speedy's shoulder and found that the smaller man had actually whipped around and stood with his back to Dick's breast. At the same time, he reached up and caught the arm of the tall fellow and bent forward.

It was really the rush of Crazy Dick himself that caused the mischief. The well-braced body of Speedy was merely a hurdle, so to speak, over which Dick flung his weight, and the downward tug on his arm was merely what flicked the feet of Dick high into the air.

He sailed forward over the hurdle. He landed on head and shoulders where the floor joined the wall. Yet, he was not knocked out! To the utter amazement of Speedy, he saw the tall man leap to his feet, turn, and stretch out his long, sinewy arms on guard!

Yes, that was the picture that Speedy saw. But a fury of incredulity suddenly overwhelmed him completely.

He told himself that his eyes saw no more than a lie. It was the mere seeming, the mere hollow shell of a man that stood there. No human being could withstand such a shock with impunity. Therefore, he ventured straight in, within the danger of those apelike arms.

A fist shot at his head and the blow seemed as strong as ever. He dropped his head to one side, and let the punch hiss against his cheek.

Then he stepped in, rose on his toes as he hit over the high shoulder of Crazy Dick, and dropped upon his heels as his fist flashed home with a thud, dropping upon the point of Cleveland's jaw.

As he struck the mark, there was a change in the attitude of Crazy Dick. His body slumped back. His shoulders were now braced against the wall. The light went out of his eyes.

His knees were still straight and his guard was professionally high. But Speedy knew what that blank, animal look in the eyes meant. He stepped back and lowered his own aching arms. He controlled his voice and made it as casual as ever.

"Some of you boys take care of him, will you?" said Speedy. "He'll start falling to pieces in a minute, and he's a good game lad. Will some of you give him a hand?"

"He don't look like he needs a hand, except on the jaw, again," said a cowpuncher near by. "But I'll take care of him if he needs care."

He approached and, at the same time, Crazy Dick began to slip along the wall and lean more and more to one side. His guard was still up, his knees were still stiff, but his whole body was falling.

The cowpuncher caught him; the whole mass of Crazy Dick collapsed and slid like water through the detaining hands, and so down to the floor.

CHAPTER 26

In the armchair which was set aside for that purpose, Speedy sat and ate his supper. He felt that his color was not good. Gripping pains clutched at his throat. The whole side where Dick's punch had clipped his ribs was sore and swollen. But he knew that he had to sit there and smile and chat, and be amiable as though that battle had been a mere nothing to him.

They had seen him slung about in the air like a throng in the hand of a mischievous boy. He must wipe that impression out of their minds.

He did not want to eat. The pain had taken all his appetite, but he had to force down the stuff. He had to praise the thin, gray, greasy beefsteak, and take a second helping. And he had to talk.

This was what it meant to be the hero of the town!

The others could hardly eat for another reason. They could not shift their eyes from the face of this slender youth who broke up big men as children break brittle kindling wood across the knee. With shining eyes they worshiped him. And all the time, his hurts were stiffening his body.

A boy came hurrying into the room.

"There's a terrible ruction over at Chambers' place. Will you come on the run, Mr. Speedy?" cried the boy.

"Oh, I'll go on over," said Speedy.

He stood up, finished his cup of black coffee on his feet. Then, amazed, as he put down the cup, he saw that every man at the long table was on his feet, also.

"Here's to the most double-barreled, gun-cotton, distilled-dynamite, boiled-down wild cat that ever walked!" yelled the miner, the lump on whose head was evidence that he had fought for the good name of Speedy.

The whole table roared out a cheer and made it three times three.

They picked Speedy up on their shoulders. They carried him with a rush across the street and down to Chambers' place, were the sounds of a near riot were beginning.

No man was at the door. They walked on into the gambling house like a river in flood, and there, behold! A long-haired monster from the hills, with a gun in either hand, was trying to eat Chambers' place like a flaming dragon.

"I want the horned toad," he was shouting, "that calls himself the boss of Sunday Slough. I wanta have a look at

Speedy. I'm gonna look at his insides, I'm gonna—"

And then he saw Speedy, dumped down before him from the shoulders of wild-eyed men; and all about him, silently, the rough men of Sunday Slough were pouring in.

His shouting stopped. He stood aghast.

Speedy stepped up to him and laid a hand upon his arm.

"If you'll let me take care of those guns of yours for to-night, partner," said Speedy, "I'll take you where you'll have a good, quiet sleep. In the morning, if you can settle up with Chambers for the damage that you've done, perhaps you'll get out of Sunday Slough all in one piece."

The wild man gave up his guns without a murmur! He had in his eyes the same stunned look that had appeared in the eyes of Crazy Dick, after the latter had been done in by the punches of Speedy. The mental effect seemed to be the same in both cases. So Speedy took the wrecker to jail.

After this the enthusiasm in Sunday Slough knew no bounds. The whole place began to celebrate, not its own virtues, but those of its deputy sheriff.

The house of Chambers, out of gratitude for destruction stopped, rolled three barrels of whisky out into the middle of the street and three bartenders ladled to all who would have that liquid fire, free of charge.

It was a fine night, a large night, a grand night. The sky rang till it cracked with whoopings and the joy that floated up to it and banged against its blue-black face from the streets of Sunday Slough.

In the meantime, the theme of all the celebration, the original tamer of wild men, the one and only Speedy, lay flat on his back in his bedroom, his arms thrown out wide, his eyes half-closed, trying to forget the bitter aching of his hurts and wondering when he could escape from the teeth of this mad town.

While he lay there, in pain of body, in the barn behind the hotel, Joe Dale kneeled at the side of the huge and un-strung body of Crazy Dick Cleveland.

Dick could lift his head from the floor, and that was about all.

From a pint bottle, Joe Dale poured a dram of whisky down the throat of the helpless man. Cleveland looked at him with lusterless eyes. When he finished coughing from the fire that had burned his throat, he said: "Who are you?"

"My name don't matter," said Joe Dale. "I'm in the same boat with you."

The other closed his eyes, opened them again, then said: "I been whanged and banged silly by a kid about a quarter my size."

"I been whanged and banged silly by the same kid," said Joe Dale.

"You ain't so big," argued the other bitterly, tasting the full shame of defeat.

"I'm big enough to have a hard fall," said Joe Dale.

"There was a crowd there that seen it all. There was a crowd that looked on and seen me go down!"

His face twisted into terrible anguish.

"Have another shot of this," said Joe Dale.

His keen eyes flickered from point to point of the face of the tormented man. He studied the increasingly labored breathing of Crazy Dick Cleveland.

"I gotta go away," said Crazy Dick. "I wouldn't dare to let nobody ever see my face again. Nobody!"

"Look," said Joe Dale, in a ringing voice.

Dick opened his eyes.

"Do you see these here marks? He picked me up just like he done you. He didn't throw me agin' a wall. He chucked me into a fire! I near burned alive. That's what he's done to me!"

Dick shook his head, staring. "I gotta go away," he repeated.

"You don't understand," said the smaller man. "We ain't gonna go away. But he's gonna go away. Look at me—I'm Joe Dale!"

"Go on," said Crazy Dick, sitting up suddenly. "It would take two of you, twice as old, to make Joe Dale. Joe Dale is the man that I—"

"I'm Joe Dale," said the boy.

Crazy Dick swallowed the words that he was about to utter. He continued staring.

"I say," went on Joe, "that we ain't gonna get out, but Speedy is."

"Gonna get where?" asked Crazy Dick, intelligence dawning in his face.

"You know where," said the other. "You and me are gonna send him."

"When?" asked Dick Cleveland.

"Tonight. Inside of an hour. Come to life. I got something to say to you. I got the job cold. Tonight he dies!"

CHAPTER 27

On the door of Speedy's room in the hotel, sounded two raps with long pauses between raps. Speedy went to the door, unlocked it and said: "Well?"

"It's me," murmured Joe Dale.

"Louder," said Speedy.

"It's me! It's me, I say."

"All right, come on in, Joe. I didn't get your voice at first."

Joe Dale stepped inside. His eyes swept around the room in a single, shifting glance, bright as the glance of a cat. Then he nodded.

"Glad to see you," explained Speedy. "Just lock that door behind you, will you?"

Joe Dale closed the door and twisted the key so that it rattled. He did not lock the door.

"There's that," he muttered, turning away from the door. "That'll be one fence for them to hurdle before they get at me."

"What's the matter, Joe? Got anything on your mind tonight?"

"Why?"

"You look worried."

"You're cast steel, Speedy," said the boy, "but it would worry even you, if you were in my boots, inside of a town like Sunday Slough. How many of the boys in this town that shoot straight and quick, would be glad to get together and hunt me down, if they knew that I was here?"

"Does anybody suspect it?" asked Speedy. "D'you think that you've been trailed, Joe?"

"I'm always trailed," muttered Joe Dale. "But I guess I'm all right. You wouldn't sell me, Speedy, would you?"

Speedy smiled.

"No, you wouldn't sell me, I guess," said Joe Dale. "But I dunno. I've seen some funny things happen in this here world, for the money."

"So have I," said Speedy. "Sit down."

"I want a drink."

"There's none in this room."

"Get some, then. Send a boy for some."

"They know I don't drink alone. You don't want them to think that you're in here with me, do you?"

Joe Dale made a face. From the water pitcher he filled a glass, swallowed a little of the liquid and made another and more bitter grimace.

"It tastes like poison," he said. "I can remember when worse slime than this tasted like heaven to me. But tonight it tastes like poison. I need a drink."

"Sit down," said Speedy. "You're nervous. Sit down, because we have to use our heads."

"I oughta carry a flask," muttered Dale.

"Don't you, usually?"

"Sure I do. But tonight I met a friend and used it up."

"You met a friend here in town?"

"Here in town? No, no, no! On the trail coming in."

"You must have been traveling high, wide and handsome," said Speedy calmly. "Letting people look you over in the open trail, eh? You must be worrying about something, old son!"

"Yeah, I'm always worrying," said Joe Dale. "I'm sick of this kind of a life that I been leading. I'm gonna quit it. I'm gonna get me a stake and settle down."

"Well, you ought to be able to make a stake. How much?"

"Oh, twenty, thirty thousand, maybe."

He glanced down toward a bulge in the front of his coat.

"You're wearing your gun slung pretty far forward under your coat tonight, Joe," said Speedy.

"That's where I keep it for a fast draw," said Joe Dale. "And that's where I keep it tonight. Now, what about business?"

"That's what I want to talk, but about guns, first. You generally carry your gat in a spring holster under the pit of the arm, don't you?"

"Yeah. You gotta do that, if you're gonna try to be good. It beats a hip holster all hollow. You get a better drop to your gun. It's faster, too. That's why I wear an extra size of coat."

"I see," said Speedy.

He stood back by the window, his head bowed a little.

"You look sick," said Joe Dale gruffly.

"I am sick," said Speedy.

"The big gent hurt you, did he?"

"Yes, he hurt me, but that's not what makes me sick," said Speedy.

"What is it?"

"It's guns in spring holsters," said Speedy.

"Whacha mean?"

"They're so fast and sure," said Speedy. "You understand?"

"You gonna start wearing guns, Speedy? Is that it?" asked the other curiously.

"Perhaps I ought to."

"Yeah, if it ain't too late," said Dale.

He looked down to the floor, so that the cold fire in his eye might not be seen. "Let me see your arrangement of that holster, will you, Joe?" asked Speedy.

"Well, why not?" said the other. But he drew back a little.

"Not if it's a patent arrangement with you, Joe," said the tramp.

"Well, you can have a look," said Joe Dale.

Speedy came nearer, unbuttoned the top button of the coat; and then his hand shot in as fast as a bird's beak dips to pick up a grain of wheat.

The grain of wheat that came out in Speedy's hand was a man-sized Colt .45.

"Hey, what's the idea?" asked Joe Dale, frowning.

The muzzle of the gun suddenly dropped against the hollow of his throat.

"Don't move, Joe," warned Speedy.

"You dirty hound," gasped Joe Dale. "You gonna double-cross me, are you? You drag me in here to double-cross me, do you?"

"I just want to see the load in your breast pocket," said Speedy, and he took out three small packages, wrapped in brown paper.

CHAPTER 28

He kept the revolver in place, the hard, cold rim of steel thrust into the hollow of Joe's throat. The tremor of Dale's cursing passed along the arm of Speedy.

In the meantime, he managed, with a forefinger, to rip the paper covering of the parcels; then he flicked the greenbacks rapidly, reading the numbers in the corner.

"Twenty, more than twenty thousand," said Speedy finally. "You said that your price might be between twenty and thirty thousand dollars. And so you sold me, Joe, did you?"

The cursing stopped. Joe Dale, gray of face, suddenly looking many years older, narrowed his eyes.

"That greasy pig, Levine, bought you up, did he?" went on Speedy. "I'm sorry about that, Joe. You could go as straight as the next fellow. You have it in you. But if you've sold out to Levine, believe me, he'll keep on using you for one job after another. Only, he'll never be able to use you for dirtier work than this—selling out a partner."

He dropped the three packages of money back into the breast pocket of Joe Dale. He held the revolver by the barrel and offered the gun to its owner.

"Here you are, Joe," said Speedy. "Go ahead with your dirty business."

Joe Dale received the weapon with a nerveless hand.

"Whacha mean, Speedy?" said he. "It's like you were askin' me to plug you!"

"I don't care what you do," said Speedy.

He turned his back and walked to the window, and stood there looking down into the thick well of darkness.

"I'm a gambler and a tramp," said Speedy, "but people make me sick. You and the rest. You make me tired of life. You're simply rotten, Joe. You could be straight, too. But you let a fat pig buy you up."

Joe Dale reached out and caught the edge of the table. He said, at last, very thickly and softly: "Speedy, wait a minute, will you?"

"Yes, I'll wait," said Speedy. "I suppose you've got some partners ready and waiting out there in the hall. Well, go out and bring them in through that door which you pretended to lock. Oh, this has been a thin job. A five-year-old child could have seen that you were crooked!"

Dale dropped the revolver into the holster within his coat. His face was whiter than ever.

"Wait a minute," said he.

"I'll wait here. I'd as soon be murdered by you and your hired men," said Speedy, "as to go on living in such a rotten world, where I have to know snakes like you. I wouldn't care about scum like Levine and Buck Masters. They're just what I expect. But you could go straight! I know you could, but you'd rather wallow in the muck!"

"I'm taking everything that you're saying," said Joe Dale. "You're right. I'm worse than scum. Go on, and say the rest. I wish you'd put a slug through my head, though. I'd rather be dead than to stand up here, Speedy, and see the sort of a thing that I am!"

"Now you're maudlin," said Speedy. "I see the way you're heading. You're going to tell me how much you repent, and that will last till your price is raised, but no longer."

"You can say anything you want to me," said Joe Dale. "You've earned the right to say it. Only gimme time to breathe. I ain't askin' you to gimme another chance. I'm just askin' you to wait and watch what I do! I don't say that I'm gonna go straight. But after Sid Levine's dead, and Buck Masters, and One-eyed Mike, then maybe you'll think a little better of me!"

"Are you going gunning for the whole lot of 'em?" asked Speedy.

"You smile, eh?"

"No, I don't smile."

"I'll get 'em or they'll get me."

"I believe you," said Speedy. "But that's not what I want. I don't want Sid Levine dead. I simply want him laid out where the law can get at him. Dying is too noble an end for Sid Levine. I want him packed away inside a jail!"

"I know what you mean," said Joe Dale. "That fat porker would die a hundred times a day, if he had to sweat off his fat working at a rock pile. But he'd never stay in prison. He'd buy his way out."

"He'd buy his way out of an ordinary place," said Speedy. "But I'm not talking about ordinary prisons. I'm talking of Federal stuff. Marshal Tom Gray is in town. He'd like to have a big carcass like Sid Levine to take to jail and render the lard out of him!"

"How'll you get Sid Levine on a Federal charge?" asked Joe Dale. "I wanta help. I wanta play the game your way, Speedy. I'll do my walkin' on my knees, the rest of my life, what I mean, if that's the sort of going that pleases you!"

"Joe," said Speedy, "you don't have to crawl to suit me. I know you. I know the stuff that's in you. That's what made me sick—thinking that even you could double-cross a partner. But I think you'll never stumble as low as that again. You'll help me to get Levine in the way that I want to get him?"

"You're right, I will. Only you tell me how the Federal marshals can get a call on him. Has he been smuggling?"

"Making the queer or passing it along," said Speedy. "Counterfeiting is Federal business."

"Great Scott," said Joe Dale. "Pushing the queer? Has he been making the stuff or handling it?"

"I don't think that he's been making it," said Speedy. "But he's certainly been handling it. If I can nail that on him, he'll go up for a long stretch. The Federal courts are pretty nasty about counterfeiting."

"They sock 'em about fifteen years, is all," said Dale. "Only, listen, Speedy. I started to double-cross you. How does it look if I turn around and double-cross Sid Levine? Yeah, and with his twenty-five grand in my pocket?"

"You didn't look twice at his money," said Speedy.

The face of the other changed. His brows twitched together into a frown. Suddenly he snatched the brown paper

136

packages from his pocket and pulled out a bill from one.

"This is all right," he said, snarling. "This is the straight goods. Wait a minute! You're right! I was selling myself for bad paper! I bump you off; then I let myself in for shoving the queer. Levine has made a clear fool out of me!"

He walked up and down the room with rapid, irregular steps. His fury turned from red to white heat.

Speedy said, "He could make a fool out of almost any one."

Dale stopped his pacing. He stood against the wall, straight, his feet braced far apart.

"You tell me what to do," he said. "I'm only a fool. I thought that I was a wise one, but I ain't. Now I start taking orders. You tell me what to do!"

"Thanks," said Speedy. "I'm trying to think it out. Where did Levine get that crooked money?"

"Out of the safe in his office."

"Seem to have plenty more?"

"He acted like he was tapping the Federal Reserve."

"Then we'll be able to get something more out of that safe," said Speedy. "That will be the proof. I want Gray along. He can be a witness."

"I can't go along with Gray," said the boy. "He wants me. They all want me!"

"He won't want you tonight," said Speedy. "Not after I've talked to him a while."

"What can we do in the Grand Palace?" asked Dale.

"Make Levine open his safe."

"You can't make him do that. Not legally."

"I'll do it illegally, then," said Speedy. "You and I will put on a pair of masks and stick him up. We'll make him open that safe and, while it's open, we'll have the marshal just happen along. You see? There may be a lot of other things in that safe that the marshal will be interested in."

Joe nodded. "It looks like pretty complicated business to me," said he. "But I'm not doubting that you're right."

"It is complicated," said Speedy. "It means, at its best, I'll only be getting Mr. Levine. And what I really want is the sheriff and One-eyed Mike at the same time. But if I get Levine, the rest of the show may fall like a house of cards. That's the bet I'm making."

"I'm ready to play, then," said Joe Dale.

Speedy went to the door of the room.

"I'm going to see the marshal," he said. "He came back this evening. I'll go to his room here in the hotel; then we'll go right down to the street. Meet you there, say, in twenty minutes. O.K.?"

"Anything you say is the right thing, Speedy. But let me go out there in the hall first."

"I understand," said Speedy. "You clear the hall, and then I'll start when you come back."

He went to the window and stood there, hearing the soft, quick step of Joe Dale as he left the room. In the hall, Speedy heard a murmur, then a snarling voice very like the voice of Crazy Dick. A blow was heard falling not on flesh but on bone. After a moment, Joe Dale returned.

He was panting.

"It's all right," he said slowly. "Take your time when you go out, though. There's a gent around here who'd like to cut your throat. I just socked him on the bean and got his guns away from him. But he can find other guns in this here town!"

CHAPTER 29

The marshal, Tom Gray, was in a sunny mood. This good humor expressed itself by a slight softening of the usually fixed, hard lines of his face. It expressed itself, also, in the rhythmical movement of his foot that swung, loosely pendent, from the crossing of his knees.

Upon his knee rested a small writing pad and he scribbled upon it the well-chosen words of an official report. He was still writing when the knock came at the door. He lifted his iron-gray head and listened for a moment.

Then he said: "Well?"

"Speedy," said the voice in the hall.

"Come in!"

The door was locked, but the marshal did not get up to turn the key. Instead, with a faint smile, he turned a bit in his chair to watch what might happen.

There was no sound of a hand trying the doorknob; only by staring with fixed intensity did the marshal, presently, see the inner knob turning.

Then, following, came the softest of clicks, a thing which no one would have noticed except by bending all attention toward the door; the door opened, and Speedy walked in.

"Good evening, Tom," said he.

He closed the door behind him and turned the key in the lock.

"I was afraid, Speedy," said the officer, "that I had locked the door; I'm mighty glad to see that I was wrong."

His smile was very faint.

"One gets odd ideas like that," said Speedy.

"Sit down," said the marshal. "I have some news for you, Speedy."

"Good," said the boy.

"It appears that here and there a few old charges rest against you, Speedy," went on the marshal, "just little things, now and then."

"I know," said Speedy, nodding.

"They're all rubbed away, now," said the marshal.

"You rubbed them out of the records?" asked Speedy

curiously.

"The government rubbed them out," said the marshal. "This government of ours appears pretty stiff in the joints and rheumatic, now and then. As a matter of fact, it can be fast and supple, when it gets started. And a good many people, high up, were interested in the fellow who caught Cliff Derrick."

"Ah?" said Speedy, with little apparent interest.

"They were particularly interested when they found out that you were not using the money of the reward for yourself. It was a comfortable fortune, that total reward."

"It wouldn't be comfortable for me," said Speedy. "I've never had blood money, and I never want to have any."

"But to give that money to Derrick's parents—isn't that almost rewarding vice?"

"There was no vice in the old people," said Speedy. "The one good thing about poor Derrick, with all his murders and other crimes, was that he supported his old folks. They never knew what sort of a rascal their son was. I took the money of the reward and bought a pair of annuities. They'll be comfortable till they die, at least!"

"That was a fine thing to do," said the marshal. "A mighty fine thing, Speedy."

"Do you really think so?" said the boy. "Well, I've had my reward for it."

"What sort of a reward, Speedy?"

The tramp took a thin wallet from an inner coat pocket and out of this pulled a slip of paper.

"Here's the reward," said he.

The marshal read:

Dear Speedy: It may be life for me, or it may be the rope. Whatever it is, I'm the only man in jail in the whole country who's grateful to the fellow that caught him. You were too keen for me; you beat me fairly.

And now you've taken all the sting out of my failure. I have letters from my mother and father. They don't know who has given them the annuities, but I was able to guess. If there's ever blood on your hands, it isn't mine. We are quits, and the debt is all on my side. The best of luck to you! May you never be beaten till the finish, and may you fall fighting hard. That's the best I can wish you, I suppose. I won't be fool enough to suspect you of ever settling down to a musty, rusty life on a farm.

Good-by.   Clifton Derrick

The marshal handed back the slip of paper.

"That's a good letter you have," said he.

"I'd rather have it than a diploma," said Speedy.

"Besides," said the marshal, "it means that all of Derrick's friends have been called off your trail."

"It means that, too," agreed Speedy.

"You're a queer lad, Speedy," said the officer. "I've given up trying to understand you. But I'd like to know this: will you take a permanent job in my department? There wouldn't be any question of taking a regular office job, you know. Your time would be your own. There would be enough excitement every week to fill a year. How does the thing sound to you? I've talked it over with the higher-ups, and I think I could get five thousand a year for you, plus all sorts of expenses, from clothes and guns, to horses!"

"I've given up horses and taken to mules," said Speedy. "I'm no rider, Tom. As for the work, hunting men is all very well, but there's something still more exciting."

"What's that?"

"Being hunted!"

Tom Gray sat up straighter in his chair.

"The mischief!" he murmured. "Is that your viewpoint, Speedy?"

"You know," said Speedy, "that some of us are dogs and some of us are cats."

"That open locked doors and walk through walls and do little tricks like that, eh?" said the marshal, smiling. "Well, I won't argue with you, Speedy. You always know your own mind. Anything serious on it, just now?"

"Levine," said Speedy.

"I know Levine is on your mind," said the marshal. "Anything new about him?"

"He's passing counterfeit money."

The marshal whistled. "That's interesting to me," said he.

"We couldn't get him on a better thing," said Speedy. "The murders he buys would be too hard to hang on him. Twelve or fifteen years in prison would be the same as life, to him."

"It would," agreed Gray. "Do you think we can catch him with the goods?"

"He passed a lot of the stuff to Joe Dale."

"There's another young man I'd like to put my hands on," said Gray.

"I'm sorry to hear that."

"Why?"

"Dale is going straight. He'll never do another crooked piece of work."

"I'll try to believe it. But he has a past behind him."

"He's only a kid," said Speedy. "He's not grown up."

"And how old are you, Speedy?" asked the marshal, with another smile.

"I was born old," replied Speedy, with a certain sad gravity in his face and voice. "I'll never change. But Dale will. He'll help to grab Levine, if you'll let him help. He can be concealed so you won't know him. Masked, even, if you'll let him."

"I'd rather catch Levine than twenty boys like Dale," agreed the marshal. "How can we go about it?"

"Dale and I hold up Levine in his office, make him open his safe, and then you walk into the middle of the robbery. Instead of taking the robbers, you haul the green goods out of the safe, and there's the testimony that will slam Levine into prison for the rest of his days."

"A Federal marshal, a robbery, masked men, evidence at the point of a revolver, that would make a pretty story, Speedy!"

"They won't break you for a job that puts Levine in jail," argued Speedy.

"When did you plan to do the job?"

"Tonight."

The marshal shrugged his shoulders. "This may cost me my job," he said, "but I think I'll tackle it. Are you starting right away?"

"In five minutes. Dale is waiting in the street."

"I'm with you, then," said the marshal.

He stood up, drew a pair of guns, looked them over with a single glance, and made them disappear again. He walked to the wall and took his sombrero from a peg.

CHAPTER 30

The office of Sid Levine, on this night, was dimly awash with the noises that rose from the different sections of the Grand Palace. To Sid Levine, reclining in his heavy armchair, nursing a cigar in his fat lips, what he heard was a music more beautiful than a symphony of many strings. It meant to him the delicious murmurings of the river of gold which continually poured out of his crooked establishment into the deep pool of his pocket.

He could sit here for hours and see visions of greater delight. The time would come when Sunday Slough was drained of all its treasure, and then he would depart to other fields. But he would go with such experience and such capital that he could afford to start on the grandest scale. He saw clearly that the way to prosperity lies over a pathway paved with golden pavements and with still richer promises. He could afford to pay in gold; he could afford still better to pay with hopes that would never be fulfilled. When he considered the greatness of his winnings in the town of Sunday Slough and the small percentages which he had delivered over to his great helpers, One-eyed Mike and Sheriff Buck Masters, he felt that he was a being especially set aside from the ordinary race of men.

He was rather annoyed when someone knocked at his door, and the voice of Buck Masters sounded immediately afterward. He felt that he had seen enough of Buck that day, but he realized that it would not do to deny entrance to the sheriff at any time.

So he swept in front of himself one of the big ledgers on which he had been working, picked up a pen and dipped it in the inkstand—all this before he called out to Masters to enter.

The sheriff came in and stamped once or twice to free his polished boots of the dust that had settled over them. His face was dark. He merely nodded at Levine, then went to the corner of the room, opened the drawer that contained the whisky, and poured himself out a large dram. He tossed it off, smacked his lips, and then threw down a second full glass before he turned toward the expectant Levine.

The latter kept his expression placid. He detested this bohemian familiarity. He loved to surround himself with a wall of dignity. As a matter of fact, he knew very well that he dared not offend the sheriff. Therefore, he maintained the expression of calm inquiry.

Buck Masters lowered himself into a chair with a grunt and a groan. It was a cold night, with a whistling wind thrusting through the flimsy walls of the building. In the office a fire burned in the stove, its open-mouthed grate dancing with yellow flames. Toward this the sheriff turned himself, eying Sid Levine over his right shoulder.

"Things look bad," said the sheriff finally.

"Bad? What way?" asked Sid Levine.

"Bad because of Speedy," said the sheriff.

"What's he done now?" asked Sid Levine.

"Ain't you heard about the fight in the hotel?"

"How would I hear about fights in the hotel?" asked Levine, frowning. "I don't have an ear in every quarter of the camp, you know. What fight?"

"Aw, there was a wild buck come down from the mountains, by name of Crazy Dick. Mean as a pair of mountain lions and strong as a pair of mules. And he started in and begun to make trouble with Speedy. But the kid started his magic tricks, they say. I dunno how he does it. He picked up Crazy Dick, which is a heavyweight, throwed him into the wall and cleaned him up. Right on top of that, there was a riot started in Chambers' place—"

"I'm glad of that," said Levine.

"So'm I," said the sheriff. "I planned the whole job. I got a long-haired idiot of a puncher and bad man to go in there and wreck the place. He had made a pretty good start, when word gets to Speedy, and the crowd, they carry him down on their shoulders to see what he'll do with the second brawl. And my gunman, the half-breed, he goes and stands like a lamb while Speedy takes his guns away and throws him into jail. I just had to go up there and turn Long-hair loose. Now the whole of Sunday Slough is boiling and humming with praise of Speedy. There never was a man invented, before he come along and showed what a real man had oughta be."

"Yeah?" growled Levine. "We gotta do something about that pup."

"We gotta do it quick," argued Buck. "He's got this town so much inside of his pocket that when we try to break his hold on it, we're gonna sprain our wrists."

"I've heard that kind of talk before," answered the great Levine. "What I wanta see is ways of taking the great man off his throne. Got any ways in mind?"

"There's Joe Dale," said the sheriff. "Maybe we'll hear something from him before very long."

"Yeah," said Levine. "Joe Dale is a man that might turn the trick. But what I don't understand is that all my boys carry guns and know how to use 'em, and this sneakin' rat of a tramp, he ain't ever carrying a gun himself. How d'you make out that he manages to handle 'em?"

"He's got 'em all buffaloed," suggested the sheriff. "They turn to stone the minute they see him. I'm gonna take a whirl at him myself."

Since the head of the sheriff was well turned away toward the fire, Levine treated himself to the luxury of a broad smile at this point. It was more of a sneer than a smile.

Then, at this moment, the sheriff said: "Levine, you handed out twenty-five thousand of green goods to that kid, Joe Dale. Look here, if that money is well made, I could pass some of it, myself."

The eyebrows of the great Levine rose to points. "You want to handle the stuff?" he asked.

"What's it worth?" asked Buck Masters. "I know some fellows who understand how to shove the queer into circulation."

"I'll sell it at twenty-five dollars a hundred," said Levine. "That's how good it is! It'll go anywhere. All most of it needs is to be a little pocket-worn, to tell you the truth. Then it'll go in a bank."

"Is that so?" asked the sheriff sarcastically. "You'd have it all deposited, if it was good enough to go to a bank."

"I mean, to most banks. But why should I step out and take a chance? But I'll tell you what, Buck. To an old friend like you, I'd make it cheaper. I'll make it twenty dollars."

"Say fifteen, and I'll take a load of it," said the sheriff.

"Fifteen? I had to pay nearly fifteen for it," lied Levine, with unction. "I want to see you rich, old son, but I don't want to go to the poorhouse."

"Call it eighteen dollars a hundred," said the sheriff. "Then, if the stuff really looks good to me, I'll take on a load of it."

"All right," said the great Levine. "There's a sample. There's a real fifty and there's a fake. You tell me which is which!"

Buck Masters studied them with care. It was some time before he exclaimed.

"This is the phony one," said he.

"Yeah, that's the phony one," said Levine.

"It's slick work, all right," said Masters, stowing both the good bill and the counterfeit in his own pocket. "How much have you got of it?"

"I've got about eighty thousand dollars," said Levine cheerfully.

"Eighty thousand dollars is good," said Masters. "If you had eight hundred thousand of this turkey, I could use it all. Shell it out, will you?"

Levine grunted as he rose and went to the safe. He could have cursed aloud, for he had not overlooked the way in which his fifty dollars had been palmed by the sheriff's absent-mindedness.

He knew, however, that he could not pay any attention to mere "details" like this. His "friendship" with Buck Masters was established upon an altogether too high a plane for that!

He counted out the packets of the counterfeit, eight neat,

tightly wadded packages in brown paper wrappings.

"Eight of 'em," he said. "That cleans me out, and it's eighty thousand dollars."

The sheriff shrugged his shoulders. "I'll take your word for that," said he.

He picked them up and dropped them in a side pocket of his coat. "I'll push these right into the market, chief," said he, and started for the door.

CHAPTER 31

A distinct shade of reddish purple overspread the face of Levine as he saw the broad back of the sheriff turned toward him.

Then he said: "Look here, brother. Hold on a minute, will you?"

"Yeah?" murmured the sheriff.

"You owe me," said Levine, "a trace under fifteen thousand bucks for that wad of the green goods."

The sheriff laughed; his laughter was not exactly natural in its ring.

"Oh, that's all right," said he. "You know that I'm good for this stuff, Sid."

"Oh, sure," said Levine. "I know that you're good for it. But you know how it is. Better be businesslike. Sloppy business methods, they don't do nothing but spoil friendships, is what my old man always used to tell me."

"He's the one that went to the pen for forgery, ain't he?" asked Buck Masters, more casual than ever.

Levine's purple turned to a darker shade.

At last he said: "Look here, brother. Fifteen thousand

bucks is fifteen thousand bucks, or I'm a liar!"

"Yeah," said Masters, "money is money. But fifteen thousand, between you and me, is just small change, Sid. You know that. Oh, I'll tell you what, I'll give you my note for it. How's that? In thirty days, eh? Here you are!"

He sat down and scribbled the IOU. Levine looked on with his eyes starting from his head. It was true that he had paid only eight dollars a hundred for the phony money, but still it represented a very considerable outlay. And a poison ran through the blood and brain of the gambler as he watched the pen carelessly wielded in the big fingers of Buck Masters. It was a worthless scrap of paper, he knew. He would never collect a penny from the sheriff; and yet he saw that his hands were tied. No matter how utterly he distrusted the sheriff, he had to pretend that all was on a basis of perfect good faith between them. He had to take the note, nod, and push it into his pocket.

Just then the knock and the voice of Mike were heard at the door, and his henchman came in.

He seemed greatly excited. "Joe Dale is out there at the back gate," he said. "He talks like he's drunk. Chief, he says that the job's done!"

All thought of the way the sheriff had beaten him out of so much money passed from the mind of the great Levine. He leaped to his feet, light as a boy of ten.

"The job's done? That means that he's bumped off Speedy and—the town ain't heard a word about it yet?"

"Knife work, likely," said the sheriff, with a grim satisfaction. "That Joe Dale is sure a handy boy!"

"I'll go bring him in," said One-eyed Mike. "I just wanted to find out—"

"Hold on," said Sid Levine. "What would he be wanting back here, anyway? Would he maybe 'ave found out—"

He paused. He exchanged eloquent glances with the sheriff. The latter said: "Well, if he comes back with anything

149

found out, you just made a mistake, brother. If the kid's bumped off, ain't it worth a real twenty-five thousand to us?"

The teeth of Levine showed as his fat upper lip lifted.

"No matter what it's worth to us," he said, "it's me that will do the paying, ain't it?"

"Why," exclaimed Buck Masters, in the tone of one who was hurt, "that's as though we wasn't all in the same boat, sinking or floating together, and—"

The door sagged softly open, making only a whispering sound, and through the open doorway came Deputy Sheriff Speedy, and with him a small fellow with a black mask drawn over his face.

Speedy carried no weapon; he did not need to; his bare hands were sufficient. But young Joe Dale, his companion, carried a big Colt of the most businesslike appearance in either fist.

It was he who spoke, saying: "Back up, Mike. Turn your back to me, Masters, you big ham. Levine, get them hands up, and stand straight. Mike, I'm watchin' you. Turn your back while you got time."

"Joe, have you gone and double-crossed me?" said Levine. "Have you gone and done that, Joe?"

There was real sadness in his voice. But Joe Dale answered: "You green-goods bum, you talk about double-crossing, do you?"

The fat man, suddenly brazen, shrugged his shoulders. "Speedy pointed it out to you, did he?"

"He pointed it out," said Joe Dale. "Unbuckle your gun belts, Mike and Buck Masters. Unbuckle 'em, and let the guns fall."

"I got a pair of hair-trigger babies that may explode when they hit the floor," said the sheriff.

"I hope they do," said Joe Dale. "I hope that they blow a leg off for you."

Each of the men obeyed the command. The two heavy gun

belts dropped to the floor.

Levine was saying: "Look what a gang of saps and thick heads I've got working for me! They send you running on an errand, Mike, and then they come on marching down the hall and walk right in on us, and get us off guard. What good are you, Mike Doloroso? What good are you, Masters? You're a pair of four-flushers, is all that you are. And I been wasting dog-gone good money on you all this while! That's what I been doing!"

He groaned as he spoke the last words. His haunted eyes glanced toward the open face of the safe. It was as though his soul were standing naked under the eyes of enemies.

"And now, boys," went on Levine, "we'll come to an understanding. I know what you want. You want to shake me down. That's all right. I know that the young hopes of the world, they gotta rise and grow and prosper. I don't mind a shakedown, I don't even mind a stiff one, boys. But let's get down to business. Whacha want out of me?"

Speedy spoke now for the first time: "We want a little quiet, Sid. Keep your fat mouth shut for a while, will you?"

And then he sat down on the edge of Levine's desk.

The fat man faced them. The other two stood still, with their faces turned toward the wall, and their hands well above their heads.

"My arms are droppin' off at the shoulders," said One-eyed Mike. "How long you gonna keep up this crazy gag on us, Speedy?"

"I ought to feed you in chunks into that fire," said Speedy cheerfully, "but I'm holding my hand a little. There's some-body else coming in here to have a look at you boys. Don't touch that bell, Sid. If you do, I'll tear you apart. You under-stand?"

Levine licked his thick lips. There was no color in his face except for those lips. They were as ashen purple.

"Who's coming, Speedy?" he asked, lowering his voice to

a whisper.

A quick step approached down the hall.

"Federal Marshal Thomas Gray," he said.

And through the door came Tom Gray in person.

The three men wilted.

It was Levine, of course, who spoke first, gasping: "Marshal Gray, thank goodness you've got here. The deputy sheriff of this here county and a masked blackguard—we think he's Joe Dale, the famous criminal—have held us up at the point of a gun."

"Then you'd better keep in place and stand still," said the marshal. "If somebody has you under a gun, it's better to be quiet."

"Gray," groaned Levine, "are you gonna stand by and see a holdup, a masked man—"

"I don't see a masked man," said the marshal, turning his back upon Joe Dale. "Speedy, what are you finding?"

For Speedy was on his knees in front of the open safe, and taking out drawer after drawer, he ran swiftly through them. Papers, account books, bundles of money, trays of silver and gold, a considerable mass of gold nuggets and finally, tied in a chamois bag, a whole mass of jewelry of all sorts, but chiefly unset stones.

Many a story must have lain behind that collection of jewels. The sight of them caused sweat to pour down the face of the great Levine.

"I see what it is," he said. "It's a plot. Gray, you're gonna be broke and ruined, for this here night's work. I'll never stop till I've got you behind the bars. You understand that?"

Speedy rose from the heap of drawers which he had taken from the safe.

"What I want isn't here," he said, "I'll fan them, and see what I find."

Sheriff Buck Masters suddenly turned from the wall.

"Gray," he said, "I'm the sheriff. I call on you as a sworn

officer of the law—"

He strode forward from the wall as he spoke and, passing the open mouth of the stove, his hand dipped into his coat pocket and cast a considerable package into the flames.

But Speedy was on it instantly. A pair of tongs stood by the stove and, reaching in with them, he pulled out the packages, while the brown paper wrappings were still blackening and burning, but with the contents almost entirely uninjured.

"These came out of Masters' pocket," he said. "Levine has passed on the rest of his stuff, I suppose. Here, Tom. Take a look at this, will you?"

The marshal received the packages, while silence deep as death fell on the room. From a brief examination, he looked up with a smile.

"Good stuff, Buck," he said. "Almost good enough to be real. This will mean about fifteen years for you!"

CHAPTER 32

The consternation of Buck Masters was great. He looked, however, not at Speedy or the Federal officer, but straight at his business associate, the great Levine.

The massive head of the latter nodded so deeply that the heavy folds of his double chin swayed forward, as he said: "This is a plant on you, Buck. No crooked marshal and thug of a bribed deputy are gonna work any deal on you. You got friends, Buck. Don't you go and forget it."

"Joe," said Speedy, aside to the gunman, "you've turned the trick in grand style. Now fade out of here. You know where Pier Morgan was cached away in the hills. Go up there and I'll meet you sometime tomorrow. I think that you've cracked the whole Levine gang wide open. You'll get a reward for it!"

And Joe Dale answered slowly and softly: "I got my reward already, if you think that I've done this right. So long, Speedy. The next time you want me, I'll be ready and under your feet."

He disappeared through the doorway, closing the door gently behind him. No gun showed in the hand of the marshal. But the disarmed trio knew his reputation too well to attempt an attack upon him, to say nothing of Sunday Slough's bit of domesticated lightning, Speedy.

They stood gloomily about, biting their lips, herded together, shoulder to shoulder, by mutual danger.

The marshal was saying to Masters: "Buck, this thing is likely to go pretty hard on you. The Federal courts are pretty mean to counterfeitors, Buck. You'll spend the cream of your life in jail. Maybe all of it for this. Partly because you've handled the stuff, and partly because you're a police officer. That makes a double count against you and a mighty black one."

"He's bluffing," said Levine. "The fact is that they ain't got anything on you. They got some counterfeit dough off of you, they say. That's nothing. That's the stuff that you picked up in the execution of your duty as sheriff of this county. What of that?"

"Yeah, that's what it was," said Buck Masters, his great jaw thrusting forward like a bulldog's as he saw the possible line of defense opening before him. "All you got off of me is evidence that I collected myself for testimony agin' crooks."

"So you threw the stuff in the fire when the pinch came, was that it?" asked Thomas Gray.

The big mouth of Masters opened, but it shut again, with no more sound than the click of his teeth.

Levine put in calmly: "Don't you do no talking, Buck.

Let a smart lawyer do your thinking for you from now on. I know the man for you, and I know where the money'll be had for paying him. You stop worrying, and let others worry for you. They're gonna wish that they grabbed handfuls of fire before they touched you, Buck!"

The arched chest of Buck collapsed as he sighed with relief.

Said Speedy: "You know, Tom, it isn't Buck that we want so badly."

The marshal nodded and said: "You're under arrest, Masters. What you say may be used against you. But I can tell you now, that we know where you got that money. If you'll tell us who passed it to you, I can promise you an easy trial and a light sentence. I might pass it off for State's evidence and get you off scot-free. You understand?"

"I understand," said the other slowly.

"Well, then," said the marshal, "talk out, man. You have anywhere between twelve and thirty years ahead of you on the two counts."

And big Buck Masters stared at Levine for the answer.

"Listen to me, Buck—" began Levine.

Speedy tapped the fat man on the arm.

"The first thing you know, Levine," said he, "you'll be resisting arrest or some such thing. I wouldn't talk, if I were you!"

The purr in his voice sent a shudder through Sid Levine. He sagged backward against the wall and stood there stunned.

The marshal went on: "Speak out, Masters! What you say now will have double weight. We know where you got that stuff. But it has to come from you before we can make an arrest. You're not going to jail and let this big swine get away free, are you? He tells you that he'll get you off with a smart lawyer. I tell you, when the Federal courts lay their hands on a case like this, they go to the bottom of it. They slam a man hard. Money won't save you. But if you turn State's evidence—"

He paused. Sheer excitement forced from the throat of One-eyed Mike a gagging sound, like that of a man choking to death.

And Buck Masters turned his heavy head from side to side like a bull at bay.

He started at the hard eye of the marshall—hard, but honest, the eye of a man who would do what he said. He looked at the almost femininely beautiful face of Speedy, now decorated with a faint smile of contented interest. He stared again at the countenance of Sid Levine.

Then he blinked.

"Ten to thirty years, it's a lot," he muttered. "It's life, that's what it is!"

Sid Levine started to speak, but the narrow forefinger of Speedy rose in caution, and the fat man was silent.

Then Buck Masters shook his head.

"You birds can do what you please," he growled. "I ain't gonna give you no information. You want me to squeal on somebody. There ain't nobody to squeal on. That's final. You don't pry no more words out of me, not even with a crowbar. Not till I've talked to a lawyer."

Levine almost fainted with relief. "Buck," he muttered, "I always knew that you was a man. I knew it from the very first time that I ever laid eyes on you."

The marshal hesitated.

Then, staring at Levine, he said: "Speedy, I hate to think of you remaining in this town with fat-faced Levine, the pig, still at liberty to buy the cutting of your throat. I'm sorry about it. I'm mighty sorry. But maybe we'll get our hands on Levine, too, before the case is over. Anyway, we've wrecked his gang or, rather, you have. You've cut Derrick away from his side. You've taken Buck Masters, now. There's no one who'll trust Levine or play with him now. He's lost everything that he built up in Sunday Slough. I wanted to throw him in jail. But perhaps it's better this way. He'll have to stew in his own juice. I can't wish him any worse luck. And he'll have the last of the seven-day men camping on his trail. Come along, Masters. You, too, Mike. I want to question you."

He took the two from the room, and behind him left Speedy and the great Levine, standing face to face.

It was Levine who moved first, and with his eyes straining blindly from his head, with his great, bulky arms stretched out before him, he tottered across the floor, with the look of a man about to die. Even the open face of the safe was unregarded now and, reaching the door, he turned slowly down the hallway.

Speedy made a cigarette and sat down before the cozy open fire to smoke it.

PART THREE

CHAPTER 33

High on a hill above Sunday Slough, in the dusk of the day, three horsemen sat side by side, two very large, and one a slenderer figure. The sun had set; twilight had descended on the long gorge of the mining ravine. From the highest of the surrounding mountains, the rose of the day's end had finally vanished, leaving only a pale radiance, and now the smallest of the three silhouetted horsemen spoke:

"Señor Levine, as you know, I've come a long distance, because it is the pleasure of a gentleman to defy miles when one of his brothers calls for him. But it is already late, and I must inform you that, instead of going to bed, I intend to change horses and return, before the morning, to my own house."

He spoke his English with the formality and the accent of a foreigner.

The largest silhouette of the three, a gross shape that overflowed the saddle, answered: "Now, look a-here, Don Hernando. I ain't the kind that hoists up a white flag before I got a need to."

"That's the one thing that he ain't," said the third member of the party. "You take Levine, before he hollers he's got his back agin' the wall."

"Aw, shut up, Mike, will you?" demanded the big man, without the slightest passion. "What I wanta say, if you'll let me, is that I ain't called for you, Don Hernando, except that I needed help. And everybody knows that Don Hernando is Don Hernando. It would be a fool that would yell for him, unless there was really a wolf among the sheep, eh?"

"Thank you," said the Mexican.

He raised his hand and twisted his short mustaches, forgetting that the dimness of the light robbed this gesture of half its grace and finish.

Then he said: "We all love to see reason according to our lights. What reason do you think you can show me, Señor Levine? This a wolf; those, sheep; which may they be?"

"The sheep," said Levine, "we're the sheep. Me and my friends down there in Sunday Slough. There was a time, not far back, when we owned the town. What we said went. But then along comes the wolf, which his name is Speedy, what I mean to say. You don't need to doubt that. Because he's the wolf, all right."

"I have even heard his name," said the Mexican, politely.

"You have even heard his name, have you?" said One-eyed Mike Doloroso. "Yeah, and you'll hear more'n his name, if ever you got anything to do with him. You'll hear yourself cussing the unlucky day that you ever bumped into him."

"One never knows," said Don Hernando. "He is not a very large man, I am told."

"Oh, he ain't so big," said Sid Levine, "but he's big enough. There was me and Cliff Derrick. Maybe you heard of him?"

"He was a very great man," said Don Hernando. "Yes, yes, some of my friends knew him very well, and one of them was honored by having the Señor Derrick steal all that he owned in this world."

"Cliff would do that, all right," said One-eyed Mike. "He'd steal your gold fillings out of your teeth, while you was saying good morning and glad you'd met him. Derrick, he was a man, what I mean."

"Yes," said Don Hernando, "I have heard that he was such a man. And he was your friend, Señor Levine?"

"Yeah," said Levine. "I had Sunday Slough all spread out, and along comes Derrick, and him and me get ready to take the scalp of Sunday Slough so slick and careful that the town won't hardly miss its hair. Then along comes this no-good, guitar-playin' hound of a tramp, name of Speedy, that looks like a worthless kid, and that turns the edge of a knife, and bites himself a lunch out of tool-proof steel—what I mean!"

"That I hardly understand," said Don Hernando.

Mike Doloroso explained: "What the chief means is this Speedy looks soft, but he's hard-boiled. He lunches on boiler plate and dynamite sticks is toothpicks for him, is what the chief means."

"Aw, shut up, Mike. Lemme talk for myself," said the chief, "will you? Don Hernando, he understands English like a gentleman, all right."

"I think I understand what you mean about Don Speedy," said the great Don Hernando. "It is to get a surprise, to meet him."

"Yeah, you said it then, Hernando," said Levine. "A surprise is all that he is. I was saying that me and Derrick, we had things planned, and then we find out that Speedy is in the way, and first Derrick stumbles over him and pretty near breaks his neck, and then along comes my best bet, which it was my old friend, Buck Masters, that I had got made the sheriff of the county.

"Why, Buck Masters was worth ten times his weight in gold to me, was all he was to me, and along comes that sneak of a wolf of a Speedy, and he picks off Buck Masters, too, and all that Buck gets is fifteen years minus hope, for pushing the queer. And there's Derrick in for life, and a matter of fact, I mean to say that there ain't any fun around here, like there used to be in the old days, when we had Sunday Slough all spread out and waiting to be scalped. What I mean."

"I seem to understand you," said Don Hernando. "I also, in a small way, have a little town at my service. It is not much. We in Mexico have not learned the big ways of you Americans. Still, it is a comfortable town. Everybody pays me a little bit, not much, partly because I love my people, and partly because they have not much to pay. But we understand one another. If my friends make five pesos, one of them they pay to me, and all is well.

"They are poor, simple people. Some of their pesos they pay to me in oil, others in wine, others in chickens, or in goat's flesh. Fine flour and cornmeal they send to me. So we understand one another. I am not one who rides down suddenly and robs a man's house. No, not I—unless the scoundrel has refused my rightful tribute to me. But I leave all of my people in peace. Like a great family we live all together, Señor Levine, and that, I dare say, is how you lived here in Sunday Slough before this accursed Speedy, whom I already despise, came to spoil your happiness!"

"Yeah," said Levine, with a sigh. "You can say that we lived like a happy family, all right. In the old days, I run the biggest gambling house in the town, and I got everything my own way. There's only one side to be on in Sunday Slough, and that's my side, what I mean. But along comes this runt of a singing fool, this here Speedy, and busts up the picture, and why, I ask you?"

"That I cannot tell," said the great Don Hernando.

"Because," said Levine, his voice warm with indignation, "because, if you'll believe it, I wouldn't let the low-down son of a sea hound get away with nothing. And there was a half-witted sap of a crooked prospector that was a friend of his by name of Pier Morgan, that claimed to own a mine, and my friend, the sheriff, he turned that mine over to a friend of mine and got Pier Morgan jailed for vagrancy, which is being a tramp, to say it in good English. And Pier Morgan starts shooting his way out of jail, and only shoots himself into the junk pile, and along comes this here Speedy that nobody had ever heard of, and he takes and picks Pier Morgan off the tin cans.

"Then he takes him off into the hills, and goes and gets him well, what I mean. And while he's getting well, Speedy, he comes down and gets himself a job as a seven-day man, I mean, as a deputy sheriff. You know how it goes. But Speedy, he goes after my scalp, unbeknownst to me, and he picks off Cliff Derrick, and then my pal, Buck Masters, that was sheriff.

"And now comes along the election for sheriff—and whacha think? If they don't go and put Speedy for sheriff! Why, he ain't got no name, even, and he calls himself John James Jones, and they laugh their fool heads off, but they get all ready to vote for J.J.J. just the same. Now, I ask you!"

"That would be hard on you, señor, to have him for the sheriff of the county?"

"It was heart failure and rheumatism to me to have him only for the deputy sheriff," sighed Levine, "so what would it be to have him for sheriff?"

He hung his head for an instant with a groan, and then he went on: "Now, I'm gonna tell you what, Don Hernando. I know how to clean out this here Speedy. There's a friend of mine called Dick Cleveland, Crazy Dick, that was smeared around by Speedy once, and he's spotted the place where this Pier Morgan is finishing up, getting well and sharpening his knife for my throat at the same time! Now, Don Hernando, if I can snatch this here fellow, Pier Morgan, away, and put him in a safe place, this here Speedy will line out after him, and that'll take him out of my path, and while he's gone, I clean up on Sunday Slough. Is that clear; I mean, is it clear if you're the place where Pier Morgan is taken to?"

"I see your reason, señor, but not mine," said Don Hernando, rather crisply.

"I got five thousand reasons for you," said Levine.

"Reasons, or dollars?" asked Don Hernando.

"Both," said Levine.

CHAPTER 34

In Sunday Slough, later on that day, Speedy, public choice for sheriff, sat in his office. In dockets upon his desk were various documents which had to do with his work, men wanted by neighboring counties. But Speedy allowed such business to roll off his back. He was interested in only one thing, and that was cleaning up the town of Sunday Slough.

The job would have been more than half finished, at that moment, except that Sid Levine was still decidedly at large. The great Levine was the major force with which, as Speedy knew, he had to contend. Though he had cut away, as it were, the right and the left hand of the gambler, there still remained the man himself, with his brain, so resourceful in evil.

He heard a light, stealthy step crossing the porch in front of the little wooden building that housed him and his office. Then came a light knock at the door.

"Come in, Joe," he called.

The door opened. Joe Dale, short, thick-shouldered, strong as a bull and quick as a cat, came into the room. He waved his hand in the dusk.

"Why not a light, Speedy?" said he.

"I like it this way. I think better by this light," said Speedy.

He began to strum, very lightly, the strings of the guitar that lay across his knees.

"What's up, Joe?" said he.

"I meet up with Stew Webber," said Joe Dale, "and the fool don't know that you've gone and got a pardon for me out of the governor. When he recognizes me, he pulls a gun. I kicked the gun out of his hand. I slammed that bird on the beak so hard that he nearly busted the sidewalk when he sat down on it. Then I told him what was what. He was gonna collect some blood money out of that, Speedy!"

"He's a fool," said Speedy. "He's a fool, though I don't know him. How are things in town, Joe?"

"Everything's so good that it'd make you laugh," said Joe Dale. "I'll tell you what. There was a bird come into the Best Chance Saloon, and he starts telling the boys that he won't vote any ex-tramp for sheriff of this here county. And the boys listen to him a while, and then they take him out and tie him backward on his hoss, and give him a ride out of town. That's what they think of you, Speedy!"

"I hope the poor fellow doesn't get a broken neck," said Speedy.

"No, he didn't get no broken neck," said the deputy. "All he got was a fall and a dislocated shoulder. One of the camps took him in off the road. He wasn't hurt bad."

"Dog-gone it," said Speedy. "I'll have to go and see him, tomorrow."

"Say, what are you?" asked Joe Dale. "A visiting sister of mercy or what?"

"Oh, lay off that, Joe," said Speedy. "What's the other news?"

"There ain't any other news except you," said Joe Dale. "It's all that anybody is talking about. All the big mine owners are gonna close up shop, that day, because they want to make sure that their men get a chance to vote for you on election day."

"That's kind of them," said Speedy.

And he yawned.

"Anything about Levine?" he asked.

"Levine is cooked. His place don't draw no business, no more," said Joe Dale. "It's a funny thing that the fool keeps hanging on."

"He'll hang on till he gets me, or I get him," said Speedy. "He's no hero, but his blood's up."

"He's beat," declared Joe Dale. "He's only a joke, now. He's got no hangers-on."

"He'll have them five minutes after I'm dead," answered Speedy. "Oh, I know how it is with the boys. They like the top dog. You say Levine is beat, but I tell you that I'm more afraid of him right now than when he was on top of the bunch, here. Bad times sharpen good brains, and Levine has a brain in his head, don't doubt that!"

Joe Dale grunted, but before he could answer, a rapid drumming of hoofs was heard, the rider stopping before the shack. Then he threw himself from the horse and ran forward.

"Speedy! Speedy!" he called, in a guarded voice.

"It's Juan!" said Speedy.

Instantly he was through the window, going like magic past the form of Joe Dale.

The panting runner paused before him.

"Juan, you idiot," said Speedy, "what are you doing showing your face in town, with a price on your head?"

Juan shook the head that had a price on it, as though disclaiming its importance, then he said: "Pier Morgan, the Señor Morgan, he is gone, Speedy!"

Speedy got him by the shoulders and backed him around until the street light fell upon his face.

"Say that again!" he demanded.

166

"The Señor Morgan, he is gone. I, señor, have a bullet hole through the side of my neck. That is why the bandage is there. I still bleed, my friend. It is not for lack of fighting, but the Evil One himself came, and took Pier Morgan from me."

"D'you know the name and address of this Evil One, Juan?" asked Speedy.

"It is Don Hernando of Segovia, señor. I saw his face only in part. But I knew the scar of his forehead. I was once one of his people. It was Don Hernando, and you will never see Pier Morgan again. He is gone to Segovia. He is gone forever."

"Where's Segovia?" snapped Speedy.

"A little on the other side of the Rio Grande. It is more than a day's ride from this place, señor! But it might as well be the journey of a life, for those who go into it never come back. They are held in the teeth of Don Hernando forever! Ah, señor, it was not carelessness on my part, but—"

"Be still, Juan," said Speedy. "You know the way to Segovia?"

"I know the way, señor."

"Will you take me there?"

"I take you within sight of it," said Juan. "I do not dare to go closer. I have been in the dungeons of Segovia. I shall never go there again!"

"I'll go all the way, Speedy," offered Joe Dale.

"You'll stay here and run Sunday Slough," answered Speedy. "I'll find out about Segovia on the way down, but I imagine that this is a one-man job. You know, Joe, that an army often can't take a place by open assault, but one crook can pick the lock of the gate!"

CHAPTER 35

Segovia stood among rocky hills, bare as the palm of the hand. The town itself was an irregular huddle of white-washed dobe, without a tree in the streets, without a bush to cast shadow. In fact, vegetable life could not exist beside the famous goats of Segovia which, men swore, could digest not only the labels of tin cans, but the tin as well.

How these people lived was a mystery which it was hard to solve. They were like their own goats, which seemed to eat the sand and the sunshine, for there was little else on the ground where they grazed. They were fierce, cruel, revenge-ful, patient, enduring. They loved their friends with a pas-sion; they hated their enemies with still more fervor. They were people to be noted, and to be feared.

All of these terrible clansmen, for like a clan they clung together, looked down on the rest of the world, and looked up to the castle of Don Hernando Garcias.

It was not really a castle. Once, to be sure, the walls had been of stone, cut and laid together with the priceless skill of the Mexican stonecutters. But the centuries had cracked, molded and eaten the big stones until they had fallen from their places, and a ragged mass of adobe finished in part the outline of the earlier walls.

Still, it remained a castle to the proud, stern peons of Segovia. For in that building, for three centuries and more, there had always been a Garcias called Hernando.

Most Mexicans are resolved democrats, but the men of Segovia preferred to be under the thumb of an autocrat. For one thing, he preserved them from paying taxes to the State, for when tax collectors came to Segovia they strangely disappeared, and finally they had fallen out of the habit of going to the mysterious little white town above the river. For another thing, according as he was a great and lordly freebooter, they themselves picked up plenty of profit from his expeditions. And the present Hernando Garcias filled all the requirements.

He was rapacious, stern, and ruled them with a rod of iron. On the other hand, since he had come into power, they rode better horses, wore brighter sashes, ate more meat. The cantinas offered them beer, wine, and distilled fire; they had money to buy it. And what other elements could they have desired in a terrestrial paradise?

The sun of this day had set, and in the twilight the white town had been filmed across with purple, and the lights had begun to shine out of the doorways. Then night gathered about the town, and it seemed to huddle, as though under a cloak, at the knees of the "castle."

It was at this time that a rider on an old gray mule came into the town, and stopped in front of one of the cantinas to play on a guitar and sing.

His voice was good, his choice of songs was rich and racy on the one hand, profoundly sentimental on the other. His hair was dark, so were his eyes; his skin was the rich walnut color of Mexico; and his handsome face seemed to fit exactly into his song of love.

So a crowd gathered at once.

He was invited into the cantina. He was offered drinks. Then they brought him some cold roasted flesh of a young kid, cold tortillas, hot tomato and pepper sauces. He ate with avidity, leaning well over his food, scooping it up with the paper-thin tortillas.

A jolly, ragged beggar was this minstrel, with a ragged straw hat on his head of the right Mexican style, its crown a long and tapered cornucopia. He had on a gaudy jacket, the braid of which had tarnished here and ripped away there. His shirt was of silk, very soiled and tattered, and open at the throat. The flash of his eyes and his white teeth as he ate, or as he sang, or as he danced, made the tawdry costume disappear, particularly in the eyes of the women who crowded about the door of the cantina to look on at the diversions of their lords and masters.

Particularly, was he a master of the dance, and it was really a wonderful thing to see him accompany his flying feet with strumming of the guitar, while he retained breath enough in his throat to sing the choruses.

The old men sat in the corners of the room and beat time with their feet and hands. Their red-stained eyes flashed like fire. The younger men stirred uneasily, nearer at hand. Sometimes one of them would dart out, with a bound, and match the steps of the visiting master. Whenever a village dancer came out to rival the minstrel, the ragged fellow welcomed him with such a grace, such a bright smile, that each man felt Segovia had been honored and flattered.

It was almost midnight before this entertainment ended. By that time the minstrel had collected, it was true, not very many coins, but ten men offered to give him a bed for the night. However, it appeared that the little glasses of stinging brandy had done more than their work on the minstrel. And now, like a drunkard, he declared that he would not bother any of them to put him up for the night. Instead, he would gain admission to the castle, where there were sure to be many empty beds!

They listened with amazement. Some of the good-hearted warned him that Garcias' household could not be wakened with impunity in the middle of the night, but the fume of the liquor, it appeared, had made him rash and, therefore, the whole lot of them flocked along to see the performance.

They even pointed out the deep casement of the room of Hernando Garcias, and then they crept away into hiding in nooks and corners and shadows among the nearer houses to watch the fortune of the rash young entertainer, as he strove to sing and dance his way into the house of the great man!

CHAPTER 36

In the meantime, Don Hernando was about to sink into a profound slumber with the peaceful mind of one who has done his duty and done it very well.

For a little earlier, that evening, he had arrived with his prisoner, the gringo, Pier Morgan, and had ridden up to his house, not through the village streets, but up the narrow and steep incline that climbed the face of the bluff and so came directly to the outer gate of the building. By this route he came home, partly because he would thus have his prisoner closer to the dungeon cell in which he was to be confined and partly, also, because he loved to impress and mystify his townsmen.

He knew that some of the household servants would soon spread everywhere in Segovia the news that a prisoner had come, a gringo. But just as surely as the story was bound to fill every house in Segovia, so sure was it that not a syllable would pass beyond. The secrets of Don Hernando were family secrets, as it were, and the whole town shared in them and rigorously preserved them.

The good Don Hernando, having lodged his captive in one of the lowest and wettest of the cellar rooms of the old house, posted a house servant with a machete and a rifle to watch the locked door. He had then gone on to his repast for the evening, content.

He had been told by Sid Levine that he would have to use

every precaution to keep his prisoner from falling into the hands of Speedy again, and this subject constituted part of his conversation with his lady, as they sat together at table. She was a dusky beauty, and now that the years were crowding upon her and she was at least twenty-two, she began to be rounder than before, deep of bosom and heavy of arm. But her eyes were bright, and she carried her head like a queen, as befitted the wife of Don Hernando Garcias.

When she had seen and distantly admired the new thickness of the wallet of her spouse, he explained the simplicity of the work which he had done. It was merely to receive from one man the custody of another, and to ride the man down across the river and hold him in the house.

"This Levine, who pays me the money for the work, is a simpleton," he said. "He seems to feel that his enemy, Speedy, is a snake to crawl through holes in the ground, or a hawk to fly through the air and dart in at a casement. But I told the señor that my house is guarded with more than bolts and locks and keys, for every man within the walls of it has killed at least once! This vagabond, had he not better step into a den of tigers than into the house of Garcias?"

The same fierce satisfaction was still warm in his breast when he retired to sleep, and he was on the point of closing his eyes when he heard the strumming of a guitar just under his window.

For a moment he could not and would not believe his ears. Then rage awoke in him, and his heart leaped into his throat. It was true that the townsmen took many liberties. It was true that they acted very much as they pleased within their own limits, but those limits did not extend to the very walls of the castle.

"A drunkard and a fool," said Garcias to himself, as he sat up in his bed.

He listened, and from the outer air the voice of the singer rose and rang, and entered pleasantly upon his ear. It was an ancient song in praise of great lords who are generous to wandering minstrels.

The purpose of the song seemed so apparent that Garcias ground his teeth. No man could be sufficiently drunk to be excused.

He bounded from his bed, and strode to the window, catching up as he went a crockery washbasin from its stand. With this balanced on the sill, he looked over the ledge, and below him, smudged into the blackness of the ground, he made out clearly enough the silhouette of the singer.

Garcias set his teeth so that they gleamed between his grinning lips. Then he hurled the basin down with all his might.

It passed, it seemed to him, straight through the shadowy form beneath!

Even the stern heart of Garcias stood still.

It was true that his forebears, from time to time, had slain one or more of the townsmen, but they had always paid through the nose for it. The men of Segovia insisted upon compensation, much compensation, floods of money. On certain occasions, they had even threatened to pull the old castle to bits and root out the tyrants!

So Hernando Garcias stood at his window, cursing his hasty temper.

For the song had ceased, or had it merely come to the end of a stanza?

Yes, by heaven, and now the sweet tide of the music recommenced and poured upward, flowing in upon his ear. At the same time, Don Hernando unmistakably heard the tittering of many voices.

"By heavens," he said, "the louts have gathered to watch this. It is a performance. It is a jest, and I am the one who is joked at."

The fear that he might have committed murder, the moment before, now died away in him. He wanted nothing so much as to shatter the head of the singer into bits. He wanted to grind him into the ground.

The washbasin had been too small. He needed a large thing to cast.

It was an old chair, the work of a master. It had been shipped across the sea. Even its gilding represented a small fortune, and on the back of it was portrayed the first great man of the Garcias line.

That was why it stood in the room of the master of the house. For every morning, when he sat up in bed and looked at the picture on the back of the chair, he was assured of his high birth and of the long descent of his line, for the picture might have stood for a portrait of himself. There were the same sunken eyes, the same narrow, high forehead, and even the same short mustaches, twisted to sharp points.

He thought not of the portrait, alas, but, catching up the chair, he hurled it out of the window, this time confident that he could not fail of striking the mark.

It did not seem to him that the minstrel dodged. But certain he was that he had missed the target entirely, for the song still arose and rang on his ears!

Then, lying flat on his stomach across the window sill, he remembered what it was that he had done. The chair must be smashed. Undoubtedly, the portrait was ruined.

He groaned. He staggered back into the room, gasping. Then he flung himself on the bell cord that dangled near the head of his bed, and pulled upon it frantically, not once, not twice, but many times.

Hurrying feet came to the door of his room. There was a timid knock; the door opened.

"Manuel, fool of a sleepy, thick-headed, half-witted muleteer, do you hear the noise that is driving me mad?"

"I hear only the music of the singer, señor," said poor Manuel.

"Music! It's the braying of a mule!" shouted Garcias. "Go

down. Take Pedro with you. Seize the drunken idiot by the ears and drag him here. Do you hear me? Go at once!"

He seized the edge of the door and slammed it literally upon the face of Manuel.

CHAPTER 37

In the meantime, he lighted a lamp and paced hurriedly up and down his room. From the windows, he heard again the tittering of many voices.

Yes, it was as on a stage, and the crowd was enjoying him as one of the actors. Rage seized upon his heart. He thought of the ruined portrait on the chair, and a sort of madness blackened his eyes.

At one end of the room hung various knives. He fingered a few of them as he came to that side of the room.

Nothing could satisfy him, he felt, except to feel the hot blood pouring forth over his hands.

Then came rough voices in the outer court and stifled exclamations from the near distance.

That soothed him a trifle.

He shouted from the window, leaning well out: "Bring up the wreck of the chair and, if you pull off the ears of the singer, I, for one, shall forgive you!"

Presently up the hall came the voices and the footfalls of Manuel and Pedro. The door opened. They flung into the room the body of a slender man, who staggered, almost fell to the floor, and then righting himself and seeing the glowering face of Don Hernando, bowed deeply.

"Señor Garcias," said the minstrel, "I have come many miles to sing for you. One of my ancestors sang for yours,

175

generations ago. And so I have come."

The master of the house glared.

Pedro, in the meantime, was presenting him with the wreckage of the chair. The old, worm-eaten wood had smashed to a sort of powder; and of the back panel, in which the face was painted, there remained no more than scattered splinters. Garcias dropped the wreckage rattling upon the floor feeling sure that he would kill this man.

He surveyed him, the dark head and eyes, the childish delicacy with which the features were formed. And suddenly Don Hernando smiled.

It was a smile famous in the history of his family. Every Garcias had worn it. Every Garcias had made that same cold smile terrible to his adherents. All of Segovia knew it. Manuel and Pedro shuddered where they stood. But the idiot of a minstrel stood there with high head.

One thing was clear. To act on the spur of the moment would be folly. The painting on the chair had been a work of art. The revenge he took would be a work of art of equal merit, a thing to talk about. And why not? The fellow was not of Segovia. He was not of the chosen people. He came from a distance!

So Garcias cleared his throat, and when he spoke it was softly, pleasantly.

Another shudder passed through the bodies of the two servants. Like all the others in the house, each of these had killed his man, but the smile and the voice of Don Hernando, in such a mood, seemed to both of them more terrible, by far, than murder.

"The Garcias family keeps an open house for strangers," he said. "We have rooms for all who come. But chiefly for such good singers. I wish to hear you sing again. Manuel, Pedro, take him down to the most secure room in the house. You, Pedro, will sleep outside of his door, armed. You understand?"

"I understand," said Pedro. "The deepest room of the

house, señor, if you wish."

"Yes, the deepest—the deepest! The one with the strongest door," repeated the great Garcias, through his teeth, "the smallest window, and the heaviest lock; the one where sleeping clothes are always ready, bolted to the wall. You understand? You understand?"

His voice rose to a high, whining snarl, like that of a great cat.

Then he added: "And in case he should want to sing, let him have his guitar. Yes, let him sing, by all means, if he wishes. I am only afraid that he shall be at such a distance that I shall not be able to hear the songs."

Manuel and Pedro grinned brutally. Their master laughed, but the fool of a minstrel was again bowing to the floor and seemed to fail to see or to understand his dreadful predicament.

That was all the better. He would learn, soon enough, what was to befall him! The guards took him to the door of the room.

"Strip him!" shouted the great Garcias, and slammed the door behind the trio.

He went back, then, to the wreckage of his precious chair and picked up, again, the splintered wood upon which the remnants of the portrait appeared. Holding them tightly grasped in his hand, he groaned aloud, with such pain that he closed his eyes.

CHAPTER 38

In the meantime, the two house servants were conducting the young singer down winding stairs that sank toward the bowels of the earth, as it seemed. Finally, they passed the mouth of a black corridor.

"Down there," said Manuel, "is the last dear guest that the Garcias brought home with him. He, also, is guarded against intrusion. Oh, this is a safe house, friend. Danger never breaks in from the outside."

And he laughed, and his brutal laughter raised roaring echoes that retreated on either hand.

The minstrel merely said: "This should be cool. But also rather dark. However, darkness and coolness make for perfect sleep in summer."

They went on, the two servants muttering one to the other, and so they came to the last hall of all, in which there was the door of a single room; and in the hallway lay slime and water half an inch thick, and the horrible green mold climbed far up the walls on either hand.

There was a low settle in the hall.

"You'll sleep there, Pedro," said Manuel, with a chuckle.

"A plague on my luck," said Pedro. "If I don't catch rheumatism from this, I'm not a man. It needs a water snake to live in a hole like this!"

Manuel was unlocking the door. It groaned terribly on its hinges and gave upon a chamber perhaps eight feet by eight, and not more than five in height. It was like a grisly coffin. A breath of foul air rolled out to meet them.

"Is this—is this the room?" gasped the poor minstrel.

"Yes, you fool!" said Manuel. "Strip him, Pedro."

They put the lantern on the floor. Between them they tore the clothes from the body of the poor singer, and flung them on the floor.

"But what does it mean, my friends?" said the minstrel. "Why am I here? Why am I stripped? Alas, I am a poor man. I have done no wrong."

"Be quiet," said Pedro. "You were told about a secure room and this is it. And you were told about bedding and this is it, perfect to fit you, like a suit of clothes ordered from the tailor!"

As he spoke, he dragged a mass of chains from the wall, and locked them around the wrists and the ankles of the trembling minstrel.

"Ah, my friends," said the youth. "This is cruel and unjust. Trouble will come upon your master, for this act."

They left the room, slammed the door upon him and turned the key in the lock.

"There's the guitar against the wall beside you. You can play and sing in the dark, amigo," were their last words.

They were hardly gone, when the minstrel raised his manacled hands to his head, and from the base of a curl, he drew forth a little piece of flattened steel.

With this, he began to work, cramped though his fingers were for space, upon the lock of the manacle that held his left wrist.

He did not work long before the manacle loosened. It slipped away, and presently its companion upon the other wrist likewise fell to the floor. The singer stooped over his anklets. They also presently fell away, and he was free in the room.

After that, he felt his way along the wall to the heap in which his clothes had been flung. When he was dressed, he went to the door and felt of the lock. To his dismay, he found that the whole inside of the lock was simply one large sheet of steel! The key did not come through the massive portal!

He stood for a time, taking small breaths, because the badness of the air inclined to make him dizzy. But eventually he had a thought.

Outside, in the corridor, Pedro the guard was already asleep, for the sounds of his snoring came like a drowsy purring into the dungeon cell.

So the prisoner found his guitar and lifted his voice in song.

He took care in the selection of his music. The ditties that found his favor, now, were the loudest, and he sang them close to the door.

It was not long before the key groaned in the lock; the door was thrust wide; and in rushed big Pedro, cursing.

From the shadow beside the door, the minstrel struck with a fist as heavy as lead, hitting home beneath the ear. And Pedro slumped forward on his face in the slime.

He was quickly secured, ankle and wrist, in the manacles which had just held the singer. And the wet filth in which he lay brought back his senses after a moment or so.

He opened his eyes, groaning, in time to feel the revolver being drawn from its holster on his hip and by the light of the lantern he saw the minstrel smiling down upon him.

Exquisite horror overcame big Pedro. Agape, he looked not so much at the slender youth before him as at a terrible vision of the wrath of the lord of the house.

"Good-by, Pedro," said the minstrel. "Remember me all the days of your life, and never forget that I shall remember your hospitality. As for your master whom you are fearing now, don't worry about his anger. He shall have other things to think of before many minutes."

And he left the room before the stupefied Pedro could answer and closed the door gently behind him.

He picked up the lantern and quickly climbed to the black mouth of the corridor down which, as he had been told, the last guest of the Garcias was housed. Presently around a sharp elbow turn the light of another lantern mingled with that of the one which he was carrying.

He went on at the same pace, dropping the revolver which he carried into a coat pocket. He could take it for granted that if a guard waited outside the door of this prison, the face of the singer would not be known to the man.

So he went on fearlessly and now saw the man in question seated on a stool. With his arms folded on his breast, he was sleeping profoundly. The minstrel laid the cold muzzle of the revolver against his throat and picked the sawed-off shotgun from his lap.

Then, as the rascal wakened with a start, he said: "Be quiet and steady, my friend. Stand up, turn the key of that locked door, and walk into the cell ahead of me, carrying the lantern."

"In the name of the saints," said the guard, "do you know that it is an enemy of the Garcias who lies there?"

"I know everything about it," said the singer. "Do as I tell you. I am a man in haste, with a loaded gun in my hand. Pedro loaned it to me," he added, with a smile.

The guard rose, with a faint gasp, and, striding to the locked door, turned the key and stepped into the gloom within.

There, stretched on a thin pallet of straw, was the prisoner. He had not been stripped; there were no irons upon him. Plainly he had not excited the wrath of the great Garcias to the same degree as the singer, who now stooped over and fastened the manacles which were chained to the wall upon the wrists and the ankles of the guard.

The latter was moaning and muttering. "The saints defend me! The saints keep me from the rage of Don Hernando!"

"Speedy!" the prisoner cried. "I didn't know you, with the color of your skin, and—"

"We have to go on," said Speedy, calmly. "There's something more for us to do, before we leave the house of the great Garcias. He's fitted the two of us with such good quarters that we ought to leave some pay behind for him, Pier. Come along with me. This chap will be safe enough here. Rest well, amigo."

So he passed out from the cell and locked the door behind him.

Pier Morgan, in the meantime, was gaping helplessly at him.

"Speedy," he said, "I'm tryin' to believe that it's your voice that I'm hearing. But how did you come here? Did you put on a pair of wings and hop in through a window?"

"Don Hernando asked me in," said Speedy, smiling faintly. "He even sent out his men and insisted on my coming in. How do you feel, Pier? Are you fit to ride a bit, and do some climbing, perhaps, before we start the riding?"

"I'm fit to ride; I rode all the way down here," said Pier. "And I can ride ten times as far in order to get away. Let's get out quickly, and let your call on Hernando go!"

CHAPTER 39

The door of the bedroom of the Garcias was locked from the inside. He had gone to bed, with the flame turned down in the throat of the lamp. Now he awoke, not that he had heard any suspicious sound, but because there was a sighing rush of wind through the room, as though a storm had entered.

To his amazement, that door was open!

He rubbed his eyes and shook his head to clear away the foolish vision, for he knew that no one in the house would ever dare to attempt his locked door. Even if there were someone foolish enough to make such an attempt, the lock of the door would itself give ample warning, for the key in the bolt could not be stirred without making a groaning sound.

He opened his eyes again and scowled at the offending door, but now the vision was more complicated. A man stood in the doorway, and was gliding with a soundless step straight toward his bed. The light of the lamp was very slight but, as he stared, the bewildered Garcias saw that it was the gringo minstrel.

He grunted. In the distance, the door was being closed by a second figure. But there was always a weapon at the hand of the Garcias, and now he snatched his favorite protection from beneath his pillow. It was a rather old-fashioned double-barreled pistol, short in length, but large in caliber. It was equipped with two hair triggers, and it fired a ball big enough and with sufficient force to knock a strong man flat at fifteen yards.

So, snatching it out, he tried to level it at the gringo.

But he found his hand struck down, a clever stroke, as it were, falling across the cords of his wrist, and benumbing the entire hand.

The pistol slipped into the sheets of the bed. A second stroke, delivered with the flat edge of the man's palm, fell upon the neck of the Garcias. He was stunned as though with a club.

Before he was entirely recovered from the effects, he found that the minstrel was sitting comfortably on the edge of his bed, toying with that double-barreled pistol with his left hand, but in his right was a short-bladed knife, the point of which he kept affectionately close to the hollow of Don Hernando's throat.

In the meantime, the second shadowy form had drawn closer and stood on the farther side of the bed. With disgust, Don Hernando recognized the face of Pier Morgan. He had received twenty-five hundred dollars for taking Morgan into the southern land across the river. He would receive twenty-five hundred more for keeping him there, or for making away with him.

This was a bad business, all around. He wished for wild hawks to tear the flesh of the minstrel.

"I see," said Garcias, "how it is. You tricked the guards and got away from them, but you know that you can't get out of the house. Every door and every entrance to the house is guarded night and day!"

He laughed a little, as he ended. His fury made his laughter a tremulous sound.

"Speedy," said Pier Morgan, "we can't waste time. We must hurry."

Don Hernando stiffened from head to foot. "You are not Speedy!" he exclaimed, through his teeth. "Your skin is as brown as—"

"As walnut juice, amigo?" suggested Speedy.

The lips of the Mexican remained parted, but no word issued from them.

Then said Speedy: "You see how it is, Don Hernando? I knew that your house was so guarded that only a bird could fly in safely through a window. And I had no wings. So I came and sang at night, to disturb you. Do you understand?"

The teeth of the Mexican ground together. He said nothing. "Then, when you were sufficiently annoyed," Speedy said, "you sent for me to get into your house and throw me into your hole of a prison. But I expected that, Garcias. I was prepared for all of that trouble, and it was worth while, because I had to reach my friend, Pier Morgan. I knew that it would be hard to hold me in a cell, because I know the language of locks."

The Garcias rolled his eyes toward the door of his own room.

"The others were no harder," said Speedy. "Besides, your men are all fools. One of your servants sleeps in one of those cells, and the other sleeps in the second. They are not happy, Don Hernando, because they are afraid of what you will do to them when they are set free."

"I will have them cut to pieces," said the Garcias, "before my eyes. I will have them fed to dogs, and let you watch the feeding, before you are cut to bits in your turn!"

"You are full of promises, Don Hernando," said Speedy, "but that's because you don't understand how simply we can get out of your house through that window, with a rope of bedclothes."

"Idiots!" said Don Hernando, "Segovia lies beyond, and

will have to be passed through. And there are always armed men there!"

"True," said the minstrel, "and I shall let them knew that I am passing. I shall sing to my guitar."

"Are you such a half-wit?" said Garcias with a snarl.

"Besides," said Speedy, "I shall have something to show them, which will prove that the Garcias forgave me for disturbing him in the middle of the night."

"What?" demanded the man of the castle.

"A ring from your finger," said Speedy.

Don Hernando gripped both hands to make fists. His fury was so great that his brain turned to fire.

"I shall believe when I see!" said Don Hernando.

"You will believe and see and hear, all three," said Speedy, "for I shall put you on a high chair to look things over. I shall put you where you'll be found in the morning. Tie his feet, Pier. I'll attend to his hands!"

Hand and foot the lord of the town of Segovia found himself trussed and a gag fixed between his teeth.

Then Speedy drew from the struggling hand of Don Hernando almost his dearest possession, his signet ring. It was merely a flat-faced emerald of no great value, but it was carved with the arms of the house of the Garcias. That ring and the portrait which had been ruined that night were his two clear claims and proofs of gentility.

He saw the second one departing in the possession of the same scoundrel; he turned blind with fury; when he recovered from the fit, he was hanging from the sill of a window of his room by the hands, his back turned to the wall. Strong cords held him at the wrists. Presently his arm muscles would weaken. The strain would come straight upon bones and tendons. And then the real torment would commence.

But what would that matter compared with the exquisite agony of being found in this humiliating position in the morning by the loyal populace of Segovia?

CHAPTER 40

In all the house of the Garcias, among all of his people, was there not one careful soul to look out a window, at this time, and see the two villains who now clambered down their comfortably made rope of bedding to the ground?

His anguish grew. He turned his head and saw the wretches standing upon the paving stones at the base of his wall. He bowed his head to stare down at them, while rage choked him, and there he saw Speedy remove from his head the hat with the tattered straw brim and sweep the ground with it, making a final bow.

Anguish, shame, fury, helplessness, fairly throttled the great Garcias.

If only he could cry out!

He had only his bare heels to kick against the wall, and he soon bruised the flesh of his feet to the bone. But no one answered. Then he heard a sound that fairly stopped the beating of his heart again.

It was rising from the lower streets of the town, and it was the strumming of a guitar, and the sound of a fine tenor voice that rose and rang sweetly through the air.

It was true, then, that the rascal had determined to do all as he had said? Was he to outbrave the fierce men of Segovia and increase the shame of the Garcias?

But Speedy and Pier Morgan did not get unhindered from the town.

It was said that the men of Segovia slept as lightly as wild wolves, which they were like in other respects, also, and when they heard the voice of the minstrel, one, then another

186

and another, jumped up in the night and went out to see what the disturbance might be. For they had seen the fellow dragged within the walls of the house, and what had happened to him in there was much pleasanter to guess than to see.

So they came pouring out, a score of those ragged, wild men, and found the minstrel, as before, mounted on the ancient gray mule, with a white man walking at his stirrup.

This was too strange a sight to pass.

There was one elderly robber, gray with years and villainy, and music did not particularly tickle his fancy.

He took the mule by the bridle and halted it.

"What is the meaning of this?" he demanded. "I saw you snatched into the door of the castle like a stupid child. Who set you free?"

"An angel, father," said Speedy, "walked into my room, wrapped me in an invisible cloak, and took me away, with this man."

"So?" said the desperado, darkening. "You will sing a new tune, if you try to make a fool out of me. You are here after midnight. So is this man. People do not start a trip at this time of the night."

"Look at his hands," said Speedy.

"Aye," said the other, "I see that they are tied together behind his back. And what do I understand by that?"

"You will understand," said Speedy, "when the Garcias knows that you have stopped me in the streets and made me explain before the people. I am taking this man to a friend of the Garcias."

"Ha!" said the man. "How will you prove that?"

He snatched a lantern from the hand of another, and held it up to examine the face of Speedy.

The latter used the light, thrusting forward his left hand with the emerald ring on the largest finger. "Do you know the signet of the Garcias?" he demanded, harshly. "Would he give it to me for pleasure, or because of an important errand in his name?"

The other was stunned.

He squinted at the ring. The face of it was well known. His companions were already falling back from the scene. They did not wish to interfere where the will of the master of Segovia was expressed in such unconditional terms as this.

The man released the head of the mule. "Well, amigo," said he, "there is a time for talk and a time for silence. This is a time for silence. Go along."

And Speedy rode on, slowly, through the last street of Segovia, and into the plain beyond.

Once down the slope, he cut the cord that confined the hands of Pier Morgan and the latter gasped: "Speedy, I thought that we were finished, when we came to the gang of 'em. I thought they'd certainly drag us back to the big house. And if they had—eh, what then?"

"Garcias would have burned us alive," said Speedy. "That's what would have happened. But it didn't happen, and the more luck for us. I thought that the ring would turn the trick, and it turned out that way."

"I've got other things to ask," said Pier Morgan. "But I'll ask 'em after we get on the other side of the river."

It was Pier Morgan who rode the mule across the shallows of the ford. It was Speedy who waded or swam behind until they struggled up the farther bank.

And there they turned and looked back over the dim pattern of stars that appeared, scattered over the face of the famous river.

Then Pier Morgan said: "Yesterday, I thought that I was ridin' my last trail, Speedy. And today it don't seem likely that I'm really here, on safe ground, and you beside me. I ain't thanking you, Speedy. Thanks are pretty foolish things, after all, considering what you've done for me; you've kept me on the face of the earth. That's what you've done. But still I'd like to ask you why you wanted to make this here Garcias so crazy mad at you. You done that on purpose, but I dunno what the purpose is."

"You could guess," said Speedy.

"Yeah, I could guess," said the other. "You got Garcias practically crazy. You wanted to make sure that he'd get together every man that can ride and shoot and come up to the Slough looking for your scalp."

Speedy chuckled a little.

"Garcias can be a pretty dangerous fellow, I imagine," said he. "He has that reputation. But I wanted to have him so blind crazy with rage that he'll never rest till he gets at me again."

"No, he'll never rest," agreed Pier Morgan. "He'll certainly never sleep until he gets a whack at you in revenge."

"When he comes, he'll come like a storm," said Speedy, "and the first thing that he does will be to get in touch with friend Levine. Isn't that fairly clear?"

"Yeah. That's pretty likely."

"And when that happens, I have a chance to scoop him up with Levine. And then the charge is kidnaping, with you and me both for proofs of what's happened. And kidnaping a man and taking him across a frontier is pretty bad and black for everybody concerned. I think, if my scheme works, I'll have Levine in for fifteen years, at least. That's my hope. And then I've done what I wanted to do—I've cleaned up Sunday Slough and given it a rest."

"All right," murmured Pier Morgan. "I'm behind you every step, but you must carry a pretty steep life insurance, old man!"

CHAPTER 41

Levine was at the breakfast table. He had a newspaper propped up in front of him, but he paid less attention to its headlines than to the conversation of One-eyed Mike Doloroso, who had just come in and made himself at home.

"Have something?"

"Nope," said Mike.

"Slug o' coffee, maybe?"

"I fed my face a coupla hours ago," said Mike. "I ain't a lazy hound like you, what I mean."

"You got nothin' on your brain to worry you, like me," said Levine. "You got nothin' but hair."

"Ain't I got Speedy to worry me, too?" asked Mike.

"Him? Aw, he don't pay much attention to you. It's me that he wants. What's that yowling out there?"

Mike went to the window.

"Aw," he said, "there's a coupla dozen poor fools walkin' down the street carryin' a big banner that says J.J.J. for sheriff."

"Close the window and shut the yapping out, will you?" asked Levine, testily. "That tramp, I'm kind of tired of thinking about him."

"Yeah," said One-eyed Mike, "you shouldn't go and get yourself into a stew about him now. But one of these days you may be rotting in the pen like Buck Masters. I got a letter from Buck just the other day."

"Why didn't you tell me about it?"

"Because you wouldn't want to see it. Buck is pretty sore. He says that he trusted you to fix things for him. He says that he's the goat and went to jail to save your scalp."

"Did the fool say that?" asked Levine, losing a splotch of color out of either cheek.

"Yeah, he said that."

"Prison letters are opened and read!" gasped Levine.

"Aw, they've all heard more than that about you a long while before this," declared One-eyed Mike. "Talk ain't gonna kill you. But Buck is sore, is what I mean."

"I spent a lotta money on that case," said Levine, sadly. "You know what I spent."

"I know what you say you spent," said Mike.

"Look," protested Levine, sadly, "are you gonna do a State's evidence, or something like that on me?"

"Aw, shut up," said Mike Doloroso. "You know that I ain't that kind. But I ain't a fool. And I'm worried. Look at Buck and Derrick, both. There was plenty of money working for both of them two, but it didn't do no good. Not a dog-gone bit."

The window that looked onto the street was thrust up with a screech. The face of young Joe Dale appeared in the square.

"Hello, boys," said he.

"Hello, beautiful," said Mike. "Whacha want here, kid?"

"I just wanted to clap eyes on you bozos, was all," said Joe Dale. "I just wanted to ask you where you seen Speedy last."

"We ain't seeing Speedy these days," said Levine. "We was good friends, once, but he's gone and got proud, since those days."

"Has he?" asked Joe. "That's all right, too. But how far south would your partner, Garcias, trail him?"

"What Garcias?" asked Levine.

But he glanced at One-eyed Mike.

"No, you never seen Garcias, did you?" said Joe Dale. "Lemme tell you, brother. I'm inside the law, just now. But I was outside of it for a long time and if Speedy don't come back, I'm gonna be outside the law ag'in. I'm gonna be outlawed for shooting the brains out of a pair of fatheads that I'm looking at, right now."

"Breeze along, Joe," said Levine. "You're all right, but you're young. You ain't got any sense.'

Another voice struck in cheerfully from the distance, down the street: "Hello, Joe! Hello!"

Levine started up from his chair. "It's Speedy!" he gasped.

One-eyed Mike grunted. There was a sawed-off shotgun standing in the corner against the wall, and this he picked up and held at the ready.

Sid Levine had slumped down into his chair again. A frightful weakness in his knees had attacked him.

The cheerful face of Speedy now appeared outside the window, at the shoulder of Joe Dale; and behind Speedy loomed Pier Morgan.

Sid Levine became smaller in his chair; a watery pulp. That window seemed to him to open upon the inferno itself, three such enemies were gathered there before his face.

Speedy said: "I took your regards down to your friend, the great Garcias, Levine. He'll be up, before very long, to see you. Just dropped in to say hello to you, Levine. And Morgan wanted to tell you that he'd enjoyed his trip with Don Hernando."

"I don't know what you mean," said Levine.

He shook his head; his fat cheeks wabbled and bulged from side to side. "You may understand later on," said Pier Morgan. "We're gonna do our best to clear up the idea in your mind, anyway. Hello, Mike! I ain't seen you for quite a spell."

But Mike Doloroso answered nothing at all. He was rather sick at heart.

And so the three outside the window passed out of view, laughing.

They left a silence behind them. Levine was resting his fat forehead in a fatter hand. Mike remained still, as one stunned by bad news. But at last he began to pace up and down along the floor.

Then he said: "Chief, it looks like we got our backs against the wall."

Levine slowly roused himself and leaned forward.

"There's one thing that we can still try," he said. "And there's one thing that will work."

"What's that?" asked Mike.

Levine beckoned, and the big Irishman came closer to him, and leaned over.

Levine whispered one word, and Mike Doloroso, though a man of exceptionally steady nerves, jumped away as though a knife had been thrust into him.

CHAPTER 42

Speedy and Joe Dale sat in the sheriff's office; Pier Morgan, exhausted by his long journeying, was asleep in the side room; and the deputy sheriff who, as nine-tenths of Sunday Slough declared, was to be the sheriff in full at the next day's election, now sat slumping in a chair.

"You ought to let the people know what you did down there, Speedy," said Joe Dale. "That'll poll all the votes for you. You'll be unanimously elected, I tell you!"

Speedy yawned.

"Ask Betsy about it," said he. "Ask her what I ought to do."

Betsy was grazing in the lot behind the shack which housed the sheriff's office. Now and then she snorted, shook her head, and lifted it to look about her.

Joe Dale went to the window and looked upon her with a

loving eye.

"Ask her about me," said Speedy.

"What about this fellow?" asked Joe Dale, pleased by the suggestion. "Come here, Betsy, and tell me about him."

Speedy went to the window as Betsy came up to it.

"Tell me about him, Betsy," repeated her owner. "Is he a good fellow?"

She stretched her head through the window and sniffed Speedy's hand, then she pricked her ears mischievously and began to nibble at it.

"She knows you're no good and she's trying to bite you," declared Joe Dale. "I'm going to keep an eye on you, Speedy. Here's Betsy says that you're no good at all. Betsy, you're a wise old girl. You know more than I do."

"I've never ridden her," said Speedy.

"You'd better not try," answered Joe Dale.

"Why? I thought that she was as gentle as a lamb."

"She's gentle with me. She's gentle with others, too, but she knows some little tricks."

"Such as what?"

"She hates spurs. One touch of 'em and she'll buck like a fiend. She's an educated little pitching witch, I can tell you! She learned young."

"Anything else that she doesn't like?"

"She's a balky brute, at heart. She even tries it on me, now and then," confessed Joe Dale. "Sometimes she doesn't like to pass a stump or a tree with a funny shape. And sometimes she'll stop dead at a bridge, and start turning in circles like a crazy thing. I can bring her out of those wrong notions with a touch. But nobody else can."

"What's to do, then?" asked Speedy.

"Get off and lead her. That's the only way. She's always as quiet as a lamb when she's on the lead. She seems to be sure that a man walking on the ground really knows the way better'n she does."

He added: "You planning to steal her, Speedy, asking all these questions?"

"I'd rather have my gray mule," grinned Speedy. "He's slow but he's sure. But some day I might want to make a fast move and need Betsy."

"You don't wear spurs, so you'd be all right on her," said the other. "And I've told you about the balking."

"How fast is she?" asked Speedy.

"She's no racer," admitted Joe Dale. "She looks a lot faster than she is. Somehow, she doesn't seem able to stretch out in a real, long gallop. But her point is that she can last all day, and all night, and she'll live on thistles and drink the wind for a week, and still be able to lope along like a wolf."

"That's the horse for this country," declared Speedy. "Next to the iron horse, that's the way to travel in this country."

"You're still a tramp," grinned Joe Dale. "You'd like to be back on the bum, riding blind baggage, and going nowheres."

"Going nowhere is the best place to go," said Speedy. "There's no place I've ever seen where I'd like to live. There's no place I'd like to drop anchor. But to drift from one spot to another—that's a good deal better."

The other stared curiously at him.

"Look a-here, Speedy," said he. "Look at Sunday Slough. The people are all proud to have you around. You could be sheriff here till kingdom come. They'd give you a fat salary. You wouldn't have to keep smiling, up here. The boys know what you can do."

"I've had a good time here, but it's lasted long enough," said Speedy. "I'm tired of having a fixed home address."

A horse beat down the street, came to a grinding halt before the sheriff's office, and a big man in shirt sleeves, rolled to the elbows, with salty sweat stains on his breast and shoulders, came clumping into the room.

"Hullo, Speedy," he said.

"Something wrong?" asked Speedy.

"You bet there's something wrong," he replied. "You know me?"

"I've seen you. I don't know your name."

"I'm Sam Jedbury. I got a claim up there at the head of the ravine and I struck it pretty good. I struck it too good for my health. Today along comes a low-down hound of a Swede and pokes a rifle into my stomach and tells me that he staked that claim a year ago. Why, there wasn't even a jack rabbit in Sunday Slough a year ago. But that's what he says. And what am I to do? Argue? You can't argue with a rifle, unless you got a gun in your hand. And I didn't have no gun. So I come in here to let you know."

Speedy sighed. "What sort of a looking fellow?" he asked.

"Big and hairy is all I can say," said Sam Jedbury. "Got a mean-looking eye, too. It was like poison to me."

"I'll go and call on him," said Speedy.

"I'll go along," said the other.

"No, you stay here. You, too, Joe."

Dale had picked a gun belt from a nail on the wall and was strapping it around his hips.

"Hold on, Speedy," said Joe Dale. "You let me tell you something. You've handled a lot of the wild men around here, but you've never handled a claim-jumper before. Those fellows know that trouble is ahead of 'em, and they plan on doing a little shooting."

"That's right," nodded Sam Jedbury. "You let us both go along."

"I don't carry a gun; everybody knows it; so guns aren't likely to be used on me," said Speedy.

"Don't be so sure of that," said Jedbury. "Neither does a wild cat or a grizzly pack a gun, but gents will go shooting for them!"

Speedy shrugged his shoulders.

"I'll go alone," he said. "Don't be surprised if I don't come back for a while. The fact is that I may have to do a little scouting around."

He turned to Dale. "Suppose that I borrow Betsy?" he asked.

"You can have Betsy," said Joe Dale, "but I'd a lot rather you'd let me go along with you. You're taking too many chances, Speedy. Some day, you'll lose your bet. Do you realize that?"

"I told you before that I wanted to be on the road," said Speedy. "Here's a trip on a side line, anyway. It may not be much, but I'm going to take it."

CHAPTER 43

Twice the beautiful mare balked, on the way up the valley, and twice Speedy dismounted and led her forward until her step became free and willing, and her ears were pricking. But he had been so delayed by these halts that it was after sunset when he got to the claim of Jedbury at the head of the ravine.

The claim-jumper was in full view, sitting on a broad-topped stone at the mouth of the shaft, which lay on top of a dump. He smoked a pipe with a quiet concentration; and he had across his knees a shining new Winchester that would hold fifteen shots—fifteen lives, perhaps!

He was what Sam Jedbury had described—a hairy fellow, with a very considerable jaw to be guessed at behind the tangle of his beard.

He paid no heed to the approach of Speedy and the mare but continued to smoke his pipe.

It was only when the deputy sheriff was a few yards away that he picked up his rifle and held it like a revolver in one hand, his forefinger on the trigger and the long barrel pointing at Speedy.

The latter spoke to Betsy and she halted.

"How's things?" asked Speedy.

"Things are fair to middling," replied the other, in his noncommittal way. "Whacha want?"

"Just wanted to have a chat with you," said Speedy.

He dismounted, and sat down on a rock near the claim-jumper, facing him. The muzzle of the rifle followed his movements like the magnetic needle pointing toward the pole.

"You go on and chat," said the miner. "Whacha gonna chat about?"

"A fellow came into town," said Speedy, "and told me a wild yarn about his mine up here. He said another fellow, who answers your description, had arrived and jumped it. It sounded like a cock-and-bull yarn, but I had to come up here and investigate. I'm the deputy sheriff, you see."

"Wait," said the other, frowning. "You call yourself Speedy?"

"Yes," said the man of the law.

"The Speedy that runs Sunday Slough?"

"I don't claim to run it."

"Hold on, now. You say that you're Speedy, and I say that you lie. Whacha think about that?" He thrust his head forward and uttered the last words with a sneer.

"Are you sure that I'm a liar?" said Speedy, smiling.

"Sure? Of course, I'm sure."

"Have you ever seen Speedy?"

"I don't need to see him," answered the claim-jumper. "I heard him described enough times. Back in the mountains they don't talk about much else of a winter evening except to swap lies about Speedy, what he's done, and what he ain't done. Why, kid, you're a plain fool if you think that you'll kid me into believin' that you're Speedy!"

The latter opened the breast of his coat and showed the

steel badge that was pinned inside of it.

"That's all that I can say," said he. "You can believe me or not, but I'll have to take you into Sunday Slough."

"You?" cried the miner.

"I'm afraid that I shall," said Speedy. "Unless you can prove that the mine belongs to you. You drove out Jedbury. He was the first to work it."

"That's a lie," said the ruffian. "I'll tell you what. I staked out this claim pretty near a year ago. Jedbury, he never would've found nothing here, except that he saw where I'd been working, and—"

He paused, scowling.

"I done enough talking," he said. "Talking ain't my style."

"I think Jedbury was telling the truth," said Speedy. "You'll have to come to town with me, partner."

"Where's your warrant?" asked the man of the beard.

"We don't bother about those little formalities in Sunday Slough," said Speedy. "Not when we have fellows like claim-jumpers to handle."

"I'm a claim-jumper, am I?" asked the other.

His teeth glinted through his beard as he spoke. Then he added: "You're gonna take me back, are you? Would you mind telling me what you're gonna take me with?"

"Yes, with my hands," said Speedy. He stood up. "It's getting toward dusk," said he. "We'd better be starting along."

The miner rose in turn and held the rifle stiffly toward the breast of the man of the law.

"I could lick you without a gun," said the miner, "except as how they say that you're a whole pack of tricks. I reckon that I don't really need a gun, but why should I throw away a bet on a sure thing? I'm gonna teach you what it means to mix up with Bill Parry, and—"

With savage satisfaction he drew nearer to the boy, so near

that the muzzle of his gun, though still out of reaching distance, was not, however, out of range of a kick.

And that was what Speedy tried. It was a difficult target, the narrow, gleaming barrel of that rifle, and if he missed, a bullet would take his life the next instant. But he took the chance.

It was a partial miss. Only with the side of his shoe did he touch the rifle a glancing blow. It exploded almost on the instant, but the force of the kick had been sufficient to make it swerve to the side, and the bullet ripped the shirt under Speedy's armpit. Half an inch closer in, it would have broken his ribs and knocked him down.

Bill Parry, as he fired, leaped backward to avoid danger, but he was far too slow of foot.

All the tangled padding of his beard was not sufficient to dull the force of a blow that clipped him close to the point of the chin and staggered him, bent his knees.

What happened to him after that, he was never quite sure. He simply knew, all in an instant of time, that he was tripped up, disarmed, half-stunned by a blow on the temple and, in general, felt as though he had been tackled by a combination of wild cat and grizzly bear.

Then he was lying flat on his back, looking up toward the darkening sky and toward the face of Speedy, who stood erect, panting.

"You'd better get up, Bill Parry," said Speedy. "As I said before, you'll have to come into Sunday Slough with me. You've resisted arrest, attempted murder and in general played a bad hand. I'll be lucky if I keep the men of the Slough from taking you out on a necktie party."

Parry did not move. He merely said: "There'll be a necktie party, all right enough!"

"I'm not threatening you," said Speedy.

"Ain't you? But I'm threatening you! You fool, we got everything set ready for you. We got you trimmed and trapped, you swine. If you don't believe me, look around you!"

Speedy, though he did not turn his head, was suddenly certain that figures had moved up behind him during the fight, and that now they were in readiness.

Then, from behind him, he heard the last voice in all the world that he wished to hear, the voice of Garcias, saying, with a tremor of joy: "Now, Pedro, now Manuel, take him on each side. If he moves a finger, fill his skin with lead!"

And, for the first time in his wild young life, Speedy made certain of death!

CHAPTER 44

Chains, irons and locks they knew better than to try upon the magic hands of Speedy, by this time. They used ropes, instead, not big ones, which may be slipped, but thin, powerful cords. They tied his hands together. They tied him across the elbows. They tied his feet and ankles together; they bound his knees. They put a stout pole down his back, and wrapped him to it with lashings.

Then he heard a voice saying: "There ain't anything he can move, now, but his brain and his tongue."

It was the voice of Levine, and the voice of One-eyed Mike broke in to add: "Yeah, he can think and he can talk."

He came and stood over Speedy, and kicked him brutally in the ribs with his heavy boot.

"You go on and tell me, Speedy. You tell me how you're gonna talk your way clean out of this, will you?"

"Oh, I'll tell you," said Speedy. "I don't at all mind telling you that I'll get out of the tangle."

"You hear that, Don Hernando?" said the great Levine, laughing softly. "He says that he'll talk his way out of this here trouble. He ain't the kind to boast, neither.

The Mexican came nearer, glaring down at the victim. Suddenly he squatted like an Indian on his heels, to bring his face closer to that of the helpless prisoner.

"You had a moment in my own house," he said, "when you could have run a knife through my throat. But you did not, Señor Speedy. Tell me why, like a blind fool, you let me go."

"Because," said Speedy, "I wanted you up here."

"And so you have me, eh?" said the Mexican.

"So I have you," agreed Speedy. "And Levine with you, and your two man-killers, there, and One-eyed Mike, also. I am only baiting a trap that will catch you all!"

Hernando sprang up and looked about him in alarm. Then he said, "Your lies are the lies of a fool! There is no danger near us. I have other men posted. They can see everything that comes near. We are alone here with you, and we intend to see you dying slowly."

"Find a death for me," said Speedy, "that takes plenty of time, because there won't be any shame in it. There'll be no shame like hanging out of a window of my own house, like a suit of old clothes, taking the air. How much do the people of Segovia laugh when they think of you, amigo Hernando?"

The Mexican, in frantic anger, fairly howled out an oath, and whirled the lash of his whip above his head.

It was caught from behind and the voice of Bill Parry exclaimed: "None of that, Garcias!"

Pedro, on one side of Parry, drew a knife; Manuel, on the other, had a revolver ready. They waited the signal from their chief before laying the rash gringo dead.

But Levine called out: "Stop 'em, Garcias. We don't want anything to happen to Parry. He's all right. We wouldn't've had Speedy now, except for him!"

Don Hernando had drawn himself up, stiff with rage.

"I have come many leagues," he declared. "I have ridden furiously with my men. I suggested this method for catching the snake when I came here. And now I am insulted by a gringo!"

"Señor, Señor!" muttered Pedro, warningly.

"Shut up, Parry," repeated Levine, but the miner was enraged in his turn, and his tongue could be as bitter as any in Mexico, for that matter.

He shouted out: "If you call me a gringo, you greaser puppy, I'm gonna—"

He reached for a gun as he spoke, but an unexpected voice broke in on the debate. It was Speedy, saying cheerfully from the ground where he lay: "Fight it out, boys. When the last of you are dead, I'll be safe enough."

This logic struck Garcias at once.

"That is true. Why should we fight with one another?" he asked. "To please this demon? We have come to dispose of him, not of one another."

"You'll never dispose of me, Garcias," said Speedy. "It's not in the cards for you. Neither for that fat-faced Levine. I know my luck that far away. But don't argue with the gringos, as you call them, Don Hernando. They have everything better than you have, stronger hands, better brains; better guns, better horses to ride on."

Don Hernando groaned with fury.

"You say four things and you lie four times," said he. "You are nothing but a lie. We have guns as good, better hands, better wits, better horses."

"You have broken-down, lump-headed, knock-kneed, sway-backed wrecks for horses," said Speedy. "They are the offcasts of the tramps and fourth-rate cowpunchers, who get tired of them, and sell them for the price of their hoofs and hides. But they're good enough for you fellows south of the Rio Grande. Plenty good enough!"

If there is any tender point with a Mexican of any pretensions to rank, it is the horse that he rides upon. Speedy already had seen the glorious animal that Don Hernando usually rode. Though it was not in sight, now, he guessed that it must be somewhere near.

Don Hernando was a mere drifting, staggering thing, so did rage buoy and lighten him. At last he managed to say: "Pedro, bring me my horse and let this lying demon see what a gentleman rides in Mexico."

Pedro went for the horse.

Levine, in the meantime, together with Mike, had carefully propped up the helpless, stiff-lashed body of Speedy against the bank of the mine dump.

He and his henchmen sat down near by. And Levine said: "Don't get too hot, Garcias. There ain't any use matching words with this here sneak. We better put our heads together about the best way of getting rid of him."

But here the horse was brought, a fine gray gelding, gleaming and dancing through the dusk of the day.

The eyes of Speedy, prepared as they were, widened a little. "Look," commanded the Garcias, "and then tell me what a liar you are. Say it with your own lips!"

"I see what you have there," said Speedy. "That's the sort of a pick-up that we give our children to ride. No man would want to be on the back of a horse like that. Take the mare, yonder. She has more brains than you and your men, put together. She'll run faster, and run farther than your gray. She is worth looking at. She has points!"

Don Hernando stared with a fixed passion. Then he said: "You, señor, being about to die, already rave. But I would like to show you how the gray would leave the mare behind him. If they ran as far as that rock and back. Then you would see!"

"Bill Parry will ride the mare and make a fool of your horse," answered Speedy. "Bill, show up the Mexican, will you, and his bragging?"

"I'll do it free and willing and glad," said Bill Parry. "It's a good mare and a grand mare to look at. Garcias, I'm ready!"

CHAPTER 45

In all parts of the world, in all times, there have been strange races, but never one under auspices more peculiar that this. Sid Levine was the only one to protest.

"The kid is playing for time," he said. "He's making fools of us. He may have something up his sleeve. You know that, Garcias."

"What can he do?" answered Garcias. "And what can his friends do? If they come near, we have horses to carry us away, unless we can drive them off with our rifles. And before we mount, each of us puts a bullet through the head of Señor Speedy. In the meantime, I shall show him that he is both a fool and a blind man, since he cannot judge horses. Manuel, take the saddle of the gray. Amigo," he added to Parry, "you ride the mare. I laugh, a little, but I will make you a bet, if you wish."

"I got fifty dollars," said Bill Parry, stoutly. "I'll lay it all on the back of the mare."

"I have a hundred," answered the Mexican contemptuously. "I offer you two dollars for one. Are you ready?"

Parry was already mounted, a big, uncouth form on the back of the dainty Betsy. Speedy looked with interest at the short spurs that ornamented the heels of Parry's boots. It was an odd miner who wore spurs at his work!

"Any tricks to her?" asked Parry of the prisoner.

"Sometimes she's lazy," said Speedy. "And if she hangs a little, just warm her up with the spurs. There's plenty in her, but she's a little petted and spoiled."

"I'll get the speed out of her," said Bill Parry savagely, "if I have to cut her heart out with the spurs. You can lay your money on that!"

"I'll lay my money on her and you, Bill," said Speedy, calmly.

"Are you ready, Manuel, you lump?" asked Bill Parry.

"Ready," said Manuel, with a sneer of satisfaction.

"I give the word," said the great Garcias. "You are both ready? Remember, to the rock and back to this place, where I draw a line with my toe. Fortune to the deserving! I raise my arm and when I drop it, send the gray on like a demon, Manuel!"

His arm fell, and the two animals shot away, side by side.

No! For the gray had a distinct head in front at the very beginning and, with every stride the good gelding shoved farther in the lead, a neck, a half length, a length.

The satisfaction of the Garcias knew no bounds. He laughed and shouted. He roared with laughter, too, when suddenly the mare, running still more slowly than before, began to buck. The curses of Bill Parry roared back down the wind to them. Even Sid Levine was laughing heartily.

Swiftly the gray flew on toward victory; and suddenly Bill Parry, for all his riding, flew high in the air, fell, and as his body thudded upon the ground, the mare cantered easily forward, carrying with her no burden other than the saddle on her back.

That instant, the Garcias, with a snarl, observed to his prisoner: "Ha? Is she a return horse? Would she run on into Sunday Slough and bring the warning?"

Aloud, he screeched in a voice like the whistling cry of a hawk: "Hai! Manuel! The mare, the mare! Stop her, rope her or shoot her down!"

Manuel heard that far-borne yell and, swinging the gray around, observed the riderless mare swinging on down the trail, while the form of her rider lay spread out far behind her.

"Shoot! Shoot!" shouted the great Garcias.

And Manuel, with an oath, drew up the gelding, slid a rifle out of the saddle holster that ran under his right knee, and fired from the shoulder. He took the head for a target and, at the first shot, she bounded high but went galloping on. At the second bullet, she tumbled head over heels and lay flat upon the trail.

Manuel, putting up the rifle, and turning his head to make sure that she was indeed motionless, turned the gray and came victoriously back toward his chief.

"And there it is," said the Garcias. "It was not I that wished to do this. It was not I. It was you, Señor Speedy. And there lies your horse dead."

"Not my horse," said Speedy. "It belongs to a man who'll follow you and cling to you like a burr. If you manage to do me a harm, I know that he'll have your blood later on."

Big Bill Parry, finally managing to get up from the ground, come back to the rest of the group, limping, shaking his bushy head. He came to Speedy, and, leaning over him, he shook a fist in his face.

"I got a mind to smash you," he said, "and I oughta smash you. I was kind of friendly to you, compared to the rest of these here. But I ain't friendly now. I'm gonna stand by and see them do whatever they wanta. I tell you what. You knew that she'd buck like a demon when she got the spur."

"Of course, I knew it," said Speedy. "Except for the Garcias, and his man Manuel—Garcias who saw what was happening and Manuel who shoots like ten demons—she would be well along down the ravine, by this time!"

"You see now, gringo, what it means to cross one of my name?" said Garcias.

"I knew that before, Don Hernando," said Speedy. "That was why I hung you like a white flag out a window of your house. I wanted to make sure that you would remember me."

Under the taunt, the Mexican snarled savagely. "There is a time," he said through his teeth, "for brave words. But your time has come to be braver still, when the fire answers what you have to say, Señor Speedy. My friends, let us sit down and consider, carefully, exactly what should be done to this man. Even the tricks of this snake have come to an end!"

CHAPTER 46

It was in the very last light of the day that Manuel had fired his shot and with every moment the gloom increased, shutting in closer and closer upon all within the ravine.

Now, as the men who had captured Speedy sat down to begin their calculations, like so many Indians around the body of a famous warrior, newly taken, Betsy lifted her head, shuddered, and rose to her feet.

She had been wounded twice. The first bullet had cut through the chin and that wound was bleeding fast. The second shot had glanced across the top of her neck, behind the ears. It was the shot which was called, in the old days, a "crease." It was said that the hunters of wild horses, men with a diabolical skill with a rifle, had sometimes brought down the mustangs with a bullet so placed that it nicked, without shattering, the spinal column, just back of the head.

So she had been struck and, thoroughly stunned, had fallen as though the bullet had passed straight through her brain.

But when she gained her feet, she was still able to take the trail. She had been badly hurt, and the blood was running down freely from both her hurts, but the instinct that guided her was as strong as ever, the impulse that had started her down the trail after she had bucked big Bill Parry from the saddle.

It was the image of her master that lived in her brain, young Joe Dale, whom she loved with devotion. Now she was in much trouble, badly hurt, and she started on toward him.

She went forward without hesitation, slowly at first, until she made sure of her balance. So it was that the keen-eared men up the valley did not hear her rise and start off through the shadows. The trees closed behind her, unseen, and now, making sure of herself, she struck into a sharp trot and then into a sharper gallop.

She grew dizzy. The effects of the blow on the spinal column could not be shaken off at once. Presently she struck a tree trunk with a force that almost broke her shoulder, barking away the skin and knocking her to the ground a second time.

She got up slowly, shuddering more violently. But she shook her brave head and then resumed the trail.

It was a strange world that she found herself running through that night. The boulders and the trees were in motion, it appeared, and swayed toward her from either side.

She got on until the lights from the town of Sunday Slough were spread out before her eyes, and then she stumbled, blinded by the swirling illumination. She fell for the third time. The constant flow of blood had weakened her. There was hardly strength enough in her head to lift it from the ground. There she lay for a time, the forelegs quivering, braced far apart.

She strove to rise. Her body heaved, and then sank back. She strove again, and this time gained her feet, only to topple over on the right side. She lay for a long moment.

Patiently she worked, until once more her head was raised from the ground. Her breathing was harsh and stertorous.

She shook violently with every effort that she made. Finally, however, the hind quarters, that had failed before, reacted to the pressure of her will and she came uncertainly to her feet.

She staggered and almost fell again from the effort, but presently she was able to walk on. And now, before, her, the lights separated and spread apart. A chasm of comparative darkness opened, and she entered the main street of the town. That street, as she turned a corner, opened upon many loud sounds of human voices and laughter.

Men came running out to her. Someone cried: "This here is Joe Dale's mare, and look at what happened to her! Somebody's shot her!"

Hands fell on her bridle reins. She shook her head, though the movement cost her pain, and broke into a floundering trot.

Down the street, two blocks, she knew that there was a large building, filled with lights, with the sounds of many human voices by day and by night. This was where her master was to be found. It was into this building that he disappeared at night, and out of it he came every morning. And now, lifting her head, she whinnied, high and sharp. Even the neigh was wrong. She snorted and tried again, and the old bugle note rang out clearly.

Almost instantly a door slammed and a step ran out onto the front veranda.

"Hello, Speedy," called a voice. "Did you get him?"

It was the voice of her master!

She whinnied again, softly, a note that he would be sure to know, for many a time on night trails she had spoken to him in exactly this manner and he had always known.

He knew now, for he came down the steps with a jump and a lunge. He was at her head. He was touching her wounds. And he was crying out in a voice sharp and wild. Other men ran in about him. "What's happened, Joe?" asked Pier Morgan, among the rest.

"They've murdered Speedy, and they've almost murdered Betsy. She's bleedin' to death," said Joe Dale, "and when I get them that done this, I'm gonna have the hide off their backs, and put a quirt on the raw underneath. They've gone and got Speedy, at last!"

The word went like lightning through the town.

There were some who were glad, in the bottom of their guilty hearts, but there were many more who were savagely annoyed and these came out, with guns. They offered themselves and their guns to Joe Dale, as the representative of the missing deputy sheriff.

He picked them with care, a stanch dozen men.

He said to the suddenly gathered posse: "I'll tell you what, boys, Speedy was never got by only one man. There's more than one. There's plenty of them that were in on his death. We ain't got much chance to nail 'em. Not hardly any chance at all, because the minute that they killed him, they're sure to've busted loose and run, because they knew that Sunday Slough would go clean crazy about the dirty job. But we'll do our best, and we'll do it on the run!"

He turned back to the veterinary who, with shirt sleeves rolled up, was busily laboring over the wounded mare.

"Doc," he said, "you'll do what you can for her. I know that."

He heard the doctor saying: "I'll fix her up, so's you'll never know that anything ever happened to her, except the scars. And you wouldn't want to rub them out. The whole of Sunday Slough wants that writing to remain on her, brother, because it'll remind us how she come in and give the alarm, and I only hope that she ain't come too late!"

Serious and deep murmurs arose.

Joe Dale patted her neck for the last time, sprang into the saddle of a gallant roan mustang, and went at a gallop down the main street of the town, heading toward the upper end of the ravine along which the mines were strung.

CHAPTER 47

High up the ravine, in their deep consultation, Sid Levine and the Garcias worked over the details of their calculations. The ideas of Levine were ingenious.

"We could do several things," he said. "There's no use limitin' ourselves. We got the time and we got the means. I've heard tell, somewheres, about lashing of a gent between two boards, and then sawing through the boards and the man. I mean, the boards keep the saw blade working straight. They clean the flesh and the blood out of the saw teeth. It took some imagining to think of that, I say."

"Well," said Mike Doloroso, "for my part, I never knew anything that much beat plain methods, like tying a gent up by the thumbs and putting a fire under his feet so as he gets tired of hanging that way!"

"Yes, and I seen a lot of funny things done by just putting a cord around the head of a man," said Levine, "and then twisting the string with a stick. That makes their eyes pop out, and they holler, you can bet!"

"He is a singer," said Garcias, savagely. "And when he screams, it should be worth seeing and hearing. His face will be good to watch, because it is a handsome face, my friends!"

Pedro said in Mexican: "Take the arm and bend it at the elbow, and then twist. It does things to the shoulder bones. Things to hear and see!"

Levine suddenly stretched his fat arms and yawned.

"We been talking for a long time," said he. "I guess we been here for about an hour, tasting this here without doing nothing. Suppose we start. Start anyway, but make a beginning."

"One moment," said Garcias. "Suppose we ask him what he wishes. Señor Speedy, what would you prefer? You have heard us talk of many things."

They had brought a lantern from the mine, and the lantern they now raised to see the face of the victim.

Speedy smiled against the light.

"Try anything you want, boys," he said. "If you can be Indians enough to do the things you talk about, I can be Indian enough to stand 'em without squealing, I hope."

"Talking game ain't the same as dying game," said Levine. "We'll get a song out of you before we finish."

"Look at the way you're winding up, Speedy," said One-eyed Mike. "A fine end you've come to! You'd live your life over again, I guess, if you could do the choosing right now! Speak up and tell the truth."

"Well, I'll tell you the truth," said Speedy. "I've had my fun, and I've had plenty of it. I've gone where I wanted to go, and when I wanted to go. I have no regrets, and I don't expect that I'll have them when I'm dying here. You can't string it out more than a few hours, at the most, and I can balance a good many happy years against all of that. Go ahead, Levine. Another day or two, and I should have had you."

Levine laughed loudly. "You would've had me," he said, sneering. "But you didn't get me. You didn't think that I'd reach this far or that I was behind that claim-jumper, did you? You couldn't see that that was all a plant?"

"I'd like to know one thing," said Speedy. "Was the other miner in on the deal, too?"

"Him? Oh, no! He's the honest man that was throwed out. I knew that he'd go straight to you. I knew that he'd get you started straight up the valley. I've beat you, Speedy!"

"The simple things will work, now and then," said Speedy, calmly. "Nobody can win all the time. But as I die, I'll be thinking of what the boys from Sunday Slough will do to you when they nail you, Levine. And nail you they will, sooner or later. Gray, and Joe Dale, and Pier Morgan, they'll never give up the work until they've cornered you and rendered down some of your fat into lard."

"Bah," said Levine, sneering, "I've matched my brains against theirs more times than I can count. I've always won before, and I'll win again. You're the only man in the world that ever bothered me much. I had Sunday Slough in my vest pocket, before you turned up. And with you out of the way, I'll go back and get the town in my hand again."

Speedy shook his head.

"You're an optimist, Sid," said he. "The town knows you now. And no decent man will ever be seen with you again. You'll have nothing but muckers like One-eyed Mike around you, and murderers, like Garcias."

He smiled again, straight through the light of the lantern and into the face of Levine.

The latter grew half purple and half white.

At last he said: "It's time to commence, Garcias. It needs the whip to make him feel something!"

Garcias arose. "We begin, then. Pedro, what's that on the wind? Do you hear anything? Like horses, coming up the valley?"

"I thought that I heard," said Pedro.

"But now there is nothing," broke in Manuel.

"Very well," said Garcias. "My men and I vote for fire, a slow fire built at the feet; roasting the feet carefully. When the fire has rotted the flesh off the bones, then move it up higher. A man will live for a long time, in flames like that."

"Build the fire," snapped Levine. "You're right, and I should've known before that I wouldn't have ideas worth the ones that you could trot out."

The wood was gathered.

There was a considerable noise of crackling in the under-brush as Pedro and Manuel broke up the fuel small. Then Manuel, with a bit of dry bark, started the fire, heaping leaves over it and the driest part of the brushwood, broken short, until the flames had gathered a good headway.

"That is enough to roast the meat," said the Garcias. "Even enough to char it, unless we keep the joint turning."

He laughed joyously, as he spoke, and Pedro and Manuel laid hands on the prisoner.

Levine, holding the lantern high, leaned close over the face of Speedy.

"Can you hold out, now that it's coming?" he asked, sneering. "Beg, you cur. Now's the time for you to talk. Beg for a quick way of dying!"

But, instead, he saw a gradual and steady smile spread on the lips and in the eyes of the prisoner.

Speedy said nothing at all!

The voice that next spoke was not from any one about the fire, but from the neighboring brush.

It was the sharp, barking tone of young Joe Dale, exclaiming: "Shoot for the legs. We want 'em alive, Garcias and Levine! The rest don't count!"

And rifles spoke like hammer strokes against the ears of the stunned group.

CHAPTER 48

When the cry of Joe Dale was heard, the men of the party gathered around Speedy scattered. Each went his own way, winged with panic. No doubt every man would have been dropped at the first volley, had not Dale issued his orders. He himself could not understand, afterward, why he had shown such stupidity, except that it seemed to him only fair that the creatures who had been about to torment his idolized friend should taste death for a time, themselves, before they suffered it.

As it was, his men strictly obeyed his orders, and fired low. But the light was bad. The glimmer of the flames of the fire danced before their eyes and, though every one was a chosen marksman, the execution was surprisingly slow.

Big One-eyed Mike, with a howl, ran straight for the nearest trees opposite to the line of firing. A bullet knocked off his hat. Another sliced through the calf of his leg. But these hindrances did not keep him from running at full speed. He flattened the brush before him like a charging elephant, and went on, dashing and crashing.

Sunday Slough saw him no more.

Pedro and Manuel, running in exactly the same fashion, ducked and dodged right and left, heading for the same trees. Pedro reached them without a scratch. But luck was against Manuel. A bullet, flying far higher than the marksman intended, broke the back of his neck and he fell dead on the verge of safety.

Big Sid Levine, screaming like a woman, and like a woman throwing his arms above his head, rushed off in such blind panic that he ran straight into the enemy. A gun butt wielded by Joe Dale with infinite relish struck him fairly on the mouth and knocked out his breath and most of his teeth.

He fell down like one who had received a mortal wound. He had fallen in a dead faint, from which he did not recover for half an hour.

Bill Parry, running for safety, stumbled midway in his course, fell flat, and rolled headlong into tall grass. He had sense enough not to rise again, but crawled away.

He would have been taken, had there been any pursuit, but there was none.

Something else was happening beside the fire that attracted attention that way, and all the guns.

For of all the men who had surrounded Speedy, only Don Hernando, in the pinch, remembered the work at hand rather than the preservation of his own life.

It was not a blind passion on his part.

The men of Segovia were a part of him, and he was a part of Segovia. He had been shamed in the eyes of all of his people, and he dared not return to them unless he could say that the insulting gringo had fallen by his hand.

The moment that the alarm came, he knew what he had to do, and started to do it. He sprang straight for his victim.

The first hindrance was purely accidental.

Big One-eyed Mike, turning toward his blind side, with his massive shoulder struck the Mexican and knocked the slighter man spinning with his charge.

As Garcias recovered his balance and darted forward once more toward Speedy, young Pier Morgan came plunging in between. He was still very weak. The riding of the last two days and the strain of the excitement had been too much for him, but he placed himself instantly between Speedy and the danger, standing with his legs braced well apart.

He saw Garcias coming like a tiger, and fired, but missed with his shaking hand. The second bullet clogged in the revolver. He hurled the weapon itself at the head of Garcias, but it flew wild in turn, and Garcias, holding his own bullet with a terrible fixity of purpose, avoided wasting a shot on the body of poor Morgan, merely knocking him senseless with a blow from the barrel of his gun.

That removed the last screen, and with a frightful cry of triumph, he stood over Speedy, leveling his gun.

He wanted to make too sure, or he would have done his work. As it was, he saw the firelight shine into the steady, keen eyes of the prisoner and, as he was about to pull the trigger that would have banished Speedy from the pleasant ways of this earth, a rifle slug tore through the hips of the

Mexican and knocked him down.

He struggled to one elbow and strove to fire again. But Joe Dale, running in like a wild cat, broke his gun arm with a kick.

That ended the battle of Sunday Slough, as it was called from that date henceforward.

Men said that all the credit was due to the brains of Speedy, who had devised the liberation of a dumb beast as a messenger. But they gave the credit, as hero of the encounter, not to Joe Dale, or even to gallant Pier Morgan, who had been so willing to die for his friend, but to the beautiful mare, Betsy.

They paraded her through the streets of the town, the next day, decked out with garlands of flowers. For she was of a tough ancestry, and she had not lost enough blood to injure her seriously for long. She was weak, but happy with her master beside her.

As for the prisoners, they brought the Garcias, silent and composed, to the town jail, where Marshal Tom Gray took charge of him. With him they carried the great Sid Levine, fallen forever. He had collapsed completely and had to be carried on a litter, where he lay sobbing out of a broken and bleeding face.

And Speedy?

Joe Dale and Pier Morgan, literally with guns, defended him all the election day from the enthusiasm of the crowds who wanted to break into the sheriff's house.

The election itself was a joke. No man dared to vote against the hero; and in the evening, when the votes had been counted, in the rosy dusk of the day, the whole population of Sunday Slough came trooping to congratulate the hero and make him the center of such a celebration as the Slough had never known before.

Joe Dale went to rouse him from the sleep of exhaustion, but received no answer to his knock. The door was locked.

They crawled through the open rear window, and found Speedy gone.

In place of him was a letter which read:

Dear Joe and Pier, and All My Friends in Sunday Slough: Levine is down. My job is ended. My trail is the out trail. If I'm the sheriff, I resign. Good luck to everybody, but I've already stayed too long in one place.

Speedy

That was all of him.

Sunday Slough saw him no more.